"City girl." Brian shook his head.

"If that means I want my eggs in a carton, pasteurized milk, my chicken deep-fried and all the sheep behind a fence, you got it."

"Shh, the chickens'll hear you."

He and Kim shared a smile, and for a minute Brian saw what their life might have been like if she hadn't hated everything he loved. But he'd had foolish dreams once—dreams where she'd loved him enough to stay. He would never be so foolish again.

"You thought I was going to leave, didn't you?" she said.

He tilted one eyebrow. "It crossed my mind."

"Mine, too," she admitted. "But I'm not. I said I'd stay until you were able to take care of yourself, and I will. Don't think you can get rid of me by making things tough, either."

He hadn't considered that. In truth, he wouldn't have to make things tough. Everyday life on the farm was tough enough. Maybe it would be good for him to see firsthand how incredibly wrong for this life she was now and had always been....

Dear Reader,

Since my mother was an Illinois farm girl, I spent one week out of every summer on my grandparents' dairy farm. I fell in the mud, got scratched by a tomcat, was chased around the front yard by a bull and became irrationally terrified of mice. But all those summer weeks gave me plenty of fodder for Kim Luchetti's return to the family farm.

From the minute I met Kim, a secondary character in my novel *Leave It to Max*, she intrigued me. Why did she party so hard? Why did she date only brainless bimbo boys? Why was her past such a well-kept secret? I discovered the answer to these questions and many more during the writing of *The Farmer's Wife*.

Kim wanted to be a lawyer and live in the big city. But she also loved Brian Riley, and Brian loved the farm. She couldn't have it both ways; she couldn't decide what to do. Then fate intervened and made the decision for her.

The Farmer's Wife is the story of Kim's journey home, with my usual array of quirky characters, both human and animal, as well as a secondary love story between Kim's parents, who start all over again after thirty years of marriage. I hope you enjoy the trip as much as I did.

For information on future releases and contests, check out my Web site at www.lorihandeland.com.

Lori Handeland

The Farmer's Wife
Lori Handeland

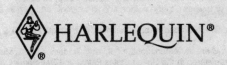

HARLEQUIN®

TORONTO • NEW YORK • LONDON
AMSTERDAM • PARIS • SYDNEY • HAMBURG
STOCKHOLM • ATHENS • TOKYO • MILAN • MADRID
PRAGUE • WARSAW • BUDAPEST • AUCKLAND

ISBN 0-373-71099-2

THE FARMER'S WIFE

Visit us at www.eHarlequin.com

Printed in U.S.A.

For my Aunt Beth and Uncle Bill.
Who always read my books and love them.
Thank you.

CHAPTER ONE

KIM LUCHETTI returned home eight years after she'd left it running.

Well, perhaps *running* wasn't the right term. But what was?

Fleeing? Crying? Aching? Dying?

Kim put a stop to those words and the thoughts they would lead to by turning up the volume of her car radio so high she could think of little else but the music. She'd become adept at avoiding memories since she'd left. So much so that the first sight of her father's silver silos brought tears to her eyes.

Eight years ago an American flag had flown atop only one of them. Now the Stars and Stripes proudly waved over three. Her father hadn't been lying when he'd said the farm was doing well. Silos cost a whole lot of money. For that reason, when a farmer paid off his debt on one he perched a flag at the pinnacle or painted an icon on the side to let everyone know the towering, grain-filled structure belonged to him forever.

"Way to go, Daddy," she whispered.

The heavy beat of "Another One Bites the Dust" shook her rented Miata sports car, the same make she drove back in Savannah. The lyrics caused a hysterical giggle to tickle her throat. Biting the dust was not something she cared to hear about with her father still in the hospital—present condition unknown.

Kim flipped to another frequency, then winced as the twang of country-and-western music filled the air. But she didn't change the station. She was almost there.

Like the silos, the stone farmhouse and bright, white outbuildings came into view from several miles away. People didn't call folks from Illinois flatlanders just to be rude. When Irving Berlin wrote "from the mountains to the prairies" he'd obviously been referring to Illinois—one great big prairie, dotted with farms and the occasional city. Even Chicago, home of the Sears Tower and various other buildings of every shape and size, was not exactly a Mecca of hills and valleys.

Kim turned onto the gravel lane that led from the main road to the house. Within seconds the sound of the engine brought the farm dogs running. While most farmers employed canines with herding tendencies such as sheepdogs and collies, or mutts because they were tough, smart and free, on the farm of John Luchetti purebred Dalmatians ran with the cows, pigs, cats and chickens. Her father had always been an original in more ways than one.

Kim's eyes burned with tears she had yet to shed. "Dear God, let him be all right," she murmured, and made the sign of the cross for good measure.

She hadn't talked to God much lately. Not since the last time her fervent prayers had gone unanswered—

eight years ago, to be exact—but she'd do anything, beg anyone for her father's life. She'd already done the unthinkable in coming back here.

Kim parked next to a line of pick-up trucks in an array of colors. From the display she calculated three of her five brothers were present. No big surprise that two were still MIA.

Colin—brother number three—was a foreign correspondent, usually lost in some godforsaken hellhole, reporting from a cave. Brother number two—Bobby— had escaped long before Kim, joining the army in a desperate attempt to get out of Dodge. He'd thrived in the military, entering the Special Forces and rising through the ranks. Speaking of godforsaken hellholes, Bobby had seen quite a few. He was probably stuck in one right now.

Kim's estimation of which family members were present proved correct when she glanced at the porch. Brothers one, four and five leaned on the railing and smirked as she fought her way out of the car.

Jabbing a fire-engine-red spike heel at the nearest dancing Dalmatian, she waved her purse at another and ordered, "Get!"

While Dalmatians were known for their polite and aloof manner with strangers, once they recognized a friend they could be as friendly as any puppy. When Kim had left, Bear and Bull—their names tributes to her brothers' favorite sports teams, quaintly known as Da Bears and Da Bulls in local lingo—*had* been puppies. They must have amazing memories, or maybe amazing noses, to remember her for so long.

At any rate, her attempts to disperse the dogs only caused them to prance faster, wiggle harder, jump higher. Her brothers laughed. Eight years hadn't changed them. They'd never been much good for anything beyond torment.

She made the mistake of glowering at the men and taking her attention off the dogs. Bear promptly placed his manure-encrusted paws on her shoulders. Since it was Kim's misfortune to stand under five feet tall, the four-inch heels only allowed the animal to kiss her on the mouth rather than the forehead. He needed a Tic Tac in the worst way. Bull took the opportunity to rub his ice-cold, slimy nose across the back of her sheer stockings.

"Aargh!" She shoved at one and sidled away from the other. Unabashed, they trotted toward the barn, tongues lolling with idiotic doggy joy. Brothers and Dalmatians had a lot more in common than one might expect.

Kim wiped the remnants of the kiss from her lips and glanced down. Her heels had sunk into the gravel about an inch. Her cream blouse sported smelly paw prints. Her black skirt was coated with a layer of dust and… She wrenched her neck and looked at the back of her legs.

Yep, there was dog drool running down her calves.

She must be home.

FROM THE SOLITARY WINDOW of her bedroom on the third floor, Eleanor Luchetti watched her baby return.

"All grown-up," she said aloud. "I must have blinked and missed it."

No one was in the room, but that no longer bothered Eleanor. Five sons, a dairy-farming husband and a daughter who would rather live anywhere but here had made her okay with talking to herself a long time ago. Someone had to talk to her.

Eleanor turned away from the window. Where had she gone wrong?

Shaking her head, she continued to sort the socks spread across the bed. How many mothers had asked themselves the same question since time began? Had any discovered the answer?

Not likely. Children were a mystery, and children like Kim more so than most.

When Eleanor had finally borne a daughter she'd been so excited. At *last* another female in the house. Pink instead of blue, quiet instead of loud, gentle instead of rough. She'd envisioned cuddles, giggles, shared joys, dreams and memories—a fellow cohort in the all-male, testosterone-humming Luchetti household.

However Kim had never behaved as expected. Eleanor loved her daughter, but she did not understand her. What drove the boys was always near to the surface and easily detectible. But from the beginning Kim had been driven by forces beyond Eleanor's comprehension. Her brilliant mind, lofty ambitions and restless nature had proved too much for her own, or anyone else's, good.

John had said that their daughter had her own drummer and Eleanor hers. The two of them should accept that and move on. Kim *had* moved on—right out of the house, the state, their very lives.

Now she was back. But how long would she stay?

The familiar routine of sorting socks soothed Eleanor. She'd been doing it for over thirty years. Sometimes she thought the ebb and flow of her life could be found in the size, style and number of socks in the wash basket. She'd begun with man's socks, then added itty-bitty baby socks. The baby socks had slowly grown until all of them were man-size—except for the socks of a tiny girl, who became a petite young woman.

Eleanor closed her eyes. She really missed those itty-bitty pink things. She missed babies and toddlers; she missed busy days and people who needed her.

Her children were grown, her husband, even before his heart attack, seemed to have forgotten she was there. Her life, which had turned out exactly as she'd planned, was not at all as she'd hoped—

The door creaked behind her. "Mom?"

Eleanor didn't have to open her eyes to know which one of her sons stood there. Aaron, her oldest, most serious, quiet and responsible child *would* be the one to walk upstairs and make her come down.

"She's here."

"I know."

"She asked for you."

"She did?"

Eleanor pressed her lips together, annoyed at the hope in her voice. Why did she still long for the love of a child who was unable to give it to her?

Aaron shuffled his big feet and cleared his throat. She turned, and from the look on his face, Eleanor knew the truth. "She didn't."

He shrugged. The shortest of the five boys, despite being the oldest, Aaron still wasn't small. But with a father who was over six feet of lanky, sinewy muscle and a mother who resembled the hardy farmwife she was, all the boys had become big, rugged men. She had no idea how Kim had ended up petite, unless they'd produced their limit of strapping offspring by the time she had come along.

"Kimmy wants to see Dad."

Eleanor smiled. The boys had always referred to their little sister as Kimmy. She hated the nickname, which was why they continued to call her by it.

Twenty-six years ago, John had not wanted another baby, had not been thrilled with a girl—what did you do with one, anyway?—yet he had formed a closer relationship with Kim than he had with any of the others.

When she'd left, he'd said it was for the best. His baby girl was made for better things than the farm. Eleanor had been a bit hurt at the intimation that her life, her work as a wife, mother and helpmate, wasn't something to aspire to, but she hadn't said anything. What would be the point?

John hadn't meant to insult her. He'd only been trying to make them both feel better about losing their youngest to the allure of the big wide world. But she didn't think John had ever felt better; he'd only pretended that he did.

"Mom? You okay?"

"Of course," she said briskly. "Are we all going to the hospital?"

He shook his head, frowning. "Dean has to stay and milk."

Eleanor resisted the urge to smack herself in the head. She *knew* someone had to stay and milk the cows. And Dean, her fourth son, was a farmer the caliber of his father. Farmers were not made—they were born; and from the cradle Dean had been her child of the earth.

Eleanor glanced at the clock on the nightstand— 3:00 p.m. She'd lost track of time again. Ever since she'd found John on the floor of the kitchen, coffee cup shattered around him, breath shallow, skin gray, she hadn't been very good at keeping track of anything but the socks.

"Evan is milking for the Dwyers," Aaron continued, a bit more slowly and surely than usual. He must think she was losing her mind. Sometimes Eleanor thought so, too. "They're in Mason City visiting their daughter."

Evan, her youngest son, hired out to many of the local farmers. He lived alone in a small cabin on their back eighty. The contrast between Evan—so laid back at times Eleanor wanted to stick him with a pin just to get a reaction, and Kim, so wired she could light up the Las Vegas strip with her energy—astonished Eleanor.

"I'll be right down, honey," she murmured.

Aaron hesitated. Like her, he wanted to take care of

everyone. Unlike her, he possessed a gentle soul, a quiet, unassuming, peaceful manner.

He'd gone off to college, majored in theology and flirted with the priesthood. Though she'd been proud to claim a son with such devotion to the church, she'd also been secretly relieved when he'd returned home at the end of his freshman year and hadn't left since.

Devotion to God was one thing; devotion to your life was another.

"Mom?" he pressed. "You're sure you're okay?"

"As okay as I can be with your father just out of ICU."

"He's going to be all right. It wasn't that bad. This time."

"This time," she echoed.

Aaron continued to hover in the doorway. He'd remain there until she did what he wanted. Aaron was like a brick wall—steady, sure and immovable—a person could lean on Aaron and he would never crumble.

Eleanor dropped the unmatched sock she'd been wrapping around her palm back into the basket. She'd felt very much like that sock over the past few years. Complete and of use only with a mate; lost, alone, useless without.

John might be physically present, but he was emotionally unavailable. Had that been the case from the beginning? Perhaps. It *had* been over thirty years since they'd been two and not three, four or more. Eleanor couldn't remember if he'd always been distant or if she'd merely noticed now that she no longer had children to raise and no one who needed her.

He'd never been much for words of affection. In their youth whenever she'd asked him to tell her that he loved her, he'd always said, "I'll show you," which was how they'd ended up with a child a year for a whole lot of years. She'd learned to live without the words and make do with actions, instead. But lately there hadn't been much of either one, and she'd started to wonder why.

They'd never talked about their hopes, their dreams, their feelings the way folks did on television. Did anyone? As a result, she wasn't sure how to ask if the man she loved loved her any longer.

Such reflections on the heels of John's heart attack, combined with the return of the prodigal child, had made this a hellish week. But then, an entire week without a disaster of some kind on a dairy farm was a miracle the likes of which Eleanor had never seen.

She turned her back on the laundry and smiled at her too serious son. "Let's go see your sister."

THE ONLY CHANGES in the house were the pictures on the wall, Kim discovered, and not the content of those pictures, but the pictures themselves. Her childhood memories were of a century-old gray stone farmhouse, large yet quaint, but devoid of any wall decorations or knickknacks made of glass.

Five boys in five years had taught Eleanor Luchetti not to bother with froufrou adornments unless she wanted them busted. Chasing, wrestling, the banging of doors and the throwing of every shape, size and color of ball were the order of each day. The first thing

Kim had done when she'd bought her own place was cover the walls with pictures and the tables with glass.

In the midst of that memory, she was suddenly swept off her feet and spun round and round. Gasping for air, Kim clutched at her brother Evan's shoulders. "Put me down, idiot!"

He ignored her order. Nothing new there. She wrapped her arms around his neck and held on tight, lest he get it into his head to fling her at Dean like a beach ball. That would be nothing new, either. One of her brothers' favorite games had always been Toss the Little Sister.

Evan stopped spinning, and shortly thereafter, so did Kim's head, but he continued to hold her aloft, feet dangling over one of his rock-hard arms. The youngest of the boys, Evan was also the tallest. Though not as handsome as Dean—who cornered the market on looks if not personality—Evan had a special *something* that endeared him to most of the female population. Perhaps it was the brooding expression in his heavily lashed blue eyes.

"Glad you finally made it home," he said.

After eight years in the South, the sound of a flat midwestern accent grated, as did the characteristic bluntness that would be considered outright bad manners below the Mason-Dixon line.

"Did you think I wouldn't?"

"We had a bet."

Dean lounged in the doorway. He didn't appear all that happy to see her. She had a pretty good idea why.

"Who won?"

"Me." Evan set Kim on her feet and patted her on the head. Why that still made her want to kick him in the knee, she wasn't sure. But she refrained. Barely.

Instead, Kim reached up and touched the auburn streaks that ran the length of his dark-brown ponytail. "What does Daddy say about this?"

He lifted one shoulder, lowered it. "I look like a thug, a drug dealer, a hippie. Depends on the day and his mood."

Evan and their father had never gotten on. Daddy was driven, Evan laid back. Not that Evan didn't work just as hard; he merely did it in his own time and on his own terms.

The two struck sparks off each other. To tell the truth, her father struck sparks off of all his sons except Aaron, and then only because Aaron wouldn't let him. It appeared that the house wasn't the only thing that hadn't changed.

"Gotta go." Evan paused in front of Dean and held out his hand, palm up. With a labored sigh, Dean made a show of pulling out his wallet and handing Evan a twenty.

"You really didn't think I'd come home?" she asked as the door closed behind Evan.

"Nope." Dean pushed away from the doorjamb and strode to the window. Even after he'd jacked it up a few inches, he continued to stare out, pointedly ignoring her.

Dean was still angry, and Kim couldn't say that she blamed him. But the crimes she had committed had not been against him, and the one she'd hurt the most would never tell the entire truth, especially to her brother. But since she wasn't going to explain why she'd left to Dean, or anyone for that matter, Kim moved on. She was very good at moving on.

"How is Daddy—really?"

Dean turned, his expression revealing that he knew what she was up to and thought less of her for it. However, he couldn't think any less of Kim than she already thought of herself. "He'll be all right if he changes his habits."

Relief flowed through Kim, strong enough to make her dizzy. He was going to be all right if—

She frowned. "What habits?"

"Less red meat, eggs and milk for starters."

"Sacrilege to a dairy farmer."

"You got that right. But what he really isn't going to like is less alcohol and no more cigarettes."

Kim winced. Each childhood recollection of her father—riding the tractor, milking the cows, leading a bull around by the ring in its nose—was accompanied by the familiar sight of a cigarette hanging from his lips. Every time she caught the scent of sun, wind and cigarettes, Kim thought of Daddy.

Her favorite memories were of summer evenings, waiting on the porch for the first sight of him returning from the barn or the fields. She'd race inside, grab the beer she'd put into the freezer a few moments earlier and meet her father coming up the stairs.

The weariness would fade from his face as he pressed the icy aluminum to the back of his neck. Then he would crack open the can, and together they would watch the sun go down. Before they went inside to join everyone for supper, he would make her laugh with foolish, corny knock-knock jokes that he'd made up while riding his tractor or operating one of his other huge, expensive pieces of farm machinery.

"Who's going to tell him?" she asked.

"I vote for you."

"Me?" Kim squeaked. "Why me?"

"The rest of us have been here. You haven't. It's your turn to do something."

"Bobby and Colin haven't been around, or Evan half the time either."

"They visit. They spend vacations with us. We haven't seen your face in eight years."

She narrowed her eyes. "I'm here now."

"Big fricking deal, Princess."

Kim's hands curled into fists. How long had she been here? Fifteen minutes, and she was contemplating murder. Not bad. Her brothers could usually send her from zero to pissed off in two point five seconds. Funny, but in her other life as a paralegal she was well-known for never losing her temper. If her colleagues could only see her now.

Kim crossed the short distance between her and Dean until they stood toe to toe. Then she tilted back her head, and she tilted it some more. No wonder she never came home. She'd forgotten that living with the Luchetti brothers gave her a constant crick in the neck.

"You don't know anything about me."

He leaned down, putting his face nearer to hers. "And whose fault is that?"

She could smell the farm on him—cows, grass, hard-earned sweat, the autumn wind in his short, dark hair—and while the scent should be unpleasant, instead it reminded her of—

"I call every week," she blurted. "Daddy understands."

"I don't think anyone understands, Kim, least of all—"

She slugged him. She didn't mean to. It just happened. But she'd made him stop. He hadn't said *that* name.

"Kimberly Marie Luchetti! How many times have I told you not to hit your brothers?"

Dean straightened. His smirk shouted "Gotcha!" without him having to say a word.

Kim stuck out her tongue at him. Eight years gone and nothing had changed. Her brothers were still the bane of her existence and her mother...

She turned, blinked, stared. Her mother had changed.

Oh, she was the same tall, sturdy, stoic farmwife. Her face tanned, the same life lines creased the corners of her blue eyes, though a few new worry lines bracketed her mouth. But her hair...

Her long, ebony hair had turned snow-white.

"Wh-what happened to your hair?"

Dean made an impatient sound. "Goddammit, Kim. Is that all you can say?"

"Watch your mouth, young man!" Eleanor snapped, though she continued to stare at Kim. "You will not take the Lord's name in vain in this house."

"Yes, ma'am." Dean slammed out of the house without a backward glance. Through the open living room window Kim heard him cursing all the way to the barn.

She caught a glimpse of Aaron in the hallway before he, too, escaped. For big manly men, her brothers were amazingly chickenhearted. What did they think was going to happen? An immediate resumption of the same old conflicts between mother and daughter? Kim certainly hoped not.

"I'm sorry, Mom. I didn't mean to be rude."

Her mother's smile was serene, though Kim could see tension in the way she wrung her hands. "I'm sure my hair was a shock. But then, if you'd been home recently it wouldn't be."

Kim sighed. She'd known when she got on the plane that this visit would not be easy for too many reasons to count. She just hadn't figured her first half hour would be chock-full of contention.

She didn't acknowledge her mother's comment. What defense did she have against the truth? "Can we go and see Daddy now?"

"Can I have a hug first?"

Kim resisted the urge to shake her head, jiggle her ear. She couldn't recall the last time Eleanor had requested a hug. "Uh, sure."

For a moment, her mother seemed to cling. But Kim must have been mistaken, or merely hopeful, because in the next instant she was alone again.

That had always been the way. Eleanor Luchetti had too much to do in any given day to waste time cuddling. Kim had satisfied her need to be held elsewhere. And therein lay the root of a whole lot of problems.

A horn sounded from the yard. "Aaron's ready to go," her mother said, then eyed Kim up and down. "You want to change first?"

Though she was no doubt referring to the dust and the manure on Kim's clothes, still Kim felt judged and found lacking. True, her short skirt and high heels were completely inappropriate for the farm, but she owned very few clothes that weren't.

Kim grabbed her suitcase. "I'll be quick."

In the downstairs bathroom she dusted off the skirt, swept a damp washcloth down her stockings and donned a fresh blouse. Minutes later she stepped onto the porch, where her mom stared at the Miata.

"Nice car," she murmured.

Kim frowned, uncertain if she was being facetious or complimentary. "I, uh, have one like it at home. Figured it would be easier to drive the same kind while I'm here."

"Home?" Eleanor descended the steps, snarled at the Dalmations when they danced too close and headed for the American model SUV idling nearby. "I thought this was home."

Kim glanced at the cows behind the barn, the pigs in the pen and the dogs that now cowered behind a bush, hiding from her mother.

Home? *Ugh.* Never.

But she knew better than to say so.

CHAPTER TWO

THE HOSPITAL IN Gainsville was new—or at least new to Kim. When she'd left, the closest medical facility had been in Bloomington, an hour's drive away.

Heck, when she'd left, Gainsville had consisted of two bars, a post office and a feed store. As Aaron drove through town, she saw that more had been added than just a hospital. Fast food restaurants, dentists' offices, a strip mall and two gas stations vied for space. The bars had multiplied, the feed store expanded, but the post office was still the same. One could always trust the federal government to be slower to change than even a midwestern farm community.

Gainsville Memorial rose like a great, gray Mecca out of a displaced farmer's field at the south end of town. "Does the community really need a hospital this big?" she wondered aloud.

"It's hopping all the time." Aaron made two passes through the visitors' lot before he found a parking place. "Lucky for Dad it was here."

"I wish it had been here years ago," her mother murmured.

Kim stepped out of the car, then followed the others into the overly bright lights of the foyer. Her mother's wry comment made her recall a few mad rides to the hospital. Aaron's cracked collarbone when he fell—or got shoved, the truth of that had never been determined—from the haymow. Bobby's broken foot—cow stompage. Colin's sprained knee—Fourth of July greased-pig contest. Dean had lost a thumbnail in the corn picker. Evan sported a nasty scar on his back from a nighttime-encounter with barbed wire. Which was what he got for sneaking across the fields to meet a girl—or ten.

Through every medical emergency, Eleanor Luchetti had always remained calm. Familiarity no doubt did breed contempt, or at least the ability not to run screaming into the night at the sight of blood.

They stopped in front of a hospital room with the nameplate Luchetti, J. As Kim had learned on the drive over, her father had been removed from ICU the day before, when his condition was upgraded to fair.

Expecting to walk right in, Kim was surprised when the others hovered outside the closed door. She glanced at her mother.

"You go on, Kim. He's been waiting for you. I-I'm going to talk to his doctor, see when we can take him home." Without another word, she headed for the nurses' station.

"What's with her?" Kim asked.

"She's having a hard time with this."

"Hospitals never bothered her before. Nothing bothers her. Except me."

"You're wrong."

Kim raised her gaze to her brother's. "I don't bother her?"

Aaron's steady, calm, blue eyes were very much like his mother's—both in shade and expression. "You drive her insane, Kimmy. Just like she drives you." He softened his comment with a gentle smile. "What I meant was, things do bother her. She's just learned not to show it."

For the first time Kim considered that her mother's calm exterior might merely mask a churning, roiling, hidden heap of chaos. Perhaps buried fear not only produced ulcers but turned the hair white.

"What good would showing it do?" Aaron continued. "Would that change anything?"

A sudden memory of a dark night full of tears, dead dreams, hidden hopes, unanswered prayers flashed across Kim's mind. No, showing your pain certainly didn't change anything. She agreed with her mom there, which was new.

"Kim?" Aaron put his big, rough, heavy hand on her shoulder. "Why did you leave? Why didn't you come back?"

Aaron had always had an uncanny ability to cut to the heart of the matter. He'd known when Kim was upset; he'd often tried to shield her from the others. But even though he was the oldest, and for a long time the biggest, four against one usually meant that he lost.

"I am back," she whispered.

"But you aren't going to stay."

Kim took a deep breath and she thought of the past, of her family, the farm, her life—what it had been and why it had become what it was. She thought of all the men she'd known, the men she'd been with trying to forget the only one who mattered, and she knew nothing had changed, even though at times she tried to convince herself that everything had.

"No, I'm not going to stay." She released a long, resigned sigh. "I can't."

THE DOOR TO John Luchetti's hospital room closed with a sharp click. He didn't need to open his eyes to know who had come. Each of his sons had his own way of walking. Aaron's tread was heavy, burdened; Bobby's, light but confident. Colin shuffled, lost in his own world; while Dean's clomp reflected his annoyance with... Well, pretty much everything and everyone. Then there was Evan, who never moved faster than slow motion in reverse.

Over thirty years of shared joy and hardship had made John able to sense the calm, sure presence of his wife. She could practically read his mind, and he liked to think that he could read hers. Words were rarely necessary between them. Together they could just *be*. Ellie was John's rock, and she always had been.

The snick of the door was followed by a step so full of energy, life pulsed in the air to the beat of high heels against a tiled floor. His lips curved. No woman in Gainsville wore *clickety-click* high heels.

"'Bout time," he murmured, and opened his eyes.

She stopped a few feet from the bed and bit her lip, concern washing over her face. His baby had grown up—gone from pretty to stunning in the space of eight years. He shouldn't be surprised, but he was.

In John's mind, Kim was forever eighteen, hopeful and happy, with a roundness to her cheeks and chin and laughter in her eyes. The woman who stared at him now was twenty-six, her chin pointed, her cheeks defined and her eyes... Her eyes still laughed, but not in quite the same way.

John sat up and held out his hand. "If I'd have known all it would take was a trip to the hospital to get you home, I'd have had an attack years ago."

"Not funny, Daddy," she said, but she came closer and linked her fingers with his.

"You want funny? Knock-knock."

She groaned. "I just got here."

John raised his eyebrows and waited. They had always shared a goofy sense of humor that no one else in their family could bear. Ellie was his rock, but Kim had always been the light and the laughter in his life. When she'd left he'd tried to share his jokes with Ellie or the boys. They would listen with varying degrees of impatience, then coddle him with a lame, stilted chuckle. It wasn't the same. There was no one on earth who laughed quite like Kim.

"Oh, all right." She winked. "Who's there?"

"Aardvark."

"Aardvark who?"

"Aardvark a million miles for one of your smiles."

She stared at him. For a minute he didn't think she was going to laugh. Then she snorted, coughed and... He held his breath.

A giggle erupted, followed by a great big belly laugh. From the time she was a baby, folks had smiled at the mere sound of Kim's laughter.

But when she continued to snicker until tears ran down her cheeks, he frowned. "It wasn't that great."

"You—you—" She held up her hand, took a deep, shaky breath, then choked and started all over again.

Concerned, John tried to sit up straighter. She waved him back and moments later managed to get herself under control.

"You don't understand, Daddy. No one tells knock-knock jokes where I come from. I didn't realize how much I missed them."

"You come from *here,* and I tell them all the time." Or at least he used to, but she didn't need to know that.

"I come from Savannah now. I spend my days with lawyers, judges and criminals. They aren't very funny."

"No? What do you call a hundred lawyers at the bottom of the ocean?"

She rolled her eyes. "A good start. Come on, Daddy, that's an oldie."

"But a goodie."

She smiled and wiped her cheeks.

"You come alone?" he asked.

"No. Mom went to talk to the doctor." She frowned. "And speaking of Mom—"

"You two didn't start already, did you?"

"No."

He gave her a long, knowing look.

"Not really," she amended. "But what happened to Mom's hair?"

For a minute he wasn't sure what she meant, thinking maybe Ellie had cut off her glorious hair. Then he remembered. "Oh, the white. That came on sort of gradual-like."

"Gradual? She had hair as dark as mine."

"You've been gone awhile, baby girl. You wouldn't remember, but your grandma's hair was white long before she was fifty. Seems to be a family trait."

"Swell," Kim muttered.

"Did you and your mom drive in alone?"

"No. Aaron drove, but he discovered a sudden and undeniable need for coffee. I think he wanted us to have some time alone."

John grunted. She was no doubt right. Aaron was always trying to make things easier for people. Trying to understand their feelings. Make everything all right. His eldest son was as much a mystery to John as the rest of them. He couldn't fathom how he felt at odds with five sons, yet in harmony with a single daughter. But then, Ellie and her boys were one big happy family. Ellie and Kim...

Oy, vey, as his good friend Mose Feldman liked to say.

"So, besides the lack of knock-knock gems, how's Savannah, the business, your friends? Tell me everything."

"Savannah's still there, probably always will be. Business is booming, and my one and only friend—"

Kim broke off with a scowl. "Never mind that. How are *you?* That's why I'm here."

"I'm fine," he snapped. "Don't I look fine?"

He was heartily sick of being babied. For a man used to running a major dairy operation, sitting in a hospital bed chafed like a cheap pair of boxers.

What was this about her one and only friend? That didn't sound like Kim. At Gainsville High she'd been the center of the social whirl, forever busy, always laughing and happy. Sure her excessive exuberance frequently got her into trouble, but that was just because there was no one as full of fire and life as Kim.

"You look great, Daddy. Why, I'll be able to get back to Georgia in no time at all."

She'd just arrived, yet couldn't wait to leave. John had a pretty good idea why.

"Can't you stay a few weeks? I'm sure there are a lot of people who'd like to see you after all these years."

She tensed, then glanced away. "And I'm sure everyone has forgotten all about me."

"You think Becky Jo's forgotten you?" He paused, considered, then dropped the bait. "What about Brian Riley?"

She flinched and her face paled.

John sighed. *Riley.* Well, he couldn't say he hadn't known.

Kim stood, turned and became overly interested in the get-well cards taped to his wall, which gave John a few moments to think.

Brian and Kim had been the golden couple of

Gainsville High. Then a week after graduation they had eloped. In a community the size of Gainsville, the scandal had been enormous. The only reason to run off and get married was a reason for which John had planned to kick Brian Riley's ass.

He had raved; he had rambled, but as Ellie pointed out, there was nothing to be done. They were of age, and most likely already married.

Then the two of them had returned to town a few days after they'd left, not only unmarried but barely speaking. Kim had denied she was pregnant, and that appeared to be the case.

Relieved that she'd come back safe and sound, and thrilled to learn she hadn't ruined her life, John left further questions for later. Kim hadn't been herself— quiet and reserved—and he'd figured she and Brian had fought, then broken up. She needed time to get over her first love.

Though John and Kim were close, he just wasn't the kind of guy who liked to talk about feelings. He especially didn't want to talk to his baby girl about her relationship with a boy. John shuddered. Particularly not a boy she'd run off with.

Call him a coward; that was what he was. He'd been too uncomfortable to ask her the questions that needed to be asked, and thus had never been able to ask her anything about that time at all. Because a week after she returned, Kim was gone.

His own theory had been that Brian wanted to stay and Kim just had to go. Brian loved the farm; Kim had always loathed it. And though John had missed her, he had wanted more for Kim, because more was what Kim had wanted for herself. But now he wondered if the more she'd gone searching for had in fact turned out to be less.

Brian had never been the same. John glanced at the rigid back of his daughter, and he remembered the lesser light of laughter in her eyes. Maybe Kim had never been the same, either.

"I need a cigarette," he mumbled.

Kim returned to the chair at his bedside. Her eyes no longer laughed at all, not even a bit, and that made him nervous. "What?"

"No more cigarettes, Daddy."

"Not here, I know." He waved his hand at the oxygen. "I could blow myself up."

"No more cigarettes, period."

His head became light and his fingers itchy. John could only stare at her blankly. The words *no more cigarettes* did not compute.

"Daddy?" She snapped her fingers in front of his face. He scowled at her. "I'm just going to get this all over with at once, okay?"

"All what?"

"No more smoking." She held up a thumb, then proceeded to tick off horrible news with each successive finger. "Less drinking, less cholesterol, less work."

"Why don't you just say, less life? That's what you mean."

"There'll be *no* life if you keep on the way you have been."

"This life was good enough for my father and his father before him."

"Grampa stroked out at sixty and Great-grampa dropped dead in his living room at fifty-eight."

"Happy as clams with a beer in one hand and a cigarette in the other."

"Daddy…"

"Fine. I take it this comes from the doctors."

"No, I made it up."

He'd forgotten her smart mouth, which had always gotten her into trouble with her mother and amused the hell out of him—though he'd tried his best to hide it. Right now, he could understand why Ellie had wanted to smack Kim stupid from the age of thirteen until… Well, knowing Ellie, she still wanted to smack Kim. She never had, never would, but she'd probably always want to.

"Not going to be easy," he observed.

"Nothing worthwhile ever is."

True enough. Getting her to stick around wasn't going to be easy, either, but it would be worthwhile. If only to erase the shadows from her eyes, which the longer he looked at them the more they reminded him of the shadows that haunted Brian Riley's eyes, too.

KIM WENT TO BED EARLY. Not only because she was exhausted from flying halfway across the country, then driving a few hours more, but because she was weary of trying to be nice. She'd lived alone too long, or maybe not long enough.

She walked on eggshells with her mother. She'd

never been sure what to say to her. They had nothing in common but a blood type.

Her brothers were loud. They always had been. But even with just three of the five at the table, the volume was so much more than Kim was accustomed to these days that she had to fight the urge to press her palms over her ears.

So she'd pleaded exhaustion and fled. The bright fluorescent bulb in her room revealed too many things—pictures, pom-poms, purity. She snapped off the light before rooting out an oversize T-shirt from her suitcase, putting it on, then climbing into bed. Tomorrow was soon enough to face the past, wasn't it?

But her mind had other ideas. She came awake in the tiny space of time between night and day with a damp trail of tears from her eyes to her neck.

Memories flickered; voices drifted from the past; feelings she'd tried to deny, prayed to forget came back to haunt her in the place where everything began.

How long had it been since she'd had the dream? Not long enough.

Experience told Kim she wouldn't sleep any more, so she tugged a pair of sweatpants over her legs and crept downstairs. Planning to make coffee and watch the sun rise, instead she became sidetracked by a photograph on the wall in the hall.

Senior prom forever frozen in time. She'd worn a red dress and black patent leather slings with three-inch heels. Even so, the boy in the black suit and red cummerbund towered over her. Tall and slim, he nevertheless had amazing muscles beneath that suit. She could still recall the shape of every one, the texture of his skin, the beat of his heart. Those memories had tortured her for months after she'd left. Until she'd learned how to make them fade with a combination of loud music, tequila and pretty men.

Eight years had passed, but she hadn't forgotten Brian Riley's face. How could she when saw it so often in her sleep? In the picture he stared at her as if his world lay right there in her eyes. His expression had always thrilled Kim, even as it had frightened her. She couldn't live up to that, and she'd only proven it in the most horrific and painful way.

Kim frowned and stepped closer, peering at the photograph. She blinked, then blinked again, but what she saw in the picture did not disappear. She'd never noticed that she looked at Brian the same way that he looked at her.

"What are you starin' at?"

She gave a squeak of alarm and leaped away from the wall, spinning around and slamming straight into Dean.

"You always were a sneak," she whispered fiercely.

"I wasn't sneaking. You were just too fascinated with your boyfriend to hear me."

"He's not my boyfriend," she snapped before she realized he was baiting her. Honestly, the next thing she knew she'd be chanting, "Na, na, na, na, na," and ducking behind the sofa when Dean threw something at her.

"In that case, you won't need to see him at all while you're here. If I were you, I'd be afraid to face him."

She was, but to let one of her brothers smell her fear was to beg for trouble. Kim had learned that lesson very young. Once they had discovered her aversion to mice they'd devised many ingenious ways to ensure that she became outright and irrationally terrified of them.

She might have lived in the laid-back South for eight years, but that didn't make her brain dead. Never let them see you sweat was a very good motto for the little sisters of the world.

"I'm not afraid of anyone," she lied. "How are they? The Rileys?"

Dean hesitated just long enough for Kim's heart to thud with dread. "Well, hell, now that you're here, you'll find out anyway. His parents died about six months ago."

She gasped, shocked and saddened. The Rileys had always been kind to her. Much kinder than she had been to them. Why on earth had no one told her?

"Car crash," Dean answered before she could ask. "Brian wanted a very quick, very small, very *private* funeral."

"But—"

"He's had a hard time. So stay away from him, you hear?"

She wanted to stay away. Oh, how she wanted to. But she couldn't. Kim turned toward the stairs.

"You're going over there?" Dean's voice was so

incredulous she would have laughed in his face, were she capable of laughing anymore.

"It's the decent thing to do."

"Since when have you been decent?"

Though she deserved that, it didn't make the words any easier to take. The truth only intensified her guilt.

Kim ran upstairs so that Dean wouldn't notice how just the thought of seeing Brian made her want to crawl back in her bed and mewl like a newborn kitten.

CHAPTER THREE

BRIAN RILEY BEGAN his day as he had begun every day for the past twenty years—milking cows.

Of course, a few things had changed over time. As a child he'd followed his father from cow to cow while he swabbed off udders and attached milking machines. Dad would pour the milk from the machine into a pail, change the filter, toss the used one to a barn cat, then methodically hook up another cow before dragging the full pail to the milk house and emptying it into a cooler.

In the intervening years, a genius had come up with the idea of bringing the cows to a milking parlor and pumping the milk from the machine directly to the cooler.

Brian stretched his back. The new way was worlds better than the old one, but it still meant bending to hook up the milking machine. New and improved dairy farming still hadn't figured out how to move the udder any higher on a cow.

The sun was just peaking over the horizon, spreading golden fingers of dawn across his shorn cornfields, when Brian slapped the last bovine rump and lifted his face to the sun.

The red barn proved a stark contrast to the bright-blue sky. The weathervane at the highest point turned slowly. There was a bite in the air this morning. He smelled snow in the future. Better repair the hole in the barn roof while he still could.

He had just hoisted himself onto the far side of the building when a car turned into his lane. The crunch of gravel beneath tires grew louder as the vehicle came closer.

Since the visitor had to be Dean, one of Dean's brothers or another area farmer, he shrugged and got to work. Whoever had come would search for him or leave him a note.

Brian didn't have many friends, which was just the way he liked it. He had a farm to run and little time for fooling around. Not that he was the fooling-around type—at least, not anymore.

His fingers clenched on the hammer as memories of when life had been full of fun, and so had he, flickered. His throat went thick; his stomach churned. He slammed the hammer onto a nail with undue force, and then he did it again.

As always, when he began to remember, began to feel and to mourn, Brian turned to the farm, to his work, to his legacy. Over the past eight years this place and his responsibilities to it had saved him more times than he cared to count.

The sudden and strident bleat of a sheep made him pause, lift his head, frown. Ba sounded seriously pissed, which meant trouble.

His mother had started raising Shetland sheep as a

hobby. The breed had been placed on the endangered list in 1977 and Clara Riley had taken up the cause, becoming one of the premier breeders in the Midwest. Brian had continued the tradition, unable to get rid of the animals his mother had doted on.

Most Shetlands were calm and easygoing, no problem to raise or to keep. But Ba had been different from the beginning. Though she did like to be petted, even wagged her tail when he did so, with strangers she was cranky and often aggressive. Such behavior was more common in a ram than a ewe, but even so, unusual in a Shetland. Still, Ba could distinguish friends from enemies better than any watchdog he'd ever had.

Since enemies were few and far between in the Illinois countryside, Brian moved nearer the edge of the roof. He leaned forward, trying to get a glimpse of the visitor just as a black sheep butted a woman around the corner.

Suddenly he couldn't breathe; he couldn't move; all he could do was stare.

Oh, God, no, he thought. *Please, not now. Not ever. Don't make me see her again.*

As if she'd heard him begging, Kim looked up and straight into his eyes. He stiffened. His foot slipped.

Suddenly he was falling down. Brian grabbed for the edge of the roof, caught it for an instant, slowing his momentum, but he couldn't keep a grip, and over the edge he went. Right before he struck the ground with a bone-breaking thud, Brian remembered.

God had started ignoring him a long time ago.

KIM SCREAMED as Brian tumbled off the roof and hit the stretch of cement beneath. He landed face first, his hands taking the brunt of the blow. Still, the force with which he'd fallen brought his head forward, and his temple connected to the ground with a sickening thunk. He lay still.

Kim took one step, and the psycho black sheep butted her back.

"*Baaa,*" the thing admonished.

"*Baaa* yourself."

Kim sidestepped the walking wool ball, and when it would have butted her again, she shoved the animal with her hip. The sheep's hooves scrambled and slid on the cement and Kim made good her escape.

She might be small in stature, but she'd learned how to best bigger animals than this. Eighteen years with the Luchetti brothers had honed her survival skills. Kim glanced over her shoulder and smirked as the hunk of mutton retreated around the corner of the barn. She hadn't lost the hard-won talent.

Brian turned over with a groan. Though Kim's heart beat so fast she couldn't think, couldn't hear, could scarcely breathe, that he was moving on his own calmed her a bit.

But when she knelt at his side and he reached up to touch her cheek, her composure fled. She'd feared coming home would bring back all the pain. Then this morning as she'd stared at the last picture ever taken of them together, she'd discovered the true danger was in remembering the joy. Now she realized a more potent threat. His touch could still make her yearn.

"A dream," he murmured. "Gotta be."

He looked so much the same, yet incredibly different. His light-brown hair curled tightly—something he had always hated and she had loved. How many times had he shorn his curls ruthlessly away, only to have them curl ever tighter as soon as he washed them?

Her fingers had often tangled in those curls, straightening then releasing, allowing their softness to brush at the sensitive junctures where one finger curved into the next. She wanted to touch them now, trace a fingertip along the streaks left by the sun.

His eyes were an odd shade of gray that could turn blue or hazel depending on his mood and the depth of his tan. Right now they were astonishingly light against his summer-bronzed skin.

He was older; so was she. Experiences they had shared and those they had not marred his face and flickered in his eyes. He was taller, broader, stronger, but he was Brian and she remembered...everything.

She reached up, not sure if she meant to press his palm closer or pull him away before she begged. But as she touched his wrist he caught his breath on a hiss of pain and jerked his arm in toward his belly.

Lustful thoughts fled, chased away by mortification that she could feel such things still, and feel them for a man who'd just tumbled fifteen feet to the ground. She was pathetic.

"Where does it hurt?"

"Where doesn't it?"

"Where does it hurt the most?" she clarified.

He tried to sit up and collapsed again. "My wrists. Damn."

She glanced at the hands he cradled protectively against his body. They were scraped from the cement, but they hadn't started to swell. Yet.

She lifted her gaze to his face, which was another story. "You've got a goose egg on your forehead the size of Chicago."

"Well, that explains the headache. I hate Chicago."

Her lips twitched. Brian had always been able to make her laugh—one of the things that had drawn her to him.

Maybe this reunion wasn't going to be so awful after all. Maybe they could be friends, or at least civil. Maybe he'd forgotten what she couldn't seem to, gotten past what she would never overcome.

"I'll drive you to the hospital," she offered.

"No, thanks."

"You can't drive yourself. Let me help you up." She reached for his arm and he flinched.

"Don't touch me!"

She gaped at the fury in his voice and on his face. The Brian she'd known would never have spoken to her, or anyone, like that.

Her eyes glanced off the knot on his head. "Do you know who I am? What month is this?"

He gave her a withering glare. "You're Kim Luchetti. Or at least you were when you walked out on me. And it's October. I haven't lost my mind, not since I fell in love with you, anyway."

Kim sighed. He hadn't forgotten. He hadn't forgiven her, either. Could she blame him?

"What the hell are you doing here, Kim?"

"I—I came to say hello."

"Hello."

He struggled to stand, the task made difficult by the fact that he couldn't use his hands, and he didn't want her help. As soon as he gained his feet, Brian strode away.

"Goodbye." He tossed the word over his shoulder without so much as a glance.

Kim stood there a moment, uncertain. She wasn't sure what she'd been hoping for when she'd come here. Absolution? Perhaps. What she hadn't expected was to find an angry and sarcastic man inhabiting the body of her once joyous and gentle Brian. He'd obviously been spending far too much time with Dean.

"I just want to help you," she murmured.

He stopped, gave a sarcastic snort and shook his head as he turned. "I needed your help once and you weren't here. I learned to live without you, Kim. I'll take care of myself now, just like I did then."

He continued around the side of the barn, presumably in the direction of the house and his truck. Kim followed more slowly.

He'd learned to live without her? That stung. But had she expected him to sit around moping? She certainly hadn't.

The memory of how she'd managed to survive the death of so many dreams made her uncomfortable in the presence of the one who had given them to her.

She never wanted Brian to know what she had done on certain dark and lonely nights over the past few years. She had never learned to live without him—at least not sober.

She slipped, slid and stumbled across the gravel driveway in her completely inappropriate lemon-yellow platforms. Before she could reach her car, the black sheep barred her way.

"Baaa." The animal lowered her head.

"So help me, if she butts me again, Brian, she's going to have intimate knowledge of a yellow high heel."

"House, Ba. Go on."

Amazingly, the animal clomped away, climbing the steps and collapsing in a wool heap on the porch. Kim had never considered sheep the brightest of beings. That was why people with no minds of their own were referred to as one of them.

"What happened to Rebel?" she asked, alluding to the Rileys' cow dog.

She'd thought Brian's face was expressionless before, but it became shuttered now. "He chased one too many cars."

A common ailment of farm dogs. "I'm sorry. And I'm sorry about your parents, too. I didn't know until I came back."

"Why would you?"

Though she could understand Brian's pain, his continued gibes were beginning to make her fingers curl into fists again. She took a moment for a deep breath and deliberately shook her hands loose. Ignoring his rhetorical question, she jerked a thumb toward the porch. "What's with the sheep?"

He shrugged. "Her mother died at birth. I bottle-fed her, kept her in a dog cage in the kitchen. When she got bigger, she followed Rebel around. Started doing what he did—announcing visitors, keeping them away from the house, herding the cattle to the barn. It was weird. But she's an excellent watchdog."

"Watch-sheep, you mean."

"Whatever."

"And her name is Ba?"

"So she says."

He reached for the door handle on his truck, then released it with a muffled curse. Kim stifled her instinctive need to touch him, soothe him, hold him. She crossed the remaining distance to her car, opened the passenger door and raised a brow in his direction.

He sighed, defeated, and came around the front, frowning at the hood the entire way. "Ever hear the term *American made?*"

"Ever hear the term *bite me?*"

He blinked and for a minute she thought he might laugh. Kim wanted to hear him laugh so badly she even leaned toward him, wishing it so.

Instead, he clamped his lips and folded his long length into her little foreign car.

THE RIDE to the hospital was blissfully silent, except for the thunderous pain inside Brian's head and the whimper coming from his wrists.

He couldn't believe he'd taken one glance at her

and fallen on his face. It was every adolescent nightmare come true.

Brian found himself staring at Kim's ridiculous excuse for shoes. His gaze wandered up her legs—she had always had spectacular legs, among other things—taking in her orange skirt and flamboyant, Hawaiian-print blouse. Only Kim would wear yellow high heels and a short skirt to a dairy farm.

What had charmed him once only proved to him now that though she'd been born here, just as he had, she had never truly belonged. Kim had no allegiance to the land, no fondness for the farm; she did not share his devotion to the legacy.

Her leaving had probably been the best thing for everyone, but the fact remained, she had walked out on him when he was in agony—an open, aching, bleeding wound where his heart had been. He'd had no one to talk to, no one to share his grief with. He'd tried to forget but been unable to. Just as he had not been able to forgive.

"You never did learn how to dress for the farm, did you?"

"If you mean overalls and boots, damn straight. They make me look stumpy."

"And how you look means so much in the scheme of life."

"My scheme of life is none of your business, Brian Riley."

"You made that clear a long time ago."

Kim took the turn from the back roads onto the main highway fast enough to make gravel spray across a grassy ditch. He cut a glance her way, waiting for the explosion. Though her jaw worked in agitation, none came.

In the old days Kim had been a volcano forever on the verge of eruption—to anger, to laughter, to passion. Apparently she'd learned to keep her emotions under control, as he had.

They reached the hospital in short order. She pulled up to the emergency room entrance and parked in a loading zone. Her blatant misbehavior made him as uneasy now as it had in the past.

"My legs are fine." He pointed to the visitors' lot several hundred yards away. "We can park over there."

"I see your raving only-child syndrome is still in full force." She flicked on the hazard lights and clipped around the car to let him out.

Only-child syndrome had been Kim's phrase for Brian's "toe the line, follow the rules, always be a good boy no matter what" personality. Kim's disregard for such run-of-the-mill concerns had fascinated him, excited him, ruined him.

Brian managed to get out of the car without her help, though it wasn't easy. He was being foolish and stubborn, but the thought of her touching him made Brian's stomach dance with panic. He tried to blame the pitch and roll in his belly on the ache in his head. He could not still be susceptible to the hold she'd always had on him. He *would* not be.

She ushered him into the Gainsville ER. Her gaze flicked around the room. A few words to the nurse at the desk and people scurried to and fro. Kim ordered a wheelchair; a wheelchair she got. She wanted a private room; he had one. A doctor? Shazaam! A doctor appeared.

Brian watched in amazement. She looked the same; she even acted the same—laughing, smiling, touching people in that casual way she had that made them feel special—but she was also very different. She no longer asked for things; she expected them. She knew who to talk to, what to say to get what she wanted with minimal trouble or time. Kim was in charge from the moment she entered the building.

"Mr. Riley, did you lose consciousness at any time?"

With difficulty Brian pulled his attention from the sight of Kim working the emergency room to the doctor at his side.

Lose consciousness? He remembered falling, hitting the ground, pain in his head, his wrists, the sight of Kim, pain in his chest, believing she was a dream, then—

"I must have," he muttered. There was no other excuse for touching her face and wishing she were real.

"Humph." The doctor scribbled something on his clipboard.

"Is that bad?"

"I think we'll keep you here for a few hours, just in case."

"In case what?"

But the doctor had already strode away to join Kim

outside the open door, drawn like a fly to an open can of pop, willing to drown in sugar just for a taste of her mouth.

Brian rubbed his eyes. He had definitely hit his head too hard if he was waxing poetic about flies—hell, if he was waxing poetic about anything. He was not now, nor had he ever been, a poetic man.

"I'll have someone bring his insurance card." Kim smiled and touched the doctor's shoulder. The man practically fell to the ground and kissed her yellow shoes. "You just order him that little old CAT scan, hmm?"

Kim had matured into a take-charge woman. He shouldn't be surprised. She'd always wanted to be a lawyer, which Brian had thought an odd choice for a girl who didn't care to follow the rules. But then again, how many juvenile delinquents wound up as cops or preachers?

When she was fifteen, Kim's maternal grandmother had left her enough money to achieve her dream. But in the end, Kim had become a paralegal not a lawyer, then bought into a law practice in Savannah. He had to wonder what had changed her mind.

"Looks like you did a number on those wrists."

He glanced up. Kim watched him warily from the doorway. Suddenly he remembered what she smelled like in a haymow at dawn, what she tasted like at midnight in the cool, silvered grass of a meadow. He shook his head to make the images go away and wound up with a slice of pain for his foolishness.

"I figured that out two minutes after I fell," he muttered. "How bad are they?"

"One's broken, maybe both. They're going to take you to X ray in a minute. But it's your head he's worried about."

"Me, too." He had to be insane to be thinking about the scent of her skin and the taste of her lips.

"He doubts you cracked your skull, and so do I."

"Why's that?"

"It would take something harder than cement to bust that head."

"Nice. Kick a man when he's down."

Brian had meant to be funny, but he hadn't been in so long, he seemed to have lost the talent. Something flickered in her eyes, and for a moment he thought she might cry. Instead, Kim straightened her shoulders and took a step backward out of his room.

"That seems to be one of my specialties," she said, and then she was gone.

"DOES EVERYTHING you touch turn to shit?"

Kim considered slamming down the pay phone hard enough to give Dean a ruptured eardrum. But then she'd just be proving him right.

"Brian needs his wallet." She was proud when her voice didn't shake. "And he could probably use you, too, since you're his best friend."

Lord knows why.

"Hey, someone had to be."

She ignored that gibe. She was getting very good at

it. "Just go to his house, get his wallet and get over here."

"Who died and appointed you princess? Oh, wait, you were born one." He slammed down the phone, and then Kim was the one with the earache. Would she ever learn?

She and Dean had never been pals. He had resented her relationship with their father and deplored her inability to get along with their mother. Nothing she did had ever been right enough for Dean. Leaving his best friend had no doubt been the last straw. Dean was nothing if not loyal—to a fault.

Though Kim and Brian were the same age, she'd been just a nuisance to both him and her brothers until their junior year of high school—when everything had changed.

Dean had graduated and started to work full-time for their father. Brian had suddenly noticed Kim wasn't so annoying after all, and they had become inseparable. Dean had made his displeasure quite clear. But hormones were a powerful thing.

Kim had never understood what Brian saw in her cranky, sarcastic brother, but they'd been friends since they were old enough to follow their fathers around milking. Maybe that was what bound them together— the love of the farm, the land and the animals—things she could not fathom.

With Brian at X ray and nothing to do but wait, Kim traversed the bustling halls of Gainsville Memorial until she reached her father's room, then stepped inside.

At the sound of the door closing, he glanced up from the notepad in his lap, Creating knock-knock jokes again, no doubt—a man had to have a hobby.

An immediate smile of welcome creased his face. The panic that had been pulsing in Kim's throat since she'd watched Brian fall, the sadness and the guilt she'd been fighting, threatened to break free.

Her father's smile became a frown as he sensed her distress. "What's the matter?"

To her mortification, Kim burst into tears. He opened his arms, and she went into them gladly. She couldn't recall the last time she'd cried. Since leaving here, she'd found very little worth spilling tears over.

He let her wind down before he asked her again. "What's the matter?"

She didn't want to talk about it, but he'd hear the story soon enough.

Kim raised her head, plucked tissues from the box on his nightstand and scrubbed half the makeup off her face. When she was certain she no longer resembled a waterlogged raccoon, she took the chair next to the bed.

"I went to see Brian."

"How did that go?"

"I just brought him into emergency."

Her father's eyebrows shot up. "Not well, then."

She shook her head and quickly explained what had happened. "Dean is right. Everywhere I go, disaster follows. I should have stayed away from Brian."

For more reasons than one. Ever since she'd seen him, touched him and he'd touched her, her body tingled, her mind remembered and her heart yearned. She felt alive in a way she hadn't for a long, long time, and that was more dangerous than a gainer from the roof of a barn.

"You know what you have to do, don't you?"

Her father's solemn question brought Kim's head up with a snap. "Do?"

"To make this right."

For an instant she thought he knew the secret that had sent her running. But there was no making that right. Not ever.

"How is Brian going to take care of his place with two broken wrists?" he asked.

Her eyes widened. She'd been feeling so guilty she hadn't thought past the initial tragedy. "He might not have *two* broken wrists."

Her father waved off the rationalization. "One is enough."

"Dean can help him."

"In the barn. But he's going to need help in the house, and Dean won't be able to stay. He's going to have to help me."

"I'll help you."

"That's sweet, honey, but when was the last time you drove a tractor and spread manure?" Since the answer was never, and they both knew it, he continued. "Brian won't be able to cook or clean. He won't even be able to dress himself for a while."

Kim's cheeks burned. She'd had plenty of practice *undressing* Brian Riley. "Not me, Daddy."

"If not you, then who?"

"Anyone but me." Her voice was too loud. Her father was looking at her too closely. If he kept staring at her like that she just might tell him everything. She'd never been very good at keeping secrets from her daddy. Another reason she'd had to run.

"I think it would be best if you helped Brian, don't you?"

No! Helping Brian would be a disaster. Just as it had been a disaster to see him. But Kim knew the inevitable when she heard it.

Until Brian was able to care for himself, she was going to become exactly what she'd always feared.

A farmer's wife.

CHAPTER FOUR

"I HAVE NO IDEA where she went." Dean yanked the wheel of his pickup truck to the right and bounced onto the gravel lane leading to Brian's place. "Knowing Kimmy, as far away from trouble as she could get."

Brian winced, then pretended he'd bumped one of his wrists against his belly. He had a knot the size of a golf ball on his head, two splints held on with Ace bandages and a matching set of slings. He'd been provided with plenty of drugs and orders to keep his wrists above his heart as much as possible for the next several days to reduce the swelling. Only then would he receive two casts.

He *had* broken both wrists, and according to the doctor he was lucky. The breaks weren't bad enough to need surgery, and he could very well be dead. But right now, with his wrists screaming, his head pounding and his stomach churning, dead didn't look half-bad.

"I wouldn't be surprised if she hightailed it back to Georgia," Dean continued. "She came, she saw, she screwed things up. Her work here is done."

Dean stopped in front of the house, shut off the

truck, glanced at Brian and sighed. "Sorry, man. I should keep my mouth shut."

"You should. But you won't."

Silence descended. Dusk hovered, heavy and damp. When Brian stepped out of the car, his breath would smoke the air, icy dew would bathe his cheeks and the honk of geese in the distance would make him think of how lonely he would have been these past few years without Dean.

Of course he would never put such feelings to words—he was a guy, after all. But truth was truth. He and Dean were pals—always had been, always would be—no matter what. Friendship like theirs didn't come around every day, sometimes not even in every lifetime.

"I'm sorry," Dean repeated. "You know Kim and me—we've never seen eye to eye."

Brian snorted. "Is that what you call it?"

"What would you call it?"

Brian wasn't sure. He'd never understood the anger between Dean and Kim. Of course, he'd never had a brother or a sister, but still, if he had, he liked to think that he would have befriended, not belittled, him or her. As long as Brian could remember if there was a puddle, Dean pushed Kim into it. If there was a clever put-down to be had, Dean was certain to be the butt of it. Brian had tried to make peace, and in the end only made things worse.

"I don't know," Brian admitted. "But I do know I'm tired of it. Can't everyone just get along?"

"No," Dean said simply, and climbed out of the

truck. He came around and opened Brian's door. But he knew better than to help him out. He did, however, stand close enough to catch Brian if he fell, once again, on his face.

"Baaa!" The black sheep scampered around the side of the house.

"Some watch-sheep you are," Dean sneered. "I could have cleaned the place out by now. And what would you have done?"

Ba tilted her head in a fair imitation of a dog that recognizes a word in a conversation, but isn't quite sure which one it is. *"Baaa!"*

"Exactly." Dean turned his attention to Brian. "When are you going to get a dog?"

Brian remembered burying his last dog, after burying his parents, after burying his—

"I'm not," he snapped. "Dogs are overrated. Ba and I get along just fine."

"But you're not fine, and you haven't been for a long time."

Already headed toward the house and an overdue date with his couch, Brian paused. "What are you talking about?"

Dean glanced longingly at the barn, even leaned in that direction. Heart-to-heart talks were not his style. Then his shoulders slumped, and he kicked the gravel with the toe of his knee-high rubber boots. "I'm talking about you. You don't go anywhere. You don't do anything. You won't even name your animals."

"What?"

"Ba? What kind of name is that? I suppose you call the cats Meow and the cows Moo."

Brian looked away. "So?"

"You do, don't you?" Dean cursed beneath his breath. "Have you touched a woman since Kim left?"

Brian gaped. Dean might not know when to shut up, but he did know better than to ask personal questions. Which was why they were still friends.

"Piss off," Brian said, and headed for the house again.

Dean's heavy hand landed on his shoulder. Rather than struggle and end up in more pain, Brian stopped, then turned.

"I'll take that as a no," Dean murmured.

Brian made his face go blank—something he'd become very good at.

"There!" Dean waved a finger in Brian's face. "That's what I mean. You used to be a different guy. Happy. Funny. Cheery, even. No one could be sad when you were around. But not anymore."

"If you don't like how I turned out, then why do you hang around?"

"I never said I didn't like you just the way you are. In my opinion you were always too cheerful. That yippy-skippy stuff used to drive me nuts. Only idiots are that happy."

Brian's lips twitched. Trust Dean to put everything in perspective. He *had* been an idiot back then. Just call him a fool for love.

"I don't want you to backslide," Dean continued.

"Maybe if you'd nail someone else, you'd get over her."

And trust Dean to take the most wonderful experience of Brian's life and reduce it to smut. But then, Dean had never been in love. Considering his suave manner and charming vocabulary, one had to ask why. Brian snorted.

"That's better." Dean reached out to punch Brian in the shoulder, then thought better of it and let his fist drop back to his side. "I'll go and milk your cows before they explode. Then I'd better get back to mine."

He trotted toward the barn, leaving Brian alone as the cool night mist settled in his hair. He glanced up to discover a full-moon rising. No wonder this day had been nothing short of insanity. There was something to be said about full moon madness. Animals and people behaved differently when the moon hung bright and heavy in the sky.

"*Baaa!*" The ewe butted his hip, angling for a pat, but Brian was fresh out of arms. Instead, he rubbed her head with his elbow, letting her lean against him as he contemplated the moon and his life.

In the world of men, what was never said had never happened. Therefore, because Dean and he had never discussed his sleeping with Kim, he never had. Lucky for Brian. Because even though Dean might not want to hug and kiss his sister, that didn't mean he wouldn't be happy to kick the ass of anyone who had done that and more—even if that someone was his best friend. He'd be honor bound. It was a guy thing.

Dean's question about sex since Kim suggested that he knew there'd been more between Brian and Kim than snuggling in the back seat of a Chevy Nova. But once again, if Brian didn't tell, Dean would continue to pretend it had never happened. Brian wished he could do the same.

There *had* been other women since. Not many, but enough to know he'd had something special with her. Kim had been his first; she wouldn't be his last. She was merely his only.

He might still love her.... Brian sighed and turned away from the bright, shiny moon. But that didn't mean he couldn't hate her, too.

KIM WAS ABLE to get home, throw what she'd taken out of her suitcase back in and escape before anyone saw her. She left a note for whoever might care and got back into the car.

Tempted to put the top down and let the fresh air stream through her hair, across her face—anything to release the tight, trapped feeling in her chest—she refrained. The temperature was near freezing, with a freezing drizzle expected before morning. She might be tired, sad and a bit scared, but she wasn't stupid. She did not need a cold on top of everything else.

Five minutes later, she parked her car next to Dean's truck. Her lip curled at the sight, and the desire to flee nearly overwhelmed her. But she wasn't going to run. Not this time.

She owed Brian. Not only for what had happened today, but for what had happened before. Maybe if she could do something for him now, she might be able to get over what had happened then.

Kim climbed the steps, suitcase in hand and knocked. Then, remembering Brian's injury, she turned the doorknob and stepped inside.

He leaned against the wall, directly across from the door, arms crossed over his chest, not by choice but because of the slings supporting them. A frown creased his forehead as he contemplated the suitcase in her hand.

A dizzy sense of déjà vu swept over her. Though this particular situation had never happened, she must have imagined it a thousand times.

He raised his gaze from the suitcase to her face. His frown was gone, replaced by an expression she was beginning to loathe. Complete blankness, utter stillness, as if there was no one home behind those eerie gray eyes. This was a man she did not know, a man far different from the one she had loved, and he scared her.

"Leaving so soon?" he murmured. "And saying goodbye? My, my, times have changed."

She deserved his sarcasm. But that didn't make it any easier to take.

"More than you think," she snapped. "I'm moving in."

His eyebrows shot up. His shoulders came away from the wall. At least he was moving; at least he had some expression on his face, some life in his eyes.

"Like hell."

"Yes, I'm sure it will be."

She plowed past him and into the kitchen. There wasn't much he could do to stop her with both arms strapped to his chest.

"I don't need your help."

Kim set the suitcase on a chair. "We've already had this discussion. You needed me once and I wasn't here. Blah, blah, blah."

His eyes narrowed; his lips thinned. Why was she baiting him? Because seeing him angry was so much easier than seeing him indifferent.

"I'm here now," she continued. "And I'm not leaving."

"Until things get rough, anyway."

Now her lips tightened. "Listen, I feel responsible."

"Responsible? You? Since when?"

"Dammit, Brian!" she exploded. Then she saw him smirk and realized he'd been baiting her as much as she'd been baiting him. She took a deep breath, counted to ten and tried again.

"I'll stay until you can take care of yourself. Someone has to."

"Why does it have to be you?"

"My question exactly." She rubbed between her eyes with her thumb. "Do you have a better idea?"

"Yeah, anyone but you."

The silence between them was so complete she heard the cows lowing in the barn.

"*Is* there anyone else?" she asked quietly.

Brian had been a late-life miracle for the Rileys— his mother in her forties when she had her first and only child, his dad in his fifties. Brian was all that was left of them both.

Her eyes burned, and she blinked hard and fast. Now was not the time to bring up the loss of so many things.

"You know there isn't," he said.

She nodded. "My family will help as much as they can, but with Dad out for a while, they're going to be shorthanded, too. I'm dispensable."

"I wouldn't say that."

She cast him a glance, but he had already turned away and she let the comment go. This was going to be difficult enough without analyzing every little thing.

"I'll put my suitcase in the extra room."

He grunted, which she took as a yes because it wasn't a no. She grabbed her bag and went into the room off the kitchen, once reserved for a cook or a hired man. The quilt on the bed was an heirloom, handmade by Bridget O'Riley in the land of Eire and brought to the New World, where some smart-ass clerk on Ellis Island had dropped the *O* and rechristened her Bridget Riley.

The first Rileys in America had worked as domestics. They'd built a railroad and fought for the Union in the Civil War. Kim had always loved to hear stories of Rileys past. That they'd known where they came from had fascinated her.

While her own family tree obviously had roots in Italy, the branches were somewhat tangled. No one knew, or much cared, when the seeds of the Luchettis had hit the shores of the good-old USA. Her mother's family—White by name—was even worse. When Kim had once asked her grandfather where the Whites had come from, he'd said, "Paduka," and that had been the end of that.

Kim tossed her suitcase onto the bed and let her gaze wander over the room. The cracks in the ceiling had been patched; the walls, recently painted. The furniture was heavy, dark and old, but it shone with loving care and a good coat of polish. The floor was clean; the bathroom, too. Not only was Brian a superior farmer, but he appeared to be a superior housekeeper, as well.

Kim wasn't much good at either one. Her mother had tried to mold her into a farmwife, but Kim had resisted every inch of the way. As a result, she was one step above awful when it came to anything domestic. That hadn't mattered a whit in Savannah, where she was a respected career woman. But here…

Kim shook her head. Here her lack of skills in the home would be a serious problem. The more she thought about it, the more stupid the entire plan became. But she'd agreed, and she would stick this out. If only to prove that she could.

The Rileys' farmhouse was even older than the Luchettis' and had been in Brian's family for four generations. The first Riley to farm had been Conner, Brian's great-grandfather. He had bought the place with money earned from working the stockyards of Chicago. After half a lifetime dealing with the end of a cow's life, Conner had dreamed of starting with the beginning. He had made that dream come true and given everything to his son, and the son of his son, and then the son after that.

Kim's eyes were caught by the mirror atop the vanity. Time rolled back and she could see herself sitting on the bench seat, staring into the antique fogginess of the glass.

"Mirror, mirror on the wall, who's the one I love most of all?"

The words echoed in the room. Had she actually said them? She wasn't sure. But childhood games were best left in childhood, along with the answer to that question.

Kim backed out of the room and returned to the kitchen, where Brian stared out the window at the bright lights of the barn. She could tell by the set of his shoulders that he wanted to be out there with the animals instead of in here with her.

"I'll fix you something to eat."

"I'm not hungry."

"Too bad. Because you're eating."

"You can't make me."

She laughed and he turned around. She lowered her gaze to his arms. "I can't?"

Annoyance sparked in his eyes, turning them a darker shade of gray. "I never took you for a bully."

"Yeah? I had some very good teachers. Sit." She dragged a kitchen chair back from the table. The legs scraped loudly across the yellowed linoleum, and they both winced. "The only way you're going to get better is to take care of yourself. And the only way you can do that, is if I do it for you. So you're eating. You're sleeping. You're not lifting a finger—''

''As if I could.''

''Exactly.'' Kim jerked her thumb at the chair. After some hesitation, he sat.

Standing behind and above him, she could see every streak of sunshine in his hair, the whirls and the curls. His neck was brown, smooth, strong. Her fingers ached to touch him as she had so many times before. She even took one step closer and reached out—

''Well, hello, Princess, what brings you out slumming?''

Dean was back from the barn. Kim snatched her hand away and hid it behind her back. But from the cool calculation in Dean's eyes, he'd seen everything. She tilted her chin and met those eyes. ''I'm staying.''

Dean's gaze flicked to Brian's, narrowed, then returned to Kim. ''I don't think so.''

''I don't care what you think. He needs live-in help. Here I am.''

''I'll stay.''

''Daddy says no.''

Dean muttered something vile that would have once earned him the mouth washing to end all mouth washings if Mom had heard.

''Never mind,'' Brian said. ''I already tried to get rid of her.''

''Figures that when you want her to go, she just has to stay, and when you want her to stay—''

The wet dishrag hit him in the face. From Dean's expression, Brian didn't hold with rinsing the thing overly much, if at all. Dean choked and wiped droplets from his cheek.

"Kim, behave," Brian admonished, though his voice sounded suspiciously choked, too.

She smirked at her brother and sidled to the side of the chair, keeping Brian between them. Not that he'd be able to do anything if Dean decided to retaliate, but she felt better anyway. She took a gander at Brian's face and sighed. He might have sounded as though he was laughing, but he didn't look like it. Would she ever be able to make him laugh again?

"What she says makes sense," Brian continued. "She's got time on her hands. And I don't have any hands."

"Princess, you don't know the first thing about working a farm or tending a house."

"I'll learn."

"You never wanted to learn before. Hell, you left him because you were too good to be a farmer's wife."

She winced and glanced at Brian. "Is that what you told him?"

"I didn't tell him anything."

That surprised her. But then again, what could Brian tell? Certainly not the truth.

However, his words explained why Dean seemed to loathe her now even more than before. He thought she'd left Brian for selfish, foolish reasons, and it was better for everyone if he continued to believe that.

"Why don't *you* tell me what happened, Kimmy?"

Brian watched her without a hint of expression on

his face. She closed her eyes so she wouldn't have to look at him as she lied.

"You're right. He had to stay—I just had to go. No farmer's life for me."

"Princess," Dean muttered.

"It wasn't her fault," Brian said.

Kim's eyes snapped open, but Brian had stood and turned toward Dean. She couldn't see his face. She had to sidestep just to see her brother's.

Dean rolled his eyes. "You always say that."

Kim blinked. He did?

"What happened between Kim and me is between Kim and me. And she isn't the only one to blame for what went wrong. It takes two to make—" His voice broke. Kim's eyes burned. She wanted to touch him again, but she knew better.

As one they took a deep breath. "It takes two to make a relationship," he said. "And it takes two to ruin it."

"You're a lot more forgiving than I am."

"There's a surprise," Kim murmured.

Dean shot her a glare, opened his mouth, then shut it again. "Do whatever the hell you want." He threw up his hands. "You always do anyway."

The door slammed behind him, and seconds later his truck roared to life. Gravel spun; the sound of the motor receded until only silence remained.

"Was he talking to me or to you?" Kim asked.

"Not sure. Does it matter?" He sat down as if standing any longer was too much of an effort. His head hung between his shoulders as he stared at the tips of his boots.

"Brian?" He raised his head, tilted it until he could meet her gaze. "Why is he so mad about what happened between you and me?"

"You weren't here when you left."

"By definition."

"Very funny," he said, but he didn't smile. "When I found out you were gone... It wasn't pretty. You broke me, Kim. I didn't think I'd ever put the pieces back together again."

Though his words tore at her, his voice and his expression reminded Kim of a robot in a B-grade sci-fi movie. Brian had always been able to share his heart; he'd been very good at putting feelings into words and into actions. It seemed he hadn't lost his touch with words, only the feelings behind them. Perhaps that was what he'd meant by "broke."

"I'm sorry," she whispered.

"Yeah, well, sorry and a dollar fifty will get me a cup of coffee these days."

Once again not a speck of emotion flickered on his face. He hadn't managed to put himself back together yet, either. But then, despite appearances, neither had she.

"You know, behind all of Dean's sarcasm and crabbiness is a soft heart."

Kim found that hard to believe, but she remained silent.

"He bled for me. I'll never forget that when I was the most alone I've ever been, Dean was here."

"Never forget him, never forgive me."

"Should I?"

Kim didn't bother to answer. Why should he forgive something she could not?

"You never told him the truth," Kim observed.

"I don't *know* the truth. You seemed perfectly happy to marry me one minute, then the next you were gone."

"There was a little more to it than that."

His sigh echoed her own. "I know. So it's easiest to say, if I say anything at all, that we didn't want the same things. We didn't, right?"

She glanced away. "Right."

She'd left and only she knew the reason why. But Kim wasn't going to confess her deepest, darkest guilty secret. Not now when it was too late. The truth would only hurt him more.

Needing something to do with her hands, Kim opened the refrigerator and found herself peering into a great big empty. "Huh," she muttered. "Looks familiar."

Kim rarely cooked, because she couldn't. When she wanted something other than PB and J, she got a date, felling both the hunger bird and the loneliness bird with one stone. Too bad neither one flew away for very long.

She snatched a half-empty jar of jelly from the shelf, opened a cabinet, found the peanut butter, then the bread. She didn't even have to think about where to find a knife. She'd been in this kitchen a hundred times before. Nothing had changed—at least in location.

Moments later she plopped a sandwich in front of Brian and sat down across from him with another for herself. "Mmm, good," he murmured.

"You don't give a girl a lot of options."

She'd meant his lack of food made it difficult to cook, but as soon as she heard her own words Kim caught her breath.

"Shut up, Kim," he said. But there was no heat in the words, no expression on his face to reveal she'd stuck in the knife and twisted it.

She didn't bother to apologize. What could she say? Neither one of them had had any options back then. Or at least they hadn't thought that they had. They'd learned differently soon enough.

He continued to sit in his chair, not eating, almost as though he were waiting for the sandwich to leap up and bite him. The light dawned.

"Oops." Kim jumped to her feet, came around the table and picked up the sandwich. Then she held it to his lips as if he were a baby. Her mind cringed at the thought; she nearly dropped the bread.

Why did the past creep up on her when she least expected it...while performing commonplace tasks that had little to do with the past at all?

His breath brushed her knuckles. He opened his mouth, took a bite, swallowed. His throat convulsed, drawing her gaze to his neck, his collarbone. A single memory was replaced by a hundred others. The spike of that bone against her mouth, the taste of his skin on her tongue, the sound of her name on his lips.

Heavy with PB and J, the sandwich sagged in her hand. Without thought, she tore it in two and placed one half on the plate, then returned the other to his mouth.

The sweet scent of jelly, the tang of yeast, the salt of skin, filled her senses. The response of her body to his was soothingly familiar, yet enticingly new.

There had never been anyone for her but him—in theory, anyway. In practice, she'd tried to prove that what they'd had was just great sex, and that could be had with anyone. She'd only failed miserably, over and over again.

Seemingly unaffected by the intimacy of their situation, Brian took another bite, then another. His teeth grazed her thumb and his lip slid along her finger. A shudder bolted through her body.

She gasped, dropping the sandwich into his lap. He jerked his head back, leaped to his feet, and the bread landed on the floor with a wet plop, an instant before his chair fell over with a clatter.

Their eyes met. He no longer appeared indifferent. She took one step toward him.

"I'm going to bed," he said abruptly.

"I—uh—" She paused, confused. There was something she had to do.

Touch him, kiss him, hold him.

"No!" Her voice was too loud. She took a deep breath, tried again and made a bigger mess of things. "I mean…your shirt—uh—the buttons. Your pants…"

"The zipper?"

She rubbed her forehead. "Let me help you get undressed."

"As tempting an offer as that is, no."

"You can't sleep in your clothes."

"Sure I can." He strode toward the stairs that led from the front hall to the bedrooms above.

Kim scurried after him. "At least let me take off your shoes."

He ignored her and started up.

"Please, Brian. Let me do something."

Maybe it was the *please*. Maybe he really wanted his shoes off. Whatever it was, he stopped, turned and sat on the third step.

Eagerly she rushed forward, knelt and tugged at the laces of his ankle-high boots. She'd done this many times before for her father, but right now her fingers shook, and several minutes passed before she worked the laces free; then she had to tug and tug to get the boots off his feet. When the second one came loose she stumbled backward, nearly fell.

For an instant, Brian's lips quirked. Until she began to smile back and he froze, scowled, stood.

Kim straightened. Even if he hadn't been standing on the third step and she on the floor, Brian would have towered over her. His height, his strength, his gentleness had always made her feel protected.

The considerable breadth he'd added to that height in the past eight years, combined with his new stoic demeanor, ensured that she no longer felt protected, yet still she did not feel endangered. Because she knew instinctively that no matter what she had done, no matter what she might do, Brian would never hurt her physically.

He didn't have to. Just looking at him cut into her soul.

Her eyes lowered to the pulse that fluttered at the hollow of his throat. She wanted to taste him there, open his shirt and discover if his chest was still silky smooth, or if a fine down of hair trailed across his belly and disappeared into his jeans.

She'd known him intimately in the past. She would touch him forever in her dreams. But the man he had become was far different from the boy he had been and resembled not at all the person he'd once hoped to be.

Brian turned and disappeared upstairs without a *good-night*. Kim sat on the steps and held his boots in her lap and wondered how she could still want him when she no longer knew him at all.

CHAPTER FIVE

"THEY TELL ME your heart attack didn't affect your brain, but I have to wonder."

Thinking he must have fallen asleep during a rerun of *ER,* John opened blurry eyes and frowned at the television, which flickered blue light across the ceiling of his darkened hospital room.

No, not *ER,* his guilty little pleasure. Instead a news channel spewed disasters from both the mouth of an anchorwoman who wore more makeup than Bozo the Clown and from a continuous line of blather across the bottom of the screen. Where had the news media come up with the brilliant deduction that the public needed to listen to *and* read the news at the same time? Wasn't life complicated enough already?

"I woke you."

The door to his room was open, spilling artificial light across the floor and framing his Ellie in the doorway like an angel.

"What time is it?" he asked.

"Six-thirty."

The flood of the overhead lights made him curse. She crossed the room and jabbed the television remote at the screen until it went blessedly black and silent.

"Is something wrong?" he asked. "Shouldn't you be home fixing supper?"

She gave him a narrow glare. "There's no one to fix it for. Aaron went to some foot-in-mouth meeting."

"Foot *and* mouth."

"Whatever."

"There isn't any in this country." He frowned. "So what's the meeting about?"

"Helping other countries that *do* have the problem."

Considering Aaron, that figured.

"Where's Evan?"

She shrugged. Evan did what Evan wanted. He always had. As long as he wasn't in jail, they considered themselves lucky.

"Dean milked at the Rileys'," she answered before he could ask. "Then he did ours, then he explained why my daughter has already moved out, before he disappeared, too."

"Brian needs help," John said quickly.

"So I hear. I also hear you're the one who suggested Kim help him." She leaned over and felt his forehead.

John jerked away. He was so tired of being poked and prodded, tested and touched. "What's that for?"

"I have to assume you're running a high fever to suggest something like that."

"What are you talking about? I found a perfectly logical solution to the problem."

"It's logical to send a woman who knows nothing

about farming or housework or cooking to tend a man who can't do anything for himself?''

''Are you worried about Kim or Brian?''

She didn't answer right away; instead, tucked the already skintight corner of his sheet more tightly against the mattress, then smoothed the covers and plumped his pillows. John ground his teeth.

''Both of them,'' she said at last. ''You know what happened last time.''

''No, I don't.''

''He broke her heart and she ran away.''

''You think?''

''I don't know what to think. I never knew. If she was going to talk to anyone, it would have been you.'' She took a deep breath. ''Not me.''

And that preyed on her mind, but just as John couldn't force the relationship he wanted with any one of his sons, Ellie couldn't make Kim into the best friend she'd always wanted.

He reached for her hand, but she turned to straighten the jumble of pills, plastic, books and cards strewn on his nightstand, and he let his arm fall back on top of the now pin straight bedclothes.

Ellie was always in motion, doing two things at once, all the while behind on something else that needed to be done. She was a good farmwife, a great housekeeper and cook and a top-notch mother. But to be honest, her nonstop energy was starting to get on his nerves.

''Knock-knock,'' he murmured.

She didn't even look his way. ''Not now.''

"You'll like this one. I thought of it just for you."

She glanced at him then, rolled her eyes, but her hands kept straightening even as she asked, "Who's there?"

"Ellie."

"Ellie who?"

"Ellie-phants never forget."

She didn't even smile. Instead she slapped his books into a stack, one by one, with a little too much force. What did a guy have to do to get a laugh around here?

"Can't you just relax a minute?" he snapped. "Sit still. Quit touching everything. Quit touching me."

She flinched and he heard what he'd said. "Ellie, I didn't mean—"

Her fingers clenched, crushing the plastic cup in her hand. Then she turned to him, bright spots of color high on her cheeks. "*Don't* call me Ellie," she shouted. "I'm not an elephant or a cow."

Shocked as much by the fact that she'd yelled as by her words—he'd been calling her Ellie for over thirty years—John blurted the first thing that came to his mind. "But I like cows."

"Really? That might explain why you've spent the majority of our marriage with them."

He frowned. What *was* she talking about? He'd tended the animals and the farm; she'd tended the children and the house. That was what they did.

"Is it hot in here?" she muttered, yanking at the collar of her pink floral T-shirt.

The sight of that shirt—short sleeves, light cotton—made John frown some more. Ellie—excuse me,

Eleanor—was always cold. In the early days of their marriage—hell, for *most* of their marriage, just not lately—he'd spent many enjoyable hours warming her up, if not thinking about it.

If the ticker tape on the news had been correct, the temperature outside was thirty degrees. Yet here she stood in a summer shirt and no coat, complaining that she was hot. What was going on?

John was at a loss what to say, what to do. He'd felt like that a lot since waking up in here. When a man's heart failed him, it seemed that pretty much everything else did, too. John had to admit he was a bit nervous to discover what was going to go bad next.

"You feel okay?" he asked.

She growled at him. There was no other word for it. His cool, calm, capable Ellie growled. And John's certain world shook beneath his hospital bed.

"No, I don't feel okay. I feel as if squirrels are running around in my head. Like mice are running all over my skin. I itch. I ache. I feel as though my whole universe is falling apart while my husband thinks up knock-knock jokes about *ellie-phants*. Does that answer your question?"

"Not really."

Her cheeks were flushed; her eyes, bright blue and wild; her hair, silky, long and white. He might have no idea what was the matter with her, but she was still the most beautiful woman he'd ever seen. Because she was his Ellie.

Make that Eleanor.

"Stop worrying," he ventured. "Take a rest. This

hasn't been easy on either one of us. But it's almost over.''

''This is far from over, and I can't rest. You need help. Kim needs help. The boys—''

The panic of a woman who never panicked was not a pretty sight. That was the only reason John spoke foolishly and rashly. He was scared.

''Leave her be,'' he ordered. ''Leave me be. Just leave *everyone* be.''

She blinked and all the color drained from her face as she backed slowly away from him.

''But then what will I be?'' she whispered, and ran from the room.

THE PAIN PILLS mercifully knocked Brian out for most of the night. But long before dawn he rolled onto his wrists and woke both the pain and himself.

He was alone. No surprise there. He always slept alone. No dogs, no cats, no Ba in the house. That way he never awoke in the middle of the night, warm body pressed to his side while sleepy confusion brought hope to his heart, only to have reality dash it dead.

Even if his wrists hadn't howled and his head hadn't ached, the fact that the hard-on he'd been trying to hide from Kim last night was still glaringly present only made Brian certain he would not get back to sleep this morning.

All she'd done was take off his shoes and look at him, and he'd wanted to lay her down on the stairs, bury his face in her hair and his body in hers.

He knew the texture of her skin, the scent of her

neck, the secrets in her heart—because her secrets were his. Secrets they'd buried, secrets they'd discussed with no one, so they'd festered and bled. He could talk about those things with Kim and no one else. That possibility was nearly as seductive as the temptation of her body.

It shamed him to want her after she'd shown him so plainly, so publicly, so painfully that she no longer wanted him. Would the desire ever go away?

There was an alternative method to relieve desire— unfortunately, he was fresh out of hands. Perhaps a shower, preferably ice-cold, would do the trick. But even if he could manage the removal of his clothes and the mechanism on the shower, he wasn't supposed to get his splints wet.

Hell, he was lucky he didn't have to pee, though that would not be the case forever. The enormity of what he could not do swamped him.

That was the *only* reason he'd agreed to let Kim stay. As soon as he was on the mend, he'd get rid of her. It wouldn't be difficult. Getting rid of Kim had never been the problem.

The distant low of a cow, the bleat of a sheep, the murmur of a man's voice tugged Brian out of bed and to the window. Lights sprang to life in the barn, their yellow glow spreading through the windows and across the hood of Dean's truck.

Brian let out a sigh of relief. Help had arrived.

A BANG FOLLOWED by a muffled curse woke Kim out of a sound sleep. From the slant of the sun through the window, she'd overslept. Some farmer's wife she made.

Kim groaned and pulled the quilt over her head. She had not fallen asleep easily, and once asleep, her dreams had not let her rest.

What did she expect? To lie in Brian's house and know peace and understanding even from herself? That would be more of a fantasy than any of the others she'd been having.

Resolute, she threw back the covers. She'd slept in flannel man-style pajamas, nothing sexy or revealing there, so she stuffed her feet into her slippers and padded to the bedroom door. A glance in the kitchen showed Brian using his bare foot and a paper towel to mop up spilled milk.

"Need a hand?"

His head came up like a pointer that had scented a grouse. His eyes were wary; his shirt, sopping wet.

Kim tilted her head. That shirt wasn't the one he'd gone to bed in. The pants were new, too. Sweatpants instead of jeans. Good idea. In those he should be able to manage personal tasks with the use of his fingertips and thumb.

She scowled. His arms were not in the sling, instead they hung at his sides, where they ought not to be. She stepped out of her room and into the kitchen. His hair was damp. What was going on here?

"How did you get a shower and clean clothes?"

"No shower." He held out his splints. "Can't get these wet. But Dean helped me wash and change before he left."

Trust her Dudley Do-Right brother to show up at dawn and make her look bad.

"What time is it?" she asked

"Eight." Brian continued to mix the milk and the paper towel with his toe.

"In the morning?" Kim peered at the clock. Why did it feel so much later?

"Sun's out. Yep. Morning."

She chose to let the sarcasm slide. She wasn't up to banter at 8:00 a.m. Instead, Kim bent and swiped up the remaining milk. Cloudy white droplets sparkled on the pale arch of Brian's foot. Reaching out, she smoothed them away with her thumb.

"Shit." He jumped back, bumped the counter with his tailbone and cursed some more.

She didn't recall him being so sensitive. She'd once spent hours learning every inch of his body. His feet, his palms, the back of his neck, the crease of his elbows, the bow of his knee, the ridges of his stomach. She'd explored every sensitive juncture with her hands and her mouth, marveling at the way his skin rippled beneath her touch.

Kim crossed the room to place the paper towel in the trash. Would she ever quit thinking about his body? It didn't appear promising.

"What were you trying to do when you spilled the milk?"

"Make cereal." Brian wiggled the tips of his fingers. "They don't quite work like they used to, and when I picked up the milk, my wrists hurt so bad—" he shrugged "—I dropped it."

"Why did you bother?"

"Hunger?"

"You could have woken me."

"Figured you must be tired to sleep half the morning."

"Half the morning? It's 8:00 a.m.!"

"City girl," he muttered.

"You say that like it's a bad thing."

"Around here, it is." He sighed. "Just like this is a bad idea."

"This?"

"Your being here."

"Last night we agreed there wasn't much choice."

"There's always a choice."

She didn't think they were talking about the same thing anymore. But she hadn't the courage to say so.

Lack of courage about the past made Kim determined to show courage in the present. She resolved to make Brian, Dean and everyone who doubted she could take care of the Riley farm and Brian Riley himself eat their words. She'd faced harder challenges than this and survived. In fact, she had thrived.

"Fine. There's always a choice and mine is to stay." All business now, she brushed her palms together and eyed his milk-sopped shirt. "First things first. Let's get this off."

She reached for the buttons and he knocked her hands away. "It's all right."

"You spilled milk, Brian. Even I know that in a few hours you're going to smell like unwashed feet."

He raised a brow. "You smell a lot of unwashed feet?"

"Not if I can help it."

His reluctant smile charmed her. Brian might be different, dark and sad, but his smile could still reach into her heart and squeeze just a little.

And because her heart hurt and her stomach danced, she didn't smile back. Instead she did what she did best. She analyzed; she categorized; she reduced what hummed in the air to a list she could manage.

"We'll change your shirt. Get your arms back in the sling, where they belong. Then I'll make you eggs instead of cereal and…"

He was watching her too closely, too solemnly, and the smile was gone. Though she missed it, she was glad. His smile reminded her far too much of things that were dead and gone.

"What?" she asked when he continued to stare at her.

"You'll have to get the eggs."

"You don't have any eggs?" Why was she surprised? "Fine, I'll get dressed and go to the store."

He made a scolding click with his tongue as he shook his head. "City, city, city girl. Eggs come from chickens."

"I thought chickens came from eggs."

"Funny. The eggs are in the henhouse, underneath the chickens."

"Oh." *Duh,* her mind taunted—with Dean's voice. "Right."

"I can have cereal," Brian reiterated. "I don't mind."

Kim was tempted, but if she let herself be intimidated by something as simple as gathering eggs, she'd never win her own personal war.

"No. You like eggs. Scrambled."

His face closed; the memory sprang between them. Scrambled eggs at midnight. Sharing the plate, the fork, each other. Laughing, talking, loving. Living, crying, dying.

Kim snapped her mind as closed as Brian's face and hurried on, trying to fix her blunder. "Better yet. Over hard."

His eyes widened. Her cheeks flamed as she heard what she'd said. She wished she had, literally, put her foot into her mouth; maybe then she could shut up.

Desperate to make amends, Kim returned to her list. "First the shirt, then the eggs."

She stepped closer and quickly released the buttons without looking at his face. The heat of his skin warmed her chilled fingers. The sight of his chest, broader, stronger, but still just as smooth, just as supple, made her throat go dry. She muffed taking the shirt off, catching the sleeve on a splint and tugging impatiently.

His hiss of pain drew her gaze from his arm to his belly, where the muscles rippled a line to the bruises beneath his ribs. The sight of them brought back memories that refused to let her be indifferent any longer.

She touched him, palm to waist, fingertips along his

back. He went still, watching her as prey might watch the predator—or perhaps it was the other way around.

"Did you do this yesterday?"

Something flickered in his eyes. Anger? Pain? Or merely the past?

"I didn't do it playing football."

He remembered. How could he forget? How could she?

Brian had been the quarterback; Kim, a cheerleader. They were nauseatingly adorable and perfect. The month had been September; the air, cool; the night, silver and blue.

He'd made the play, won the game, gotten the girl. They'd gone to a party in someone's woods. Bonfires and beer cans. The laughter too loud, the population too dense. She'd only wanted to be with him. He'd held out his hand, and she'd gone into the darkness with him gladly.

They'd walked. Talked. Kissed. Sat on the hood of his car, then crawled into the back seat. She'd touched his side and he'd grimaced with pain, just like today. And like today, she'd slowly unbuttoned every button to reveal every bruise. He'd watched her then, too, his eyes hungry, not far different from the predatory cast in them now.

She hadn't understood what she was seeing, why or how he'd been hurt. Then he'd shrugged. "The pads only do so much."

Shock had taken the place of confusion. "This happens every game?"

"More or less." He winked. "No guts, no glory."

To a seventeen-year-old girl, his strength, his bravery, his willingness to put himself on the line for the team had seemed epic. She'd put her mouth to the bruises, put her mouth on him, and that night he had become her first, just as she had become his.

The past faded, but the bruises remained. His belly quivered beneath her hand, and before she could stop herself, she stroked him—just one brush of her thumb against his skin. No one's skin had ever been as smooth or enticing as Brian's.

His splint smacked her hand, heavy and awkward, pinning her to him even as his fingertips struggled to pull her away. But he was as helpless right now as she.

She tilted her head back, and the stark memory of his face made her reckless.

"No guts, no glory," she repeated.

Their lips met—she was never sure afterward if she'd kissed him or he'd kissed her—it hardly mattered. The first touch of his lips and she dove.

Open mouth, open palms. Open heart, open mind. The spirit of Brian washed through her. Colors swirled behind her closed eyelids—crimson to garnet, sage become emerald, cerulean into sapphire.

The kiss was everything she'd known, yet nothing at all of what had been. Gentleness banished, softness consumed, the embrace was him—hard and dark—his flavor a claret of sadness at midnight.

She'd loved him, lost him and so much more. She'd gone on, but she couldn't seem to stop missing what had never even been.

CHAPTER SIX

BRIAN HAD LOST HIS MIND. There was no other explanation for what was happening.

Only a crazy man would beg to be crushed again by the very same woman who had crushed him before. But then his sanity had been in question more than once in his lifetime.

Since he was already halfway down the path to insanity, he might as well enjoy the journey, so Brian stepped in closer and he kissed her some more.

She tasted the same; she smelled the same, too. Of snowflakes on evergreen branches, holly, ivy and brown sugar.

Her lips were just as soft; her tongue, as eager. Her body slid along his in both new and familiar ways. Her hands on his bare skin knew exactly where to touch to make him moan. But he couldn't touch her, not really, and while that was as frustrating as hell, it was also arousing.

He fought the rising tide of need, knowing he should put a stop to the kiss before it led to something more, something he couldn't control, something that might leave him more broken than he already was. But for one more moment he wanted to remember what it had felt like to be loved by her—or at least to believe that he was.

They'd learned so many things together. Spanish and French…kissing. Biology and…biology. Phys ed and baseball—first, second and beyond. Algebra and the discovery of the unknown.

He'd learned some things without her, too. That sex wasn't love. *Forever* didn't really mean forever. And desire, however pleasant, could still make a man feel emptier than he'd ever felt before. He might still love her, but how could he still want her after what wanting her had done to him?

It was that thought, that feeling, more than any other, that allowed Brian to step away and keep himself from kissing her again when she opened her eyes and looked at him with the same expression he had seen a thousand times.

"Brian?" she whispered, and reached for him.

He stumbled back, stepping on the shirt that still trailed from his splint, yanking it clear, ignoring the pain.

"Don't touch me, Kim."

The dreamy cast disappeared from her face. Her cheeks flamed. "Don't touch me. Don't touch me. You never used to say that."

"You want to talk about all the things I used to say?"

She flinched. "No."

Her arms curled protectively around her middle as she turned, shoulders hunched. Seeing Kim in such a defeated posture made Brian regret his hasty words.

She'd hurt him. Badly. But that didn't mean he had to hurt her back—no matter how many long, lonely, empty nights had been spent thinking about doing just that.

He gentled his voice. "We could do this, Kim. We could go in your room, or up to mine, fall on the bed and have sex until our eyes crossed, but it isn't going to change anything."

"What will?"

Her voice, wistful, tugged at a part of him he'd buried along with so many other pieces of himself.

"Some things can't be changed. What's done is done. What's gone isn't coming back, and our—"

"Shut up!" She spun around, her eyes wide and wild. The color had drained from her face; her lips trembled, then tightened. "You don't want me to touch you? Fine. I won't. But I don't want to talk about what happened that night. Not *ever*. Do you understand?"

She was shivering now. Brian wasn't sure what to do, what to say. They'd sworn never to tell another living soul what had happened. He hadn't, but for some reason he'd figured Kim had. A friend, a lover, even a doctor. How had she kept the secret inside herself for so long? How had he?

"No, I don't understand," he murmured. "If we can't talk to each other, then who can we talk to?"

"Talking won't change anything, either."

Brian wasn't so sure about that. The temptation of talking with Kim about what only they could talk about was nearly as enticing as kissing her had been.

He could give up the kiss, but he wasn't quite sure if he could give up talking about what they'd both lost one rainy June night.

"You say no touching. I say no talking." Kim was already backing away from him and toward the door. Running again. He shouldn't be surprised.

"That's how it has to be," she muttered, almost to herself. Then she raised her chin, looked him straight in the eyes. He blinked at the depth of pain he saw in hers. "I—I can't, Brian. I'm sorry, but I just can't."

Her hand fumbled on the doorknob. She cursed, took a deep breath, tried once more, then she was gone, fleeing toward the chicken coop as if the rickety structure held salvation or at least sanctuary.

Brian sat at the kitchen table and contemplated his thumbs. His skin was hot, hotter still where she'd touched him. But with his milk-drenched shirt on the floor and the past in his mind, a chill spread from the outside all the way in to his heart.

For eight years he'd nursed his anger, his pain, his loathing because that was the only way he could go on without her. He had to believe that she'd left him without a backward glance, that she had never wanted the life he needed, never mourned all they had lost. Kim had callously gone on to bigger and better things, leaving him to muddle through alone.

But one glimpse into her eyes had shown him a truth he had never allowed himself to consider. Kim was still raw, still bleeding.

She was broken inside; just like him.

KIM MADE IT to the chicken coop without crying. But her heart was pounding so loudly the beat echoed in her head, in time with the voice chanting, *Go, go, go. You've* got *to get out of here.*

So much for her pledge to stick this out and make all who'd ever doubted her eat their words. Of course, she'd been talking about farm work when she'd made her silly vow. She'd never considered that Brian might decide to dredge up their past and wallow in it.

What kind of *guy* was he anyway? Every other man she'd ever known—father, brothers, lovers, save one—did not care to chat about feelings, painful or otherwise. They would definitely not bring up the most god-awful night of her life and ask her to share.

But then, Brian had never been like any other man or boy she'd ever known.

A sob escaped Kim's lips before she could stop it. She clapped a hand over her mouth and stumbled inside the chicken coop.

The smell made her forget everything else. People who thought pig farms reeked had never been near a chicken farm. But the shock of chickenshit only lasted so long. An instant later all she'd been trying to forget came roaring back.

They'd been so happy, crazy with passion, drunk with devotion. They'd had problems, sure. But they'd been young and in love for the first time. They'd believed they could overcome anything. Together they'd seemed strong, invincible. They'd learned differently.

Excitement faded to fear. Fear turned to pain. Dear God, the pain. Through everything Brian had been there. He'd held her, talked to her, never let her lose hope. Until all hope was gone.

Tears ran down Kim's cheeks, reminding her of the way the rain had traced the windowpane of a sleazy little motel in Wisconsin. She scrubbed away the tears, banished every memory. They still swirled at the edges of her mind, but she was used to ignoring them. Going on, doing something, anything, staying busy. In her other life she was known as a party girl—smile, laugh, dance, drink—anything to keep the sobbing child within herself at bay.

She contemplated the chickens. Somehow, she didn't think dancing was going to work right now. Well, when in Rome—or a stinking chicken coop…

Kim snatched a basket from the wall and approached the nearest hen. She'd never gathered eggs before. With five older brothers the farm chores had been parceled out long before Kim arrived.

Her mother had always kept her close, tried to teach her wifely chores like cooking, canning, cleaning. Kim had rebelled, resenting the implication that a farmwife was all she could be. As a result, she knew diddly-squat about quite a bit, including how to get an egg out from underneath a chicken. But how hard could it be?

She approached slowly, cautiously, hand outstretched, mind focused on taking shallow breaths through her mouth and thinking of nothing but the chicken. The instant she touched feathers, the hen pecked her hard enough to draw blood.

"Ouch!" She jumped back, bumped the nesting

boxes on the other side and caused a small, cackling riot, which sent feathers shooting in every direction.

When the hens quieted, she tried again, with similar results. Annoyed, frustrated, furious, she refused to give up. One thing Kim had never been short on was stubbornness.

Ten minutes later, her hands were bleeding, her hair was full of feathers and her basket was still empty.

But at least she no longer thought about anything but chickens.

BRIAN WAITED and then he waited some more. How long did it take to grab an egg or two? He would have figured her gone, but he hadn't heard the car. Maybe she'd walked away.

And if so, what would he do? The time they'd spent together had shown him one truth. Despite the years that had gone by, they were both tormented by their memories.

It was this thought that haunted him as he waited. She was back; she was here. He wasn't so foolish as to believe she might stay, but if he could get her to talk to him, if he could talk to her, then maybe, just maybe, they could move on.

But *how* was he going to get her to talk about a past they had both buried?

Since the answer to that question was not to be found in his kitchen, Brian hauled himself to his feet, hunted out the least disgusting T-shirt in the laundry room and managed to get it over his head and his hands. Then he headed for the chicken coop.

He heard the ruckus as soon as he stepped out of the house. The door wide-open, feathers sputtered out along with furious squawks.

Brian peeked inside just as Kim crept toward a hen already fluffed to twice its size with outrage. Murmuring nonsense, she slowly reached out and got pecked for her trouble.

"You're not doing it right," he said.

Kim gasped and spun around. Her hair was white with feathers, and her hands ran rivulets of blood. His amusement faded at the sight. Blood had never bothered him, unless it was hers.

He raised his gaze to her face, and the tear tracks made him take a step toward her. Had she been crying because of the chickens or despite them?

"Forget the damn eggs," he snapped. "They're not worth bleeding over."

"If I don't get them, who will?"

"Dean."

"Uh-uh. No way. No how. No, *sir!*"

Brian was glad to see a spark of spunk beat back the dull resignation in her eyes. The shadows still hovered, but then, so did his.

He leaned a shoulder in the doorway. She scowled at the hen. The bird ruffled her feathers with disdain. Brian could almost see that chicken brain at work.

There is no way this amateur is going to get my hard-laid egg!

"Well?" Kim demanded, cutting him a sideways glare. "What am I doing wrong?"

He hesitated. If he refused to tell her, would she

give up and go inside? The set of her mouth and the narrowing of her eyes told him that wasn't likely. She was going to do this with or without his help. Brian sighed.

"Don't bother to be polite," he directed. "Just dart in. Grab the egg and get out from under before she knows what hit her. From the looks of your hand you're giving 'em too much time to think."

"Chickens think?"

"They've outsmarted you."

"Thanks." She took a deep breath. "Okay, here I go."

She darted in and yanked out an egg. It exploded in her fist. Silence settled over the chicken coop, broken only by the occasional miffed cackles of one or two hens.

"You're not doing it right," he repeated.

As egg slime slid over her fingers and dripped onto her slippers Brian held his breath, uncertain if she would burst into tears, laugh or throw a chicken at him.

She did none of them. Instead, she shook the egg off her hand, shifted to another chicken and tried again. Brian found himself reluctantly impressed with her determination. If only she'd been half as determined about their relationship as she was about the eggs.

He stopped those thoughts before they could bring back his bitterness. As he'd told her earlier, what was done was done, and he'd better start living what he preached or he might never truly live again at all.

This time Kim didn't break the egg. At least not right away. Her still slimy fingers opened to reveal it perched on her palm.

Her expression of wonder turned to horror. "Uck!" She yanked her hand out from under, and the egg dropped to the ground, where it broke.

"To make scrambled eggs, you really need to break them into a pan," he pointed out.

"D-did you see what was on that thing?"

"The usual."

"The usual? There was…was…stuff on it!"

Brian couldn't help it; he snickered. "Did you think eggs came out of chicken butts pure white and sterile?"

"I try not to think of eggs coming out of chicken butts at all."

He shook his head. "City girl."

"If that means I want my eggs in a carton, pasteurized milk, my chicken deep fried and all the sheep behind a fence, you got it."

"Shh, they'll hear you."

The two of them shared a smile, and for a minute Brian saw what their life might have been like if she hadn't hated everything he cared about. But he'd had foolish dreams once—dreams where she'd loved him enough to stay. He would never be so foolish again.

"You thought I was going to leave, didn't you?"

He tilted a brow. "It crossed my mind."

"Mine, too," she admitted. "But I'm not. I said I'd stay until you were able to take care of yourself, and

I will. Don't think you can get rid of me by making things tough, either.''

He hadn't considered that. In truth, he wouldn't have to *make* things tough. Everyday life on the farm was tough enough. Maybe it would be good for him to see firsthand how incredibly wrong for this life she was now and always had been.

"Forget the eggs," he repeated.

She shook her head. "I may be a city girl, but that doesn't make me a pansy. No chicken is getting the better of me." She wrinkled her nose at her hand. "Or chicken slime, either. I'm going to finish in here, then I'll make scrambled eggs and you *will* eat them."

As if to emphasize her resolve, she shot her hand underneath a chicken, came back with an egg and placed it in the basket without so much as a second glance. Her smirk of triumph had him smiling, too, before he stepped out of the chicken coop.

"About before."

He stepped back in. "Yeah?"

Methodically she robbed each chicken of its egg. Nary a squawk was heard and no more eggs landed anywhere but in the basket. She caught on quick—when she wanted to.

"Do we have a deal?"

"Deal?"

"Um. You know. I don't touch if you don't talk."

Understanding dawned. Brian hesitated. He could agree, but he'd be lying. He planned to talk and talk a lot. However, if he told her that, she would clam up worse than she already had.

They had several weeks to spend in close quarters until his hands were functional. Brian was betting Kim wanted to talk about the past as much as he did; she just didn't know it yet.

She needed time—preferably time free of dissension and anger. A truce was in order.

"I tell you what," he offered. "I won't talk about—" The glance she shot his way was alarmed, even fearful. He sighed. "Anything. Unless you ask me to."

"I won't," she said too fast.

"Fine. Then we're all set."

Her eyes narrowed. "So it follows that I won't touch you—except to help you—unless you ask."

"And I won't."

She muttered something indistinguishable.

"What was that?"

"Baaa!"

The sheep stuck her head into the chicken coop and absently Brian rubbed his elbow between her ears.

Kim stared at Ba with a sullen expression. "She hates me."

"Sheep can't hate."

"A lot you know. I can see it in her eyes."

"You're imagining things."

"I've never had much of an imagination."

Now, that wasn't true. Kim had been very imaginative in certain situations.

Brian straightened and backed out of the chicken coop again. Here he was saying he wouldn't ask her to touch him, then remembering all sorts of fascinating details about how spectacular she'd once been at that touching. He'd never be able to stick to their deal if he kept that up.

"I'll see you inside."

She waved and continued with her egg hunt.

"Go on now," he told Ba. "Run off and chase squirrels."

Her head tilted. Brian made a shooing motion. "Watch 'em."

She trotted toward the oak tree behind the chicken coop and stared upward hopefully. Ba had never *chased* squirrels. Some canine mannerisms were beyond her. But she did like to sit beneath the tree and pretend the ones that were up there were terrified to come down with Ba on patrol.

Satisfied that they were all where they belonged and no imminent disaster loomed, Brian headed for the house. He should have known that disaster was never far away on a dairy farm.

He had one foot on the porch, when Ba erupted with a furious, *"Baaa, baaa!"*

He froze. Ba never made that particular sound unless she was pissed off and planning to—

Brian cursed and spun about just as the ewe sprinted around the corner of the chicken coop, lowered her head and butted Kim in the back.

Kim flew forward, the eggs upward. Then she hit the dirt on her hands and knees. As if in slow motion, the basket upended, raining eggs all over Kim and the ground. Not a single one hit Ba. Every last egg broke.

Kim lifted her head. Yolk dripped down her cheek.

"Sheep can't hate, huh?" Her green eyes glinted at the retreating woolly rump. "But they certainly know how to declare war."

CHAPTER SEVEN

THE SLAMMING of a car door woke Eleanor from the deepest sleep she'd enjoyed in months. Of course, she hadn't fallen asleep until well past 4:00 a.m. and then only after she'd cried herself silly.

To top that off, her bedroom had been so hot she'd woken up several times, heart thundering, mind searching for the reason she was dripping with sweat. She needed to remember to turn down the thermostat before she went to bed, although she could have sworn that she had.

Eleanor turned over. Nose clogged, throat dry, eyes swollen, her head pounded to the beat of her pulse. If she recalled correctly, this was what a hangover felt like. Too bad she hadn't had the pleasure of a drink first.

Footsteps sounded on the staircase. Groaning, she pulled the covers over her head. She felt awful and most likely smelled worse if the slightly stiff state of her sweat-encrusted nightgown was any indication.

The door opened; silence drifted through the room. Eleanor breathed in, then out slowly, hoping the hulking lump of her body appeared asleep to whoever might be watching. At last the door closed.

She was hot beneath the covers so she threw them back, sat up and screamed. John leaned against the door, staring at her.

Her scream didn't even make him jump. Instead he regarded her calmly, curiously. She'd always loved the way he looked at her, telling her everything without saying a word. Or so she'd romanticized about his tall, dark and silent manner. Right now that stare made her want to shriek until he said something, anything at all.

He must have seen the intention in her eyes. He'd always been pretty good at reading her—back when she wasn't on the verge of madness.

"You forgot to pick me up."

"No, I didn't."

Confusion flickered across his face. "But I was released, and you didn't come. I thought maybe you were running late, though you hardly ever..." His voice trailed off. He cleared his throat, shuffled his feet, continued. "So I stood in the lobby for quite a while. Then I called Aaron."

In the end John hadn't really needed her. Did anyone? He'd called sturdy, reliable, always-there-in-a-pinch Aaron. Tears burned at the back of Eleanor's eyes, and she viciously rubbed them away.

"What happened?"

"I overslept."

"You?"

The shock in his voice reflected her own. Eleanor Luchetti never overslept. There was too much to do on any given day to waste even a minute snoozing. But lately she had plenty of time to get everything done and plenty left over to think far too much about far too little.

"Yes, me. I didn't sleep well."

"To tell the truth, El—" He broke off, shuffled his feet. "Um, Eleanor. You don't look too good."

She was sure that she didn't, but hearing him say so hardly helped matters. And hearing him call her Eleanor, even though she'd told him to, only made the distance between them loom wider. There were so many things they'd never talked about, so many things they'd never shared, and, as his heart attack had made her so viciously aware, too little time left for any of it.

"I came home to an empty house last night," she blurted.

His expression became full of concern. "You told me that at the hospital. Remember?"

He thought she was losing her mind. Yeah, join the club.

"I meant," she enunciated, "when I came *back* from the hospital."

"Oh."

Eleanor rolled her eyes. For John, *oh* meant just about anything—or maybe everything. *Oh* was sorry; *oh* was terrific, how awful, leave me alone and I'm not even listening.

In her current state, if he said *oh* one more time, she just might throw something at him, so she continued with her story.

"I walked around in the dark, and I remembered how I used to dream about being alone in the house.

It was quiet, as I'd always imagined, but also strange, even spooky. I didn't like it.''

Talking, sharing what had never been shared, felt good. She'd been the best wife, mother and farmer's helper she knew how to be. She hadn't complained. She'd done her job and kept any disappointments to herself. That was what women of her generation did. But she didn't want to keep quiet anymore. She wanted John to understand how her life had been.

"They never took naps at the same time," she murmured. "Did you know that?"

His only reaction to her sudden and—most likely to him—inexplicable change in topic, was a slow nod. Lately her mind flew from subject to subject the way birds flew between the trees.

"I would long for a single minute of silence. The closest I got to that was every afternoon at three. Do you know what I used to do every afternoon at three, John?"

His face and voice were wary. "What?"

She almost said, *Danced naked on the rooftop.*

But John wouldn't think that was funny. The only thing he *did* consider funny was his knock-knock jokes, which she considered stupid.

How had they managed to stay married for over thirty years and create six children when they had so little in common? She'd loved him, desired him, but she realized in that moment how little she knew him and how little he knew her. Could they change, or was it already too late?

"What did you do every afternoon at three?" he repeated.

She cut him a glance. He appeared interested, or maybe just concerned. She rarely went off into her own inner world as she'd just done, mainly because as a mom and a farmer's wife, her inner world had been slim to none.

"At three I would take every child who wasn't asleep—and there was usually at least one or two. I'd divvy them up between the playpens and the cribs, then I'd go outside and walk around the house ten times."

He shrugged. "Okay."

Well, at least *okay* was better than *oh,* but not by much.

Eleanor sighed. "I felt guilty about leaving them, but I put them where they were safe, and I looked in the windows every time I went by. I had to be alone for a few minutes."

"There's nothing wrong with that."

"But I felt there was. Felt I couldn't handle what was my job to handle."

"You always handled everything just fine. I never knew you were unhappy."

"I *wasn't* unhappy. Just overwhelmed now and again."

"And guilty about it."

She shrugged. "Mother's curse."

"That was a long time ago. The kids are fine. No harm, no foul."

"Are the kids fine? I worry, John. I worry a lot."

"Is that what made you cry last night?"

No wonder he continued to stare. He might not be the most sensitive man, but he wasn't blind. He had to have known she'd been crying from the moment he'd seen her puffy, old face. She had never been much for crying. What good did it do?

"No. Last night I cried because all those years I dreamed about quiet, about an empty house, and when I had it..." Her sigh was long and hitched in the middle with the echo of tears. "It was the worst thing I could ever have hoped for. The quiet..." She shuddered, remembering. "It was awful."

A door slammed downstairs. Heavy footsteps thumped into the kitchen. Chairs rattled. Outside, the purr of a tractor warred with the barking of the dogs.

"It's not quiet now, and probably won't be that quiet or lonely here ever again. There's no reason to cry any more, Eleanor."

Calm, sure, logical John. She wanted him to hold her and help her, but he didn't know how.

In her opinion, she had quite a few reasons to cry. She'd spent years wishing her children would grow up, and now that they had, she wanted them back the way they'd been. She wanted a second chance with Kim—although she still wasn't certain what it was she'd done to ruin the first chance. Eleanor wanted someone to need her, but no one did.

John cleared his throat. "Hey, where'd you go?"

She blinked—wool-gathering again. But she didn't want to admit she'd gone off somewhere twice in one conversation. So she shrugged, then she lied. "No-where."

His brow creased. "You're starting to worry me."

Eleanor didn't answer, because she was starting to worry herself.

KIM LEFT THE EGGS where they'd fallen, except for the ones in her hair. Brian watched as she picked out the shells with her fingernails. At least those daggers were good for something. They weren't going to last much longer around here.

With egg on her face, her hair, her hands and feathers pretty much everywhere, Brian had a hard time not laughing. He would have, too, if she hadn't lifted the hem of her pajama top and wiped her face.

No touching, no talking, but neither one of them had said anything about looking. Which was good, since Brian's gaze was irresistibly drawn to the firm, smooth plane of her belly. The last time he'd seen that part of her—

He closed his eyes to shut out the sight—both past and present—and when he opened them again, Kim had dropped her pajamas back where they belonged and turned away.

She tossed the empty egg basket into the chicken coop and slammed the door on the infernal squawking. Then she marched across the yard, up the steps and right past him without a glance. The sound of running water drifted from the open doorway, and he followed her into the kitchen, where she washed the blood and egg slime from her hands.

"Why don't you take a shower?" he asked.

"I will. But first I'll feed you."

"I can wait."

"Won't take long. I can do cereal like nobody's business."

In less than a minute she placed corn flakes—just the way he liked them, lots of milk, lots of sugar—on the table. That she'd remembered made him misty again and he resorted to teasing. Something that, as an only child, he'd also learned about with her.

"Eggs are good for your hair, I hear. Skin, too." He kept the smirk off of his face if not out of his voice. "But I think you're supposed to eat them, not wear them."

She tapped the spoon against her palm as her spattered slipper slapped against the floor. "You got a death wish?"

He fought a grin. "No, ma'am."

"Then sit, eat, like it."

He sat, snatched the spoon from her hand and promptly dumped the first helping into his lap.

Without comment, Kim took the utensil and pulled a chair closer. She scooped up soggy cereal and poured it into his mouth. Her face suddenly wrinkled and she sniffed, then sniffed again.

"You know we removed your other shirt because it was going to smell like old milk. Can't you find something better to wear than one that smells like—"

He swallowed. "Smells like what?"

"You don't smell that?"

He took several deep sniffs, plucked a feather out

of her hair and held it in front of her nose. "I smell chickens."

She batted the thing to the floor. "That's it?"

"Scrambled eggs?" He opened his mouth for another bite and she upended the spoonful down his chin.

In the old days he might have dumped the bowl of cereal over her head; then, laughing, they would have kissed. If his parents had been away from the house, they'd have done a whole lot more.

"Was that necessary?" he asked.

"I enjoyed it."

Brian used his shoulder to rub the milk off his chin since she didn't appear eager to do it.

"You're honestly going to tell me you don't smell manure?" she asked.

"You do?"

"I think I know what manure smells like, Brian."

"No doubt from all those years spent in a courtroom."

"Very funny. Take off that shirt."

"Uh-uh. Been there, done that. The shirt stays."

"It smells."

"Kim, that's not my shirt—it's my farm. The wind is from the east today. That doesn't happen often, but when it does—"

"Oh!" Understanding spread across her face. "The fields. You fertilized them."

"Bingo."

"I can remember Daddy spreading the fields every fall. Until the snow covered it..." She waved her hand in front of her face. "Whew!"

"Manure might not smell nice, but it has two big advantages."

She lifted a brow. "What might those be?"

"It's free and there's a lot of it."

"Both on a farm and in the courtroom."

"Now you're catching on."

The clink of a spoon against the side of the bowl was the only sound for quite a while. Brian found himself curious about her life in Savannah. He'd promised not to talk about "that night." But he hadn't promised not to talk about anything else.

"You spend a lot of time in the courtroom? That must be interesting."

Her face reflected surprise. "I didn't think you approved of bottom-feeding scum suckers."

He winced at the words he'd once used to describe her chosen profession. He'd been eighteen; she'd been picking a college and he'd been terrified.

"I'd like to know what you've been doing," he said softly.

She jumped to her feet, gathered his empty bowl, then went to the sink. Brian frowned at her stiff, straight back. Kim always ran when the going got tough, even if it was just halfway across the room. But what was tough about that question?

"Kim?"

"I would think that Dean told you everything."

"No. Dean was amazingly closemouthed about you."

"Then who…?"

"You wrote to Becky Jo Harding."

Kim gasped and spun around. "She—she told you?"

He shrugged. "You know how it is. When there's not much to do for entertainment, folks talk."

"She was my best friend."

"Probably still would be if you'd let her."

Kim shook her head. "She stopped writing a few years back. We didn't have much in common anymore."

She looked so sad and that made Brian wonder. Becky Jo Harding was now Becky Jo Sopol—wife of Patrick Sopol, dairy farmer, and mother of Cindy, Joey, Carrie and, just a few months back, Chloe Sopol. Becky had become everything Kim had feared, so why would their parting of ways make her sad? He had a feeling that if he asked, he'd only be informed of another item to add to the no-talking list, so he returned to the one subject she hadn't seemed averse to talking about.

"She told me that you're a paralegal and you live in Savannah."

"Yes."

"You like it?"

"The job or Savannah?"

"Both."

Kim leaned against the sink as she considered the question. "I'd have to say I like the job and love the place. It's beautiful there, Brian. Nothing like here at all."

Which to Brian's mind would make Savannah a bit

of hell. However, from the expression on Kim's face, hell was housed in Illinois.

"The city is old, but not broken-down old. Savannah is ancient, stately, haunted."

"Haunted? That's good?"

She smiled at his skepticism. "The ghosts add character. And there are plenty of living characters, too. You would not believe the differences that exist side by side in that city. Every day is a marvel. There's no snow. Flowers bloom in March." She spread her hands. "March? Can you believe that? And the trees…" She sighed with nostalgia. "They have a personality all their own."

Brian had a hard time understanding how trees could have personality. And no snow? What kind of winter would there be with no snow? No ice-skating, no snowmobiling, no hockey. *Bummer.* He wasn't even going to think about how depressing a green Christmas would be.

"How did you end up there?"

She blinked, and Brian could almost see her coming back from her little mind trip to Savannah.

"Um, well, after I uh…left—" she busied herself washing the few dishes in the sink "—I went south. I wanted to feel the sun on my face. I was so cold," she whispered.

Brian had to stifle his urge to go to her, put his hands, such that they were, on her shoulders, turn her around and—

Kim shook her head, almost as if she knew what he

was thinking. "I went to Atlanta. Got a job, started school."

"What kind of job?"

"Bartender." Her voice was clipped, defensive. "I had no experience, no references, no training."

"I didn't say anything."

She ignored him. "Once I finished school, I worked for a large law firm in Atlanta. I hated it."

"The job or the law firm?"

"Both. Being a paralegal is like being the bridesmaid but never the bride."

"Then why didn't you become a lawyer?"

"I couldn't afford it."

"But you had money from your gramma."

"If I'd stayed here, lived at home for my undergrad years and worked, I might have made the money stretch through law school. But on my own—" she rinsed his cereal bowl, stacked it in the dish rack "—I needed to live, pay for school and keep something back for a rainy day. I couldn't ask Daddy for help, not when I'd—"

"Run off?"

She cast him a narrow glare over her shoulder. He must have skated too close to the no-talking zone. She didn't bother to answer.

"I decided that maybe if I worked in a small office, with a lawyer who had some ideals, I'd feel better. I saw an ad in the Atlanta paper for a secretary-paralegal in Savannah. The minute I drove into town...*Bam!*" She clapped her hands. "It was love."

"You fell in love with a place?"

"Hey, Savannah isn't just a city. It's a state of mind."

He grunted. Sounded like the town slogan. Maybe it was.

"Don't you love this farm more than anything else?" she pointed out.

Once he'd loved her more, but he certainly wasn't going to bring that up. She'd run farther than Savannah this time.

"That's what I thought," she murmured, taking his silence for agreement.

"So you started working for a lawyer in Savannah."

"More than just working for. I became Livy's partner."

"Partner? But you aren't a lawyer."

"The money I'd kept back for a rainy day I invested in Livy's practice. She had a shiny new diploma and a brand-new baby. She needed help and she needed money. We became partners in crime fighting. It was pretty darn great."

Her voice wistful, her face had gone sad again. She loved and missed Savannah. Her job had once been great, and something was not right between Kim and her partner, Livy. Kim might be different, but her face still revealed whatever she felt.

"Was?" he prompted when she didn't continue. "Aren't you still partners?"

"Technically." She dried her hands on the dish-towel. "There was an incident."

"Sounds serious."

"Not really. Or at least not as serious as I made it out to be. Livy lied."

"About what?"

Kim tossed the towel onto the counter. "She said her son's father was dead. Then, surprise, he turns up undead."

"A vampire? Savannah really is full of spooky characters."

Kim giggled and the sound made Brian smile. He much preferred her laughter to her tears, even after he'd shed so many over her.

"Spookier than you can imagine," she agreed. "Anyway, when the truth came out, I didn't handle it well."

"You ran home."

Her laughter died. "Aaron called. I came *back*. My home isn't here anymore, Brian."

"I think I know that better than anyone."

In the silence that fell between them the distant cackling of the hens intensified.

"I'll take that shower now." Kim disappeared into the bedroom.

"I kind of figured that you might," he murmured to the closed door.

KIM STRIPPED OFF her egg-encrusted pajamas and kicked her ruined slippers into a corner. Feathers rained all around her. Funny, but she didn't smell chickens anymore. How long before she no longer noticed the scent of manure wafting on an eastern wind?

She had to make sure she was out of here before that happened.

She turned on the shower and, while the water heated, glanced into the mirror. A surprised snort of laughter escaped. She resembled a refugee from a fried chicken commercial. If only Livy's son, Max, could see her now, he'd no doubt write a story titled "Attack of the Chicken People." That kid had an imagination that just wouldn't quit.

Kim was very fond of Max—had been since the moment she'd first seen him. A psychiatrist would no doubt say she was compensating for the children she'd never have by bonding with Max. Whatever kept her out of the psych ward.

She stepped into the shower. The pecks on her hands burned when the water hit them. She'd broken three nails but wasn't sure how. Kim leaned her head against the faded peach tile and let the steam soothe her aches and pains. She missed Max, Livy and Livy's mom, Rosie, something awful.

Rosie—a Savannah character if ever there was one—was the mother Kim had dreamed of during many a long, silent, grounded night in her room. Free spirited, outgoing, accepting of everything and everyone—except for those who weren't as accepting—Rosie flitted from job to job, cause to cause and jail cell to jail cell. You could talk about anything with Rosie, and she'd tell it to you straight. Kim adored her.

Yet Livy and Rosie had as prickly a relationship as Kim and her mother. Rosie didn't cut Livy as much slack as she cut the rest of the world, and Livy pre-

ferred people who were dependable and law-abiding.
Rosie was neither one. Kim had often thought that
Livy would have appreciated Eleanor as much as Kim
appreciated Rosie. God's little idea of a knock-knock
joke, perhaps.

Knock-knock.
Who's there?
The wrong mother.
The wrong mother who?
The wrong mother for you.

"Har-har," Kim muttered, and rinsed her hair.

Before Kim had left Savannah, circumstances had
forced Livy to take a clearer look at her mother; and
vice versa. The two had started their relationship from
scratch. They were buddies now, and Kim was just a
bit jealous.

She frowned. Did she want to be pals with her
mother? The idea was novel…more intriguing than
she wanted to admit. So she put it out of her head—
for the moment.

What she really needed to do was call Livy and
apologize. She'd told herself that she'd been hurt and
upset over years of lies. But in truth, discovering that
Livy had been lying only brought home that Kim had
been lying, too.

Brian was right. Her guilt had made her run.

Just as it had made her run all those years ago.

Kim stepped out of the shower. If she called Livy,
she might ease her guilt over how she'd behaved, but
then her friend would want to know when Kim was
coming home. Kim would have to explain why she

wasn't—at least not immediately—and then they'd be back to the lies. Be they outright or by omission, a lie was a lie was a lie. Perhaps a letter was a better idea.

Kim unearthed her jeans, a University of Georgia sweatshirt—not that she'd ever gone there, but she'd dreamed about it—and the only pair of tennis shoes she owned, pristine white and never worn.

She curled her lip at the ho-hum tennies. Her denim-shaded, two-inch platforms with rhinestone accents would go nicely with her outfit, but she didn't want to tempt fate any more than she already had. If she continued to buck tradition and prance around in her favored footwear, she'd no doubt end up with a torn ligament, or at the very least, a tumble into the pigpen.

Kim donned the tennis shoes, considered curling her hair, and French-braided it, instead. She had a feeling that in the weeks to come she'd be doing a lot of French-braiding.

CHAPTER EIGHT

THE DAYS PASSED, marked by the slowly fading bump on Brian's head. They settled into a routine of sorts. Brian, used to awakening before the sun, continued to do so. He walked the barn with Dean, watched his friend work and listened to him grumble. Then, before Kim appeared, he'd have Dean help him dress, right down to his shoes. The less Kim touched him, even on his toes, the better off Brian would be.

She prepared a mean bowl of cereal, and often did, but she also managed to dominate the chickens after that first day. Not to say that she didn't still nurse several pecks on her hands and her fingernails were a thing of the past, but she didn't give up, and the squawking had faded to a minimum.

Unfortunately, the first time she made scrambled eggs, she burned not only the eggs but the pan, too. The smell had been horrendous, the fire alarm so loud the sheep had scattered to the far end of their field and the cows, too. From then on they ate a lot of PB and J and even more cereal.

Ba still butted her whenever she got the chance. Yesterday she'd butted Kim right into a pig wallow, ruining Kim's yellow high heels and Hawaiian-print shirt. There was also the little incident of a headfirst plunge into the compost pile wearing denim heels and a lacy white sweater.

No matter what Ba or the farm dished up, Kim took it. She didn't complain and she didn't get mad and she didn't disappear. His admiration for her was growing in spite of himself.

Brian glanced at the clock above the sink. He was exhausted, and it wasn't even noon. Most days he'd have milked over a hundred cows; then, depending on the season, plowed, planted or picked corn, barley or hay and all before lunch. He'd done nothing lately except hang out with Kim. Well, she always had been so full of energy she made everyone else tired.

Her door opened and she stepped out in what looked to be her only pair of jeans. One of Brian's Gainsville High sweatshirts enveloped her to the knees. She'd rolled the sleeves up to just below her elbows. Her tennis shoes had once been sparkling white and never worn. Not anymore.

"What should we do today?" she asked.

"Something. Anything."

They hadn't been doing much, and he was about to lose his mind.

Her glance swept the kitchen. "I could clean." The wrinkling of her nose revealed her opinion on that. "It's been quite a while since I have, but I'm sure I can manage."

"You don't clean in Savannah?"

"Nope. I work fifty to sixty hours a week. I have a cleaning lady."

The novelty of a cleaning lady made him pause. He'd never known a woman who had one, but if anyone would, or probably should, that someone was Kim.

"Never mind," he said. "I cleaned the place, top to bottom, a few days before you came."

"You?"

"You see anyone else around?"

"Good point. I could go grocery shopping. What would you like for supper?"

"You're going to cook?" He was unable to keep the fear from his voice.

She scowled. "Well, you certainly aren't."

"Can you?" He recalled the smell of burning eggs and blackened frying pan.

"Kind of."

"How do you kind of cook?"

"I can read the directions on a package and make something *kind of* close to what's on the box."

"Swell."

"Guess I should have paid attention when Mom was trying to teach me a few domestic chores."

"Wouldn't have hurt."

"It did back then."

He could imagine. Kim had hated anything domestic, everything to do with the farm. She'd wanted two things—him and out of here. They'd put off for as long as they were able to the realization that she could never have both.

"No reason to grocery-shop today," he said. "I need to go to town tomorrow and get these casted." He held up his arms. "We can shop then."

"Are you ever going to put those back in the sling?"

"Nope. Makes me feel like I'm in a straightjacket."

"And you know what a straightjacket feels like?"

"Yeah, a double arm sling."

She shook her head. "I guess we can have PB and J for supper again."

"That's for lunch. For supper we go to your parents'."

"We do?"

"Dean said your mom wants us for supper tonight to celebrate your dad coming home."

"Oh! I forgot that was today. Supper. Great," she said, but she didn't seem happy.

"Hey, you want to take a walk?"

Kim cast a dubious glance at the gray, overcast sky visible through the kitchen window. "Outside?"

"City girl," he muttered, earning a glare. "Yeah. Outside."

"Why?"

"Exercise? Fresh air?"

"It's fresh all right."

"Come on. I'm not used to sitting around twiddling my thumbs, such as they are. If I don't move around outside, I just might go crazy."

"Okay, but keep that vicious wool ball away from me. These are the only pair of jeans I've got at the moment."

"No problem." He followed her out the back door. "This time of day she's usually at the sheep pen pretending she doesn't care that she's different."

"You mean Ba is the black sheep?" She snickered. "I'm sorry. That was just too much to resist. Doesn't she think she's a dog?"

"I'm not sure what she thinks. But she's drawn to the others." He paused and pointed at the field behind the chicken coop, where about a dozen sheep clumped together on one side of the fence and a single black sheep stood alone on the other. "She likes to watch them."

"You should let her be a sheep, Brian."

"I don't think she knows how."

"Poor thing."

"A minute ago you called her a vicious ball of wool and now she's a poor thing."

"Well, just look at her. She wants to be with her friends."

"They aren't her friends. I put her in with them once. They kicked her butt."

"What? Why?"

"Survival of the fittest."

"That's the law of the jungle, George, not the farm."

"It's the law of life. Ba is different. She knows it. They know it. I saved her by taking her in, but I changed her, too. She can't ever go back with them."

"Are you sure? Maybe you didn't give them enough time to get used to one another."

"When I said they kicked her butt? I meant that

literally. Any longer and they'd have kicked her head in, too.''

"How awful," she whispered.

"Welcome to the jungle."

She gave him a dirty look, and he could almost hear her thinking how heartless he was, but Brian couldn't change the truth.

For city dwellers nature was something to be observed on the Discovery Channel, never in your own backyard. Farmers dealt with it every day, and they couldn't afford to get attached to their animals. Animals died—by accident or design—or they disappeared and were never heard from again. Kind of like people. Brian had learned the hard way not to get attached to anything at all. Sometimes he did feel heartless, but that was better than heartsore.

"Come on," he muttered, and turned away.

They strolled down the gravel lane, which curved past the barn and headed up to the main road.

Even though the weather wasn't the best—damp, cool and gray—Brian always felt better outside. In the house he was bored, trapped, lonely. But walking his land brought him peace. There were so many things to see, so much to be done, so many animals both domestic and wild, that Brian was never truly alone.

He took a deep breath. Sure, he smelled manure. But to him, that just meant he was home.

Lost in his thoughts, he didn't notice right away that Kim wasn't at his side. By the time he did, she was already in trouble.

"Hey!" he shouted. "Don't touch that—"

Raarh!

Kim leaped back from the cat she'd planned to pet, holding her scratched hand to her chest as the orange-and-white striped tail disappeared into the tall grass surrounding the barn.

"Tomcat," Brian finished. He crossed the distance separating them in three steps. "Let me see."

Wide-eyed, she held out her hand, where a new, bloody mark crisscrossed the steadily fading chicken pecks. If this kept up, there wouldn't be much left of her.

"What did you think you were doing?"

"Petting the cat. I like cats."

"Since when? I didn't think you liked animals at all."

He couldn't recall a single memory of her near a cow or a pig. Recent images of her with sheep and chickens only served to reinforce his opinion. But with five brothers, all older and bigger than she was, Kim had never been required, or allowed, to perform any farm chores.

"That's not true!" she cried. "I always wanted a pet. But Mom said we had enough animals in the house."

"I don't remember any animals in your house."

"Aaron, Bobby, Colin, Dean and Evan. Our own little herd."

Brian's lips twitched. "I suppose they caused their own kind of carnage."

"You got that right."

"You had Dalmatians."

"Outside, never in. And they weren't very cuddly, just busy."

True. Farm dogs were not pets. They were working animals. And once again, it didn't pay to get too attached to them. Run-ins with cars, tractors or cows' hooves did little to improve a farm dog's life expectancy.

Brian recalled, too, that Kim's mom had never been an animal lover. In fact, she'd always dealt so sternly with the dogs that they fled at the first sound of her step. He'd thought her manner an odd one for a farmwife, but then again, maybe not.

"Daddy let me play with the cats sometimes," Kim murmured. "I always had to wash my hands afterward, and never, ever hold them by my face. And—" her brow creased in thought "—never play with the…" Understanding dawned and a rueful twist came to her lips. "Tomcat. I forgot."

"Not the best rule to forget."

"I only played with the cats until I was five or six. Then one of my favorites was crushed by a cow." She winced.

"Unfortunately, that happens. The cats burrow into the hay to get warm in the winter, and the cows lie on them or step on them. They don't mean to."

"I know. But after that…" She shrugged. "I didn't want to get attached."

Brian could relate.

"Just remember to avoid the big, nasty toms. They're like kitties on acid. They hate everyone for no reason at all."

"Then why have them?"

He blinked, stared and waited for her trademark giggle. None came. Kim had to be the most city city girl he'd ever known. Not that he'd known so very many.

He tilted his head toward the barn. "Open the door, and I'll show you."

Confusion flickered over her face, but she did as he asked, opening the door so they could step inside. The scent of hay and autumn waning, of warm bodies, cool nights, of nostalgia, brushed Brian's chilled cheeks, making them tingle. He didn't touch the fluorescent light switch so he could enjoy the forever twilight that inhabited his barn at any time of the day.

At the far end of the structure, he paused next to an ancient barn board that leaned against the wall. Kim was about to speak, but Brian held up a splint to forestall any questions.

"Shh," he murmured. "Pull that board back."

Wariness filled her eyes. "I don't think so."

"I'm not one of your brothers, Kim. I promise nothing slimy or disgusting will leap out."

Still she hesitated, and he couldn't say that he blamed her. In their youth, he'd heard of, and laughed about, many of the rotten things the five of them had done to her. Once he'd fallen in love with her, Brian had insisted the torment stop, although he had a sneaking suspicion the Brothers Luchetti only made sure they pulled their tricks when he wasn't around. And Kim would never have snitched. He might be an only child, but even he knew that snitching only assured further persecution.

"Go ahead," he urged. "Think of this as a present. All you have to do is pull the board away from the wall to unwrap."

At last she did, but slowly, tentatively, her body stretching so that she could stay back as far as she could, just in case a monster leaped out and shouted, *Boo!*

Instead, kittens tumbled free, spilling across her tennis shoes, chewing on a toe, batting at the laces.

Her breath caught; the giggle erupted. She dropped to her knees, and her battered hands fluttered over their soft fur. When she gazed up at him, her eyes were misty despite the laughter. "They're beautiful."

"Makes even a tomcat worthwhile, hmm?"

"I suppose." She picked up an orange-and-white tiger that looked amazingly like its daddy but for size and temperament. "But won't toms—" She broke off and cuddled the tiger protectively against her chest. "Um—"

"Kill their young?"

She lifted one shoulder, lowered it, then snatched a calico from the pile and cuddled it, too.

"They will if they find them."

"How barbaric."

"Survival of the fittest again."

"If you say that one more time, I just might hurt you."

Already did, his mind whispered. But he kept his mouth shut. Needling her about the past had lost its appeal several days ago.

"I always make sure the barn is closed up tight,"

he continued as if she hadn't spoken. "And I'll let you in on another little secret about Ba." Kim raised a brow. "She hates tomcats."

Kim snorted. "You can't tell me that Ba, Ba Black Sheep knows one cat from the next."

"She doesn't like anything slinking about. She caught one trying to squeeze through a gap in the door once."

"And?"

"Kicked his butt."

"Literally?"

"There's no other way with Ba."

"Hmm. She might be a big, mean ball of wool, but I'm starting to like her."

"I thought that you might."

Kim placed the tiger kitten on the floor, where he promptly jumped on another's back, then they rolled end over end until they slammed into a cow stanchion. The two broke apart, blinking in confusion. Before they could regain their feet, their brothers and sisters attacked them, and all was forgotten in the excitement of a new game.

Grinning, Kim held the calico above her head. "I like him."

"That's not a him."

She lowered the kitten and cuddled it against her chest once more. "You know the sex of each and every one of these?" She waved a hand at the eight balls of fluff now tumbling over her feet. One climbed the leg of her jeans, and she absently plucked each needle-sharp claw from the denim until it fell back to the ground.

"Not every one. But calicos are female."

She frowned and took a peek at the flip side of the kitten. "You're right. Calicos are *always* female?"

"Ninety-eight percent of the time." He shrugged. "The vet explained it to me once. Something about genetics, chromosomes and the colors of their coats."

"What I don't know about a farm could fill a book." She shrugged. "I'll take *her,* then."

"Take?" Brian frowned. "I didn't mean you could *take* one."

"Isn't she old enough to be away from her mother?"

"Well, sure, but—"

"What did you mean, when you said there was a present behind the board?"

Brian opened his mouth, then shut it again. *Hmm.* What *had* he meant? He'd wanted to show her there was something good on his farm. Up until now, she hadn't been impressed.

"That's what I thought." Kim rubbed her cheek against the kitten's. The animal purred as loudly as a muffler-free Camaro. "I'll name her...Precious."

"Oh, no. No, you're not."

"What's wrong with Precious?"

"Besides being so cute I have to gag?"

"She is, isn't she?" Kim leaned the board back against the wall and immediately the other kittens scuttled behind it. Then she strode toward the front of the barn.

"Where do you think you're going?"

"I'm taking Precious into the house."

Panic tightened his throat. She'd bring that adorable ball of fluff inside, she'd become attached—or worse, he would—then something terrible would happen. It always did.

"No, no and no again. No cat in the house."

She stopped, turned and rolled her eyes. "You sound like my mother. Why not?"

"You said it yourself. Doesn't pay to get fond of cats."

"But if I keep her in and around the house, she isn't going to get hurt—now, is she?" Kim resumed her stride.

Brian scurried to keep up. "If you want a cat, at least pick a real cat."

She stopped and threw a wry glance over her shoulder. "This is a fake cat?"

"You know what I mean. A cat, not a kitten."

Brian was pretty sure he could resist an aloof, snooty cat.

"No, thanks. I like this one. But I'd better give her a bath." She wrinkled her nose. "She smells like manure, even without the wind." She continued toward the house, pausing on the front steps. "My parents like supper at five sharp, so I'll help you get dressed around four."

He opened his mouth to refuse her help, but she'd already disappeared inside without a backward glance.

Brian felt as if he'd been rolled over by a John Deere tractor—a common ailment when dealing with

Kim. She plowed ahead, ignoring every bump in her path. She'd no doubt learned the technique a long time ago in self-defense.

She'd never been big enough, or mean enough, to fight her brothers. Instead she'd ignored them and merrily gone on doing whatever she damn well pleased. Such behavior had always driven Dean crazy, which was undoubtedly why she had done it.

Brian sat on the porch, attempted to put his head in his hands and ended up knocking his splint against the still sore, but steadily declining, goose egg on his head.

Supper at the Luchettis'. When Dean mentioned it, Brian had eagerly accepted—anything to avoid another PB and J. But now he wished he'd made some excuse. He'd never been altogether comfortable at Kim's house. All that noise, so much conflict. In his home, life had been quiet, the arguments few. But not even his unease had kept him from being drawn to the light, life and excitement that was Kim.

He recalled the first time he'd seen her as anything other than his best friend's baby sister. He'd been tossing a soft football with Dean in the Luchettis' living room—something his mother would never have allowed—when Kim had run down the stairs in a tank top and shorts.

Though she wasn't even five feet tall, the shortness of her shorts had made her legs appear long. Her ebony hair had been tousled around her face, her skin flushed so that her green eyes shone.

He must have been gaping, because Dean hit him in the face with the football.

''Knock that off,'' Dean ordered.

''What?''

''Staring at the princess. It's my *sister,* for crying out loud.''

''Right.'' Brian cleared his throat and went back to tossing the ball.

But he couldn't forget her. He'd become obsessed, as teenaged boys will. Since he was at her house more than at his own—uncomfortable noise level or not, the fun was always at the Luchettis'—he was able to see quite a lot of Kim.

He'd never had a girlfriend. Never wanted one, in truth. Between sports, school, friends and the farm Brian barely managed to keep up.

To gather the courage to talk to her alone took him a month. She was funny, outgoing and cheerful. Everything he was not. She was also easy to talk to, and they talked a lot. Brian had never known that he needed someone to share things with until Kim had come into his life.

Another month and he asked her out. Four dates before he kissed her. Then he was lost.

Dean sneered that he was being led around by his pecker, but Brian had known better. He'd found true love.

Kim brought him out of himself. He became a different guy when he was with her, someone he'd never known he could be, someone he liked.

Life was brighter with Kim in it, fuller and faster,

too. She taught him to live on the edge, find the adventure and run full speed toward it. He'd never misbehaved in his life—chalk it up to his raving only-child syndrome—but Kim had made misbehavior an art form.

Curfew was something to be broken. The only purpose of rules was to bend them. What was forbidden was there to be explored.

She would sneak out in the night, knock on his window, draw him out, too, then she would lead him on a chase through the cornfield. Once he caught her, or she let him, they would make out for hours.

Haymows, meadows, the banks of a creek, the back of a car—anywhere was paradise if Kim lay in his arms. How many times had they watched the sun rise or the moon wane? How many mad dashes through the dawn to be back in their rooms before someone figured out they were gone?

Brian's parents considered her wild, but she was also sweet, pretty and charming. Her pranks didn't hurt anyone—at least not then—and they knew that forbidding Brian to see her would only make Kim that much more appealing. They had believed such intensity of feeling would burn brightly, then die.

But they'd been wrong.

How a tiny kitten could make such a mess, Kim wasn't quite sure. But Precious didn't like water, and she made her dislike known. Top of her lungs, thrash and slash. Kim had to admire the kitten's fury, even though she got scratched a few more times for her trouble.

When she was done with the bath, and the extensive clean-up of the bathwater all over the basement floor, Brian still hadn't come inside. Concerned that he was trying to work and might injure himself further, she went to the front window and looked out. He was sitting on the porch. She considered joining him, but Ba already had.

Kim might feel sorry for the sheep that wasn't, but that didn't mean she was going to give the animal another chance to knock her flat. In a survival of the fittest battle with Ba, Kim had a feeling she would lose.

She turned away from the sight, even though deep down something still pushed at her to go to him. Instead, with Precious wrapped in a towel and purring her way toward sleep, Kim went to her room and sat on the bed.

The days were gone when she and Brian had shared everything. He'd been a wonder to her then, so quiet and strong, dependable and certain. Being with her had taught him the value of a smile, a joke, a laugh, while being with him had shown her that sometimes following the rules might not be such a bad idea.

Sighing, she reclined on the bed, allowing the kitten to cuddle against her side. There was one rule she would forever wish she had not broken.

Images came to her of the first night she and Brian had made love. They'd been a good little boy and girl for a long, long time—nearly a year, in fact.

Most boys would have been trying to get into her pants from day one. Not Brian. Kim was always the aggressor; she always pushed things between them one step further because no one had ever made her feel as Brian did.

All her life she had craved physical affection. There was forever an empty space inside that ached to be filled. Brian seemed to sense that. Whatever she wanted, he gave. Whatever she needed, he found. He never let her go unless she let go first.

His big, rough, gentle hands had made her mindless with a longing to explore the forbidden together. When he held her, pressed his lips to her temple, as if she were priceless beyond compare, and murmured that he loved her, she wanted to give him something no one else had ever had.

The triteness of losing her virginity in the back seat of a car was overshadowed by the sweetness of the act itself. His hands shook when he touched her; his voice broke when he said that he loved her. His kiss was reverent; his face, so dear. Beneath the half-moon she'd finally found a way to make the ever present, nagging emptiness go away. With Brian deep inside her, she no longer felt alone.

Kim couldn't get enough of him, nor he of her. They made love every chance that they got, which wasn't too often, considering the size and nosiness of her family, the tininess and concern of his.

They'd possessed the teenaged gift of living in the moment, which brought about the false sense that disasters happened to someone else. Even when they tempted fate, or God, again and again and again, they were still surprised when the inevitable happened.

Kim started, opened her eyes. The room was shadowed. She must have drifted off, gone dreaming about the past and not just thinking of it.

Precious stood on her chest, prancing, purring, making a nest, then the kitten leaned over and, with a tongue the texture of sandpaper, licked the tears from Kim's cheeks.

The empty, aching loneliness was back. To be honest, it never left her anymore. Kim had tried too many times to re-create the sense of oneness she'd known then, but she'd discovered that only with Brian was she truly whole.

Because only Brian understood what they had lost one long-ago night.

The best part of themselves.

CHAPTER NINE

JOHN SAT on his porch as the sun dipped low in the sky. In the heat of summer, this would be the best time of day for a beer. But now, when the chill in the air whispered autumn waning to winter, a shot of Wild Turkey would warm his aching bones.

Unfortunately, his suddenly crazy wife, or perhaps a meddlesome son, had emptied all the liquor bottles, then drunk all the beer.

At the least a man could contemplate his day, his week, his life with a cigarette. John smirked. Someone had tried to get rid of his cigarettes, too. But his mama hadn't raised a fool. He kept an emergency pack stashed in a secret hideaway in his desk. But unearthing those had unearthed something else as well.

Proof positive that his son was plotting anarchy behind his back.

Add to that Ellie's odd behavior, the shadows in his daughter's eyes, the changes he was supposed make in his life and the gut-crunching boredom of sitting on his duff and *resting,* and John was more than a little on the edge.

He felt useless, worthless and every single year his age.

He considered smoking the single cigarette he had
secreted in his breast pocket—just having it there
helped—but the crackle of gravel at the end of the
lane, followed by the barking of Bear and Bull, announced the arrival of Kim and Brian.

John called off the dogs and sent them back to the
barn before Kim's car got scratched or they dribbled
drool on her hundred-dollar shoes.

She and Brian were arguing as they got out of her
car, so they didn't see him lurking in the shade cast
by the eaves.

"One of the reasons I'm at your house is to help
you get dressed. There's no reason for you to come to
supper in sweatpants and an old T-shirt."

"And there's no way I'm letting you undress me.
I've had quite enough of that for one lifetime, thank
you very much."

"Ahem." John cleared his throat before he heard
more than he wanted to, although he probably already
had.

"Daddy!" Kim exclaimed, and ran up the steps,
clippety-clop, in her strappy red shoes.

"Don't you look nice," he murmured as she kissed
his cheek, though he wondered about the suspicious
swelling of her eyelids, the uncommon lack of makeup
on her face and the braids in her hair, none of which
matched her smooth black skirt and sparkly red
sweater.

"Thank you. I'm down to my last few pairs of
shoes, courtesy of that walking wool ball."

"How so?"

"She hates me. Keeps shoving me into every disgusting pile of filth she can find."

John coughed to stifle a laugh. Sounded like jealousy to him, which only meant things were going his way.

"Don't mind Brian." Kim turned up her nose. "He said it wouldn't matter what he wore."

She didn't seem to realize—or maybe she just didn't care—that John had overheard something private, but Brian did. A flush rose from the collar of his white T-shirt, and the fading knot on his head turned a darker shade of purple as he avoided meeting John's eyes.

Poor sap. John had probably not done him much of a favor in sending Kim to help. If Brian was still stupid in love with her—and John was betting that he was—having Kim around had to hurt worse than those two broken wrists.

Once, John had wanted Kim to have more than what he and her mother had. But with age came wisdom—sometimes. What he and Ellie—there was no way he would think of her as anything other than Ellie, no matter what she wanted—had together was pretty damn good. Or at least it had been until his wife got weird on him.

John shook his head. Ellie was only one of many problems. Nearly losing his life had made him realize he wanted his girl near. If that meant tossing her and Brian Riley back together, then so be it. She could do far worse than a young man who still loved her eight years after she'd left him behind.

"Just glad you two could make it," John said. "How you feeling, Brian?"

"Clumsy."

John smiled, remembering why he'd always liked this boy—until he'd started kissing on John's baby girl, at least. Brian's dry wit and dependable demeanor were that of a born farmer, and there was no higher praise in John's book.

"So you still have Barbara?"

Brian cast a glance at Kim, who shrugged. "Barbara?"

"Knock-knock."

"Daddy, Brian doesn't like knock-knock jokes."

"Speak for yourself, city girl."

John smirked at Kim's new nickname and her subsequent scowl. The boy didn't plan on being a doormat. Good for him.

"Who's there?" Brian asked.

"Barbara."

"Barbara who?"

"Barbara black sheep, have you any wool?"

Brian snorted. John beamed. A snort was the proper response to the perfect knock-knock joke. Not outright laughter, but surprise that anything so foolish could be funny.

"Got any more, Mr. Luchetti?"

"Call me John."

Brian blinked. "Sir?"

"My name. It's John."

"I'm not sure if I can."

"Try. I feel old enough already without being called mister by another farmer."

"You aren't old, Daddy."

"Old enough to know we'd better get to the table before your mom has a conniption."

"Mom? Conniption? Right. That'll happen."

"You'd be surprised," John muttered, earning a sharp, suspicious glance from his daughter.

She fell back, took his elbow, and when Brian would have stayed, too, she shook her head—just a little—and he continued into the house. They might be on edge with each other. They might argue and sneer. But there was still something between them. Something strong, sure, as solid as what John had with Ellie. He wanted that for his baby girl.

"What's up, Daddy?" she asked as soon as the door closed behind Brian.

He shrugged, not sure if he should say anything, especially to Kim. It wasn't as if she and Ellie were pals. But Kim was a woman, which made her closer to Ellie—in theory, anyway.

"Your mom is acting—" he wasn't sure how to describe it except "—weird."

"Mom and weird do not go together."

"Which only makes how weird she is weirder."

"Specifics, Daddy."

"I'm not supposed to call her Ellie any more."

Kim's eyes widened. "That's it?"

John shrugged. "I've been calling her Ellie for thirty years. She could have mentioned before now that she hated it."

"What else?"

"I don't know. She's just..."

"Weird. I got that."

He stuck his hands in his pockets and kicked at an imaginary rock. "When I was in the hospital, I made up this great joke just for her."

Kim's eyes narrowed. "What joke?"

Quickly he told her his ellie-phant gem. Her lips twitched and she coughed.

"She didn't like it?"

"No. She's really mad."

"You know that Mom doesn't enjoy knock-knock jokes the way we do?"

"Who does?"

"True. So why did you bother?"

"I thought she'd like it. I used her name."

Kim rolled her eyes and gave him a look that shouted *Men!* more clearly than if she'd shouted.

"Even if she didn't like the joke, she's overreacting. To that and a lot of other things." He took a deep breath, then plunged ahead. "Could you talk to her? See if you can find out what's the matter?"

"Like she's going to tell me?"

"Please? For Daddy?" His fingers itched again. He patted the pocket with the cigarette and felt calmer, but not much. "She's making me nervous."

Kim frowned. "You shouldn't get upset. You're supposed to be resting."

"I was almost resting permanently. I've got work to do."

"And three sons perfectly able to do it."

"Able to take over and put me in the nursing home, you mean."

Kim peered at him in the fading sunlight. "Okay, you lost me."

"Never mind. I just don't like sitting around. Now, promise me you'll talk to your mother." She opened her mouth, and he could see a denial on the way. "Tonight," he insisted.

His concern must have worked its way through to her, because she hesitated, snapped her mouth shut and nodded.

SUPPER WOULD ONCE have been meat and potatoes, two vegetables, homemade bread and fresh-baked pie. Tonight the red meat had yielded to chicken, the mashed potatoes and gravy to baked potatoes and margarine, and instead of pie there was angel food cake topped with fresh fruit. Eleanor Luchetti knew how to cook for any situation.

And she *was* acting weird. Daddy was right.

But Kim's mom wasn't the only one behaving strangely. Her father kept scowling at Dean, when he wasn't scowling at the margarine and the fruit. Not that scowling at Dean was unusual, but Dean flinched every time. Usually her brother just scowled right back.

Aaron was oblivious as always; Evan, too busy eating to notice much beyond his plate.

Brian had gone silent. He was polite enough, thanking her mother for supper, answering any questions that came his way, eating whatever she put in his mouth and doing the best he could to feed himself a bit with the tips of his fingers.

But he stayed out of the conversation, almost as if he didn't want to be noticed, which reminded Kim of how he used to behave back when they'd been heating up the sheets—or rather, the back seat of the car. He'd been terrified one of her brothers would catch them— worse, her father. But no one had. They'd thought they were lucky; now they knew differently.

However, she couldn't understand what was making Brian so nervous tonight. So they'd kissed. They weren't going to do it again, or anything else. Even if they did, they were adults. He had nothing to worry about from her father or her brothers.

The phone rang and Brian jumped so high she thought for a minute he was going to get up and an- swer it himself. She cast him a questioning look, but he ignored her and went back to chasing a green bean around his plate.

"Colin!" her mother exclaimed.

They all stopped eating and held their breath, want- ing, needing, to hear about Colin. They received so little news from him.

"Where are you?"

She nodded, nodded again—as if Colin could see her.

"Where is he, Ellie?"

Eleanor glared at her husband. Kim blinked at the expression—one she couldn't recall ever seeing her mother direct at her father. Kids, yes. Husband, no.

"Sorry," Dad mumbled. "Eleanor."

Mom turned, presenting the room with her back. Kim glanced at Aaron in time to see him frown and glance at Dean, who was also frowning. Evan just shrugged and went back to eating.

"And Bobby? Have you heard from him?"

The entire table tensed. Bobby worried everyone the most. Wherever there was a hot spot in the world, Bobby was usually knee-high in the middle of it. They were all proud of him, but they were also terrified he'd get himself into something too deep to wade out of one of these days.

"Uh-huh. Uh-huh. Do you want to talk to your dad?"

John pushed back his chair, but before he could stand, his wife stiffened.

"Colin? Colin? You there?"

She pulled the phone away from her ear, shook it a bit, then tried again. "Colin!"

Her shoulders sagged and she hung up the phone, turned. "The line went dead."

Her husband nodded. Though no disappointment appeared on his face, he had to be feeling it. He often kept his emotions to himself, which, now that Kim thought about it, had to be awfully hard to live with and not exactly good for him, either.

John Luchetti's modus operandi was to tamp down every upset, every regret, every anger for as long as he could—then he would explode. From the way he'd been glaring at Dean tonight, an explosion was imminent.

Kim glanced at her mother, who had returned to her

chair and resumed eating as if the phone call had never happened.

Silence settled over the table. Wasn't anyone going to ask? Frustration made Kim grit her teeth, then finally blurt, "Where was he?"

Her mother started. "Oh. Didn't I say?"

"No, you didn't. And inquiring minds want to know."

"Don't be a smart mouth, Princess," Dean sneered.

"You aren't my father," she returned.

Brian groaned. "Here we go."

Their mother's voice stopped the inevitable argument. "He's in a country that ends with 'stan.'"

Eleanor took a sip of water, frowned as though she were having a hard time remembering the conversation that had ended two minutes ago. Kim looked at her father, who shrugged as if to say, *See? Weird.*

"Which country that ends in 'stan'?" Aaron asked gently.

"I can't quite recall. Does it matter?"

"Probably not." He patted her hand. "He's all right, then?"

She nodded. "You know how he is. Thrilled. Jazzed. The action is happening and he's right in the middle of it."

"What about Bobby?"

Concern flickered in her eyes, there and then gone the next instant. "Colin didn't know where he was. He tried to get word to him about your heart attack, John, but he hasn't heard anything back yet."

"Secret mission," Dean muttered. "Special ops. Hush-hush."

His mother gave him a silencing glare. She didn't like to think about all the dangerous places Colin visited, all the dangerous things Bobby did. Such ostrich-like behavior had annoyed Kim in the past, but right now she could see her mother's point.

There was more than enough to worry about right here at home. Why borrow trouble?

"Coffee?" Eleanor asked brightly. Without waiting for an answer, she disappeared into the kitchen.

Kim rubbed her thumb between her eyes. Her mother might be overworked and underpaid, but she wasn't a ditz—contrary to all appearances over the past few minutes.

Someone kicked her under the table. She scowled at Dean and kicked back.

"Ouch," her father said. "What was that for?"

Dean smirked.

"Sorry. My foot slipped."

Her brother laughed out loud. His mistake.

"If I were you I wouldn't be yucking it up."

Dean swallowed.

"I'm not dead yet," her father continued. "This place isn't yours, and it may never be. I've got six children."

Kim glanced at Brian, who appeared uncomfortable. She couldn't blame him. He was friend, not family. He shouldn't have to deal with the dirty laundry. Heck, Kim didn't even want to.

"I'm not interested in the place," she volunteered.

"No shit," Dean muttered.

Their father's face turned an unpleasant shade of purple. "Daddy!" she cried.

"Quiet! This is between me and him, and we're going to discuss it right now. Get everything out in the open, rather than underneath the table. Or in the bottom of a drawer, hmm?"

Kim had no idea what he was referring to, but Dean obviously did, since he paled.

"I told you I didn't want any of that fancy sci-fi nonsense on my farm. But you went and talked to the folks anyway, didn't you?"

Dean nodded.

"Everyone calm down." Aaron's voice soothed as it always did. Unfortunately, it never seemed to soothe their father.

"I'm not going to calm down! Do you know what he did?"

"No, but I'm sure I will soon enough, whether I want to or not."

Kim fought a giggle. Aaron rarely made a joke, and when he did, it was usually so subtle as to go unnoticed by anyone unfamiliar with his wry sense of humor.

"He had some slick salesman give him a quote on a robotic milking system."

Brian perked up. "Robotics? I read about that."

Her father ignored him, focusing instead on Dean, who slouched in his chair. "I told you I wanted nothing to do with that hocus-pocus. So what did you do?

Wait until I keeled over and then snuck the guy in under your mother's nose.''

"I knew he was here." Eleanor stood in the door-way with a tray of cups and a thermal coffeepot.

"What!"

"Don't shout, John. It isn't good for you." She set the tray on the table and busied herself pouring.

"It isn't good for me to see generations of work go down the toilet, either."

Dean defended himself at last. Kim was surprised he'd kept his mouth shut this long. "Just because things have gone well so far doesn't mean they can't go even better if we try something new. Why won't you listen to me?"

"Ever hear 'Don't mess with success'? 'Don't fix what ain't broke'? There's truth behind every cliché, son."

"How about, 'Keep up or you'll be left behind'?"

Kim winced as her father's expression became even more forbidding. Would Dean ever learn to skate away from the edge?

"The system will help us, not hurt us," he continued. "Once we get things up and running, once the cows are used to it, we don't have to be here 24/7."

"That's what farmers do. They don't fly off to Tahiti and leave their animals alone, or put the responsibility on someone else. Farmers farm."

"But it doesn't have to be that way anymore."

"If you don't like how it is, you don't need to stay. I've got four other sons."

Kim gasped. "Daddy!"

Dean might be a sarcastic jerk, but he loved this farm. Maybe the farm was all that he did love.

Her father barely glanced her way. Dean muttered, "Stay out of this, Princess."

But she couldn't. She'd been born the littlest and the youngest, the only girl among so many boys, and as long as Kim could remember, she had championed the underdog.

Her years in family law had only made her need to do so stronger, and even though Dean had never stuck up for her—and wouldn't thank her for doing it now— she couldn't let him stand alone against something so blatantly unfair.

"Now, Daddy," she said. "Bobby and Colin don't want the farm. You know that. And Evan will never stay put."

The man in question nodded agreeably, then grabbed the cup of coffee his mother nearly dumped in his lap while she frowned fiercely at her husband.

Ignoring everyone else, John swung his attention to Aaron. "What about you?"

Aaron tapped his fingers on the table, taking several moments to consider before he answered the question. "There's no reason Dean and I can't both run this place along with you."

"With a robotic milking system, he won't need you or me."

Aaron shrugged. "I can live with that, too."

"Sometimes, boy, you're too accommodating for your own good."

Aaron smiled serenely, and took a sip of his coffee, clearly done with his part in the argument.

"How does it work?" Brian ventured.

Dean's face lit with eagerness, before he glanced at his father and the light faded.

"Go on and tell him," John said. "I want to hear what's so damn wonderful."

Dean hesitated a moment longer, but in the end his excitement won out. "The cows are trained to come in when they want to be milked. Each wears an ID collar, which a computer reads and records. Not only is there less physical work but less paperwork."

"You expect cows to know when it's time to be milked?" John snorted.

"Don't they already? By force of habit, they all head for the barn morning and night. With the robotic system, the cows could be milked three times a day, which is ideal anyway."

"What if a cow shows up five times in one day?"

Dean shook his head. "No more than three. The computers wouldn't allow it."

"And neither will I," their father said. "I still can't believe you went behind my back like this."

"They've been using robotics in Europe for years already. Canada, too."

"What do foreigners know about dairy farming?"

"Quite a bit," Dean muttered.

Their father's eyes narrowed and his face darkened. But before he could explode, his wife intervened. "All he did was ask how much it would cost, John. Where's the harm?"

"This is my place. Not his. At least not yet."

"That's what's really bothering you, isn't it?" She stood. "That he took some initiative. But sooner or later you're going to have to let this place go before it kills you."

"*When* it kills me, you can pry it out of my cold, dead fingers. But until then—" He broke off at her shocked intake of breath. "Aw, hell, Ellie, I—"

But she was already gone, rushing into the kitchen with her hand over her mouth. The sound of her crying filled the room.

They all remained still, shock visible on their faces. Even if Kim hadn't already been apprised of her mother's odd behavior she'd know about it now. Because Eleanor Luchetti cried over nothing and no one.

CHAPTER TEN

THE KITCHEN DOOR swung open behind Eleanor. She swallowed her tears, scrubbed her palms over her face and turned.

Her eyes widened. Eleanor had expected Aaron, maybe John, though truly she knew better. Instead, Kim studied her with a wary, concerned expression.

"I'm fine," she said, and turned around again.

Eleanor plugged the sink, twisted the taps and squirted dishwashing liquid in a long, steady, wasteful stream. Then, because she felt like it, she started tossing silverware and plastic cups into the water so the suds flew up like flakes of snow before floating downward once more.

The muffled clip of Kim's heels on the vinyl floor announced her approach seconds before she grabbed a dish towel. "You wash—I'll dry," she said. "You can talk, and I'll listen."

The offer was more tempting than it should have been. Eleanor wasn't a talker. She was of the "pull yourself up by your bootstraps" generation and geographic location. Illinois farm wives did not whine; they did not go on *Oprah* and tell their secrets; they did not need to discuss every blasted twitch and twinkle in their lives.

But right now Eleanor wanted to share all the jumbled feelings and fears inside her with another woman. And in Luchetti land, Kim and Eleanor were all the women to be had.

Even though she wanted to talk, Eleanor wasn't sure how to start. So while they washed and dried, the clink of silverware and dishes were the only sounds in the room. After a few minutes Eleanor realized those were the only sounds in the house.

"Where did everyone go?"

"Brian took Dean for a walk."

Eleanor smiled. No matter what had happened between Brian and Kim, he had always been a good friend to Dean, and that wasn't easy.

"Evan said he had an appointment."

"Hmm." Evan had been having a lot of appointments lately. Knowing her son, that meant a woman.

"Aaron went to bed."

"And?"

"Daddy's on the porch."

Stiffening, Eleanor removed her hands from the dishwater, planning to sneak a peek out the front window and make sure he wasn't smoking.

Then she remembered. She'd taken every cigarette she could find and methodically broken each one in two before lighting a nicotine bonfire in the fire pit behind the house. While that burned, she'd upended all the beer into the sink and rinsed it down with the last of the liquor. She hadn't had so much fun in a long, long time.

"He's worried about you," Kim continued, "and I am, too."

The idea of having someone worry about *her* for a change was such a novelty Eleanor snickered.

"Mom?" Kim was staring at her as if she'd just belched or farted in church. The image made her choke on another laugh.

"Sorry," she said.

"You aren't yourself. Or at least the self I know. One minute you're crying, the next giggling."

"Is that a crime?"

"With you? Maybe."

She peered down her nose at her daughter. Kim grinned. "*That's* more like you."

Eleanor had perfected her evil eye over many long years of raising little boys. Unfortunately, the same look had only made Kim laugh. She'd forever been at a loss with her little girl.

"I do feel out of sorts," she said slowly.

"In what way?"

Eleanor lifted one shoulder, lowered it. "I get distracted. Forget things. I suppose I'm just getting old."

And what if, right when life should be getting better, she couldn't remember what life was all about? Could a woman go senile at fifty? She'd seen worse things happen.

"Mom?"

Eleanor started. She'd been drifting again. Washing the plates, rinsing them and rambling along happily in her own little mind.

"What else?" Kim pressed.

She tried to focus, lost the thread of the question and tried harder. How was she out of sorts? How wasn't she?

"Uh, well, I wake up with my heart pounding. Must be bad dreams, but I can't remember them. I get so hot. Especially at night. Sometimes I sweat so badly the sheets are damp."

Eleanor shuddered. She really, really hated when that happened.

"I'm tired a lot, achy, too, but then, I'm not sleeping well. Especially while your dad was in the hospital."

Kim stared at her. "I think I know what the matter is."

Dread filled Eleanor's heart. The symptoms were so common her daughter could diagnose them? That couldn't be good.

"What is it?" she whispered.

"Nothing to worry about." Kim patted her shoulder, squeezed it quick before letting her hand drop. "Just menopause, Mom. I'm surprised you didn't figure that out for yourself."

Eleanor blinked. She couldn't seem to focus— again. Something was off about Kim's diagnosis.

"But...but... No." She shook her head, hard, and the fog cleared a bit, as did the sudden, chest-compressing anxiety. "That can't be. I haven't. I mean I still—"

"Just because you haven't quit, doesn't mean you aren't about to."

"But I'm only fifty. That's too soon."

A little voice reminded her that she hadn't figured fifty was too soon to go senile. She ignored the voice; sometimes that even made it shut up.

"Not really," Kim answered. "Women can begin menopause as early as forty."

"How do you know so much about it?"

"My partner's mother, Rosie, went through menopause last year."

Eleanor's mouth sagged. "And she told *you* all about it?"

"Rosie isn't shy. She thought Livy and I should be prepared, so she told us everything. Ad nauseam sometimes."

The fondness in her daughter's voice when she spoke of this Rosie, someone else's mother, caused a twinge of jealousy to flare in Eleanor's belly. Well, she'd always known that Kim would have preferred any other mother but her.

"You need to see your doctor," Kim said. "There are medications that will make this easier on you. On everyone else, too."

"Doctor?"

The panic fluttered to life again. If she went to a doctor, that would make this real.

"Oh, no. No way."

"What do you mean no way? You don't have to suffer. Just take a pill."

"That's your generation's answer to everything isn't it? Take a pill. What if I don't *want* to take a pill?"

Eleanor could hear her voice rising hysterically, but

she couldn't seem to stop it. Kim was staring at her as if she'd gone insane. Maybe, at last, she had.

"Mom, calm down. I'm just trying to help. You could at least call your doctor."

"What doctor?"

"Yours. Dr. Halloway."

"He died, Kim. About five years ago."

"And you haven't been to a doctor since?" Now Kim's voice escalated, until the last word was very high and very loud.

Eleanor shrugged. "Haven't been sick."

"Mom, you need to get regular checkups. Blood tests. Mammograms."

"I'm not sick," she repeated.

Kim smacked the heel of her hand against her forehead. "Mom!"

Then she closed her eyes and appeared to count to ten—a familiar trick of Eleanor's from the days when Kim had lived at home. She had to smile at the similarity—the first she'd ever noticed between the two of them.

"Tomorrow." Kim took a deep breath and opened her eyes. "I *am* calling a doctor. I *am* making an appointment. I *will* take you there."

"I don't think—"

"Just a checkup, Mom. Please?"

The intensity of Kim's voice and the pleading expression in her eyes made Eleanor pause. She didn't want to go. She didn't want to hear that the one thing she'd always been very good at was over. Not that she'd planned on having any more children, but—

"I'll go if you promise me something."

Kim's forehead creased. "What?"

"Don't tell your father."

"But—"

"I mean it! I don't want him to know."

"Won't he figure it out on his own eventually?"

The question made Eleanor pause. Had he already? That would explain why he didn't touch her anymore, why the physical relationship they'd always enjoyed had gone the way of itty-bitty baby socks.

When cows could no longer have calves, John sold them. Eleanor had to wonder what John had in mind for her.

Kim patted her hand gently, but Eleanor started nevertheless. "Relax, Mom. It'll just be between you and me for now, okay?"

She nodded and Kim turned away to finish drying the dishes. Eleanor wrapped her arms around herself and admitted the truth. She'd suspected this for quite a while, but she hadn't wanted to face it. While she might not have planned on more children, she would miss the *possibility* of ever having another child. Some women looked forward to the time after menopause as a new beginning, but Eleanor would mourn all that had ended.

BRIAN WAS STILL trying to talk Dean out of packing his bags and decamping immediately, when Kim stepped onto the porch and joined her father. Framed in harsh yellow light from the front window, Brian could not see her face, but from her gestures and the way she leaned in, put her hand on her dad's shoulder, then hugged him, something wasn't right.

Dean's curse brought him back. "It's just like it was before. The minute she walks into a room you can't think of anything else."

"I can think just fine. You can't."

"Can, too."

Brian ground his teeth. If he had raving only-child syndrome, Dean was the poster boy for rabid middle-child neurosis.

"Your father isn't the kind of guy who can sit around and do nothing without feeling useless. His life's changing. He's changing. So he wants everything else to stay just the way it is, in the place he loves the most. Now is *not* the time to push the robotics. Now is *not* the time to walk out on him."

"When did you become a psychologist?"

Figuring out the Luchetti family dynamics didn't take a doctor. Only someone who'd been on the outside looking in for as long as he had.

Brian remained quiet. He'd learned over the years that if he kept his mouth shut, Dean would eventually spill everything Brian wanted to know. He didn't have to wait long.

"You heard him," Dean continued. "He wants to give the place to Aaron. Why should I kill myself for this farm if I'm going to end up with nothing."

"Because this farm is your life, and you know he would never cut you out."

"*How* do I know that?"

Brian shook his head. "The two of you are so much alike, but neither of you can see it."

"Alike?" Dean's forehead crinkled. "I don't think so."

"You're both workaholics, both brick-headed stubborn. For you and your dad, farming isn't everything—it's the *only* thing."

"Oh, man, don't quote Lombardi around Dad."

Brian smirked. "There's another similarity. You both hate the Packers, love the Bears."

"That isn't called being alike. It's called being born in Illinois."

"And you would both do whatever it takes to make this place last. Your dad might threaten—that's just the way he is—but he'd never follow through."

"What makes you so certain?"

"Because he knows that the best man for his job is you." Brian put his hand on Dean's shoulder. "Which only makes him feel outdated and replaceable."

Understanding dawned in Dean's eyes. "Kind of like the old milking parlor."

"Bingo!"

Dean glanced at the house and the anger faded from his face. The tension leaked from his body, until the shoulder beneath Brian's hand no longer vibrated with suppressed emotions. "Maybe I'll just let the robotics idea slide for a while."

"Couldn't hurt."

Brian released Dean, then couldn't help himself— his eyes strayed back to Kim. The entire time he'd been dealing with his friend, he'd known she was there. Like a match in the darkness, a whiff of fire amid the rain, like a single patch of wild iris adrift in a field of planted clover, was Kim dropped into the quiet fabric of his life.

She stood at the porch rail, her gaze searching the night. Brian stepped forward, out of the shadows cast by the roof of the milking parlor and into the halo of the spotlight glaring from the corner of the barn roof.

She saw him and she smiled. His heart slowly rolled toward his feet, and his chest began to ache.

Or perhaps she was the sore tooth that just had to be probed, the pain he knew was there, waiting to erupt at the slightest touch. Yet he was helpless to resist the temptation.

"YOUR MOM didn't say what was wrong?"

Captured by the intensity of Brian's gaze, Kim heard her father as if from a long way off. When Brian looked at her like that the years fell away. She was eighteen again, and all she could think about was how many hours she had to endure before she could be in his arms.

"Kim?"

"Sorry, Daddy." She pulled her gaze from Brian's and met the worried eyes of her father. "Mom's fine. I'm sure of it."

"She said that?"

Kim sighed. Why, oh, why, had she told her mother she'd keep secrets from Daddy? Because for the first time that Kim could recall, her mom was in trouble, and it was Kim to the rescue. Once a champion of the underdog, always a champion, and it seemed she could do nothing less for her mother than she did for perfect strangers back in Savannah.

Kim gave her dad a noncommittal mumble and kissed him on the cheek. "I have to take Brian home now. Thanks for supper."

"Kimberly..."

She was avoiding the question. Well, too bad. The only way she'd ever keep her mouth shut was to get her mouth out of there.

So she did what she'd been wanting to do since Brian had stepped into the shiny white circle of light. She ran to him.

Even across the distance of the wide front yard, he must have sensed something was wrong, because he nodded to Dean, who made a nasty face in her direction and went into the barn, then he met her halfway.

"Ready to go?" she asked brightly.

His eyes narrowed. She'd never been very good at hiding things from Brian, either.

"All right. Sure."

They waved goodbye to her father and made their escape. No sooner were they on the road and headed toward his house when the questions began.

"Your mom all right?" he asked.

"Yeah."

"She didn't seem all right."

"She's stressed, upset. She doesn't like things to be any different from what she's used to."

That wasn't a lie; just not the entire truth. Something Kim had become adept at. As Livy always said,

Kim would have made an excellent lawyer—if she'd ever learn to keep her emotions off her face.

"You know, but you aren't about to tell me."

And Brian would have made an excellent cop. He had the probing questions and the stoic demeanor down pat. Although she had to say, lately she'd seen a few softer feelings hovering in his eyes. Or maybe that was merely a trick of the shadows and a temptation toward hope.

"I promised I'd keep my lips zipped."

"You're very good at that."

Kim slid a glance his way, then returned her attention to the road. "What the hell does that mean?"

"Just what I said. You keep yourself all zipped up. You never used to."

"Brian, I—"

"I know. No talky, to touchy. I remember. I just wish...." His voice drifted off, and he glanced out the window as the fallow fields rushed by.

"You wish that things were different," she stated.

"Is that a crime?"

"I hope not." He looked at her again. "Because I wish that every day."

Silence settled between them. Kim was thankful Brian didn't press her, because she wasn't sure what she would say.

She *had* wished every day that things could have been different. But she also knew, logically, that what she'd wanted and what he'd wanted would never have come together in a way that would have made them both happy for very long. But that didn't stop her from wishing.

They reached the farm and went into the house. Kim's foot knocked against something in the hallway, which skidded across the floor and slammed into the wall.

"What the—?"

"Hold on." Brian flipped the lights with his elbow.

Kim blinked, first at the glare and then at the mess.

Precious had been entertaining herself quite well if the number of "toys" in the hallway was any indication. Plastic cups littered the floor; shoelaces draped the staircase banister; socks lay strewn in the hall leading into the kitchen.

Kim followed the path and discovered the kitten poking her paw into a tiny hole in the wood floor. "Hey!" Kim snapped. "What do you think you're doing?"

The kitten scampered across the floor and proceeded to climb Kim's leg. Her stockings sagged, snagged and ran. Kim snatched her up. "Who said you could have a party?"

Precious batted at Kim's nose with sheathed claws. Kim giggled.

"Oh, that's telling her."

Kim turned the kitten toward him. "How can you yell at that face?"

He refused even to glance at the animal, keeping his eyes on Kim. "It wouldn't pay. If you yell at cats, they'll only ignore you."

"What do you do with cats?"

"Be thankful they let you live in the house."

Kim laughed, kissed Precious on the nose, then placed her on the ground. The kitten scooted back to her fascinating hole in the floor. Had she dropped something bright and shiny down there? Kim certainly wasn't going to dig it out for her.

"You go on to bed," she said. "I'll pick up the mess."

"Okay." Brian lifted his splints. "I'll let you."

The house settled around Kim as she returned to her task. The creaks and crackles of the wood and the wind were familiar. The scuttle of the kitten in the kitchen and the slight bumps and thumps from Brian upstairs assured her she was not alone. Strange, but Kim felt at home here—something she'd never felt anywhere else.

The slight smile dissolved. What on earth was the matter with her? Home was Savannah. She had the perfect life there, one she'd carved out for herself through no small amount of sweat and tears.

In Savannah there were no cows, no pigs, no chickens. Definitely no sheep. When the wind came from the east it smelled of sunshine on the water. She had friends, money, men. No ties, no guilt, no past. Exactly the way she wanted it. Then why did she suddenly feel so sad?

Kim continued to gather the stolen items and put them away. As she did so, she remembered why she'd always enjoyed Brian's house more than her own.

The Rileys' place had been quiet, sedate, full of warmth and love and peace. She'd known Brian's parents hadn't approved of many of the things she'd done, but they'd accepted her because she was Brian's. Because he loved her, they had, too. Kim had never felt she had to change herself to please his family, as she'd believed she must to please her own.

She sighed. Water under the bridge. She really must let the past go. Tonight, while talking with her mother, she'd wondered again if the two of them could work a few things out. It wouldn't hurt to try.

Finished cleaning, Kim got ready for bed. "Precious?" she called. "Here, kitty, kitty."

But the cat had disappeared. After a cursory walk through the downstairs without a sign of her, Kim gave up. There was no way she was venturing into the basement, where the tiny, furry monsters might live; nor upstairs, where an even more frightening monster lurked.

Instead, she resolved to clean up in the morning whatever mess Precious made in the night and climbed into her cool, wide bed all alone.

But she wasn't alone for long.

Groggy, when her mattress dipped and the *pitter-patter* of cat feet approached, Kim smiled. She'd always wanted to sleep with a cuddly cat or dog. Perhaps even more than most children, because pets in bed was something her mother found abhorrent and would never allow.

"I'm a big girl now," Kim mumbled. "Cats in the bed. Dogs, too. No sheep, though. Gotta draw a line somewhere."

Precious made an odd muffled sound, as if trying to

answer. Then something small dropped onto the pillow next to Kim's cheek. That something moved.

She shot off the mattress, tapping the light as she flew by. Precious sat on Kim's bed with pride all over her sweet face.

Kim stared at the gift on her pillow, and when it moved again, she jumped onto a chair and began to scream.

CHAPTER ELEVEN

THE SCREAMING dragged Brian from sleep. Heart thundering, he was out of the bed and halfway down the stairs before he realized who was shrieking. Then he ran faster, terrified Kim was hurt. From the volume of sound, she was dying.

He slid into the kitchen, nearly tripped over the cat as she raced, tail up, paws scrambling, for safety, then stumbled into the bedroom.

The lights were on; the bed was empty—kind of. An injured mouse limped back and forth across the pillow, which explained why Kim was on top of a chair. How could he have forgotten her irrational, yet extreme, fear of mice?

At the sight of him, Kim stopped screaming, but she didn't stop shaking. She couldn't seem to talk; all she could do was point—and open, then shut, her mouth.

"Let me guess. Precious brought you a gift?"

Kim nodded, then motioned out the door.

"I'll get rid of it."

She blew a sharp breath upward, stirring the hair that had come loose from her braid and drifted across her face.

Brian tried not to stare, but Kim had worn nothing but a T-shirt to bed and the hem rode the tops of her thighs pretty high. With her standing on the chair, he kept getting glimpses of her panties. That, combined with the spike of her nipples visible through the worn cotton, made him barely able to think, let alone grab the mouse with his incapacitated hands.

After a few tries, he managed to catch it by the tail, then he headed for the door.

"Eeeh!" she squealed. "What are you going to do with it?"

He stopped and turned. "Do you really want to know?"

"No. Yuck." She covered her eyes. "Get it out of here."

He did and returned in a moment to discover she still stood on the chair, surveying the floor warily.

"You going to stay up there all night?"

"If I have to."

"You don't. The bad mouse is all gone."

"But there are more where he came from."

"Always are."

Mice were a part of farm life. They were everywhere, outside and in. Mice were the reason that cats existed on a farm. At least Precious knew that, even if Kim did not. Although Precious seemed to have been absent when her mother taught the final act in the mouse melodrama—as her live and kicking gift proved. But he doubted Kim would be any more appreciative of a dead mouse on her pillow than a live one.

She remained on the chair. And it didn't appear that she planned to come down any time soon. Brian sighed. "I'd carry you over to the bed if I could."

"What?" She'd been staring at the shadows that peeked from under the mattress. "Oh. Thanks. But there's no way I can sleep on that bed now."

"Ever?"

"Not tonight."

He could understand her unease, sort of. Brian would never let something so minor as a mouse running across his bed keep him from sleeping in it, but he suspected stuff like that didn't happen to Kim every day—or at least not anymore.

"You can sleep in my mom and dad's room if you want."

Relief washed over her face. "Thank you," she breathed.

"Shut the door and Precious can't bring you any more gifts."

She froze with one foot on the floor. "More?"

"You didn't think she'd stop, did you?"

"Uh, I didn't think." Her throat clicked when she swallowed. "She'll bring me more mice?"

"Once they start, they don't usually stop. To Precious, she's giving you the most important thing in her world. What her mother brought her."

"But after she's in the house awhile and eating kibble, won't she forget about mice?"

"Forget about mice? A cat? That's like telling a lawyer to forget about winning."

"Har-har." She hovered, half on, half off the chair,

her face scrunched in thought. "But Ba forgot about being a sheep."

"She never knew to forget. And she still does sheep stuff."

"Like what?"

"She goes *baa,* not *woof.* She likes to watch squirrels, but I don't think she'll ever chase one. And she butts people."

"Really," Kim said dryly.

Brian shrugged. "She just can't help herself."

Sighing in defeat, Kim sat on the chair, careful to keep her feet off the floor. "I guess that means more mice for me."

"I'll find Precious and take her back to the barn."

"No!" Kim drew a deep breath and placed her feet gingerly on the floor. She stood. "No. I'll just keep the door shut."

"You sure?"

"Yeah. I'm not going to lose a survival-of-the-fittest contest on my own territory."

"Your territory?"

"I'm indoor girl remember?"

"I think that was city girl."

"Whatever."

She ran across the room on tiptoe. Brian wasn't sure if the floor was cold against her bare feet or if she believed a mouse ambush might occur at any moment. Either way, once out of the room, he had to hurry to keep up, and then he had to fight to remain calm. Because watching her climb the stairs in front of him only made him remember all the times he'd dreamed of a situation just like this.

The reality was every bit as enticing as those dreams had been. Her legs, long and smooth, stretched and flexed beneath the short T-shirt. With every step she took, he glimpsed her rear end, framed by white lace panties. Her breasts bobbed; his body throbbed. He might as well be a teenager again the way he responded every time he saw her face—or anything else.

She stopped outside his parents' bedroom, turned and gazed at him with such innocence he was embarrassed by the direction of his thoughts.

"Good night," she murmured, "and thank you for rescuing me."

"Any time."

His voice was a croak. He could find no place to look that did not make him want to push her back against the door, align his body to hers and kiss her until she pulled him into the room, then onto the bed.

He could lose himself in her as he had so many times before. Having Kim here for the past several days had made him feel alive in ways he hadn't since she'd left. And while that was dangerous, it was also tempting.

If he touched her and she touched him, would that part of him that had died when she left come alive again?

No. Because the part that had died could not be brought back by sex; not even love could bring back what they'd lost.

He glanced at Kim and found her watching him

with some of the same questions in her eyes. He re-called so many nights, lying awake in the room of his childhood, dreaming of the future when Kim would be his wife and they would share a bed in this house.

They were no longer children. She was here by choice, in the house that was now his. She wanted him. He wanted her. Simple. And maybe if he took her, and took her, and took her again, he might at last rid himself of his desire for her.

But then he would never be able to rid himself of the love.

JOHN SAT on the porch until well after ten. He might as well. For the first time in as long as he could recall, he did not have to crawl out of his bed before the sun.

He'd hoped that once Kim and Brian left, Ellie would come outside and tell him what she and Kim had talked about. Why he'd hoped that, John had no idea. Even if Ellie had been behaving normally, she probably wouldn't have told him. They had never sat around chatting. That had never bothered him, until now.

Not only did his wife shun him, but Dean went around the back of the house and up to bed without even saying good-night.

John sighed. He supposed he deserved that.

He shouldn't have come down on Dean so hard, especially in front of everyone else. But he'd never been very good at holding on to his temper once he reached a boiling point, and since going into the hos-pital, damn near everything grated on his nerves. Of

course when a man had no means of letting off
steam…

He patted his shirt pocket. The cigarette was still
there, and it no longer helped just to know that. Right
now his mouth watered so badly for a taste he was
light-headed with hunger.

John glanced up at the house. All dark. If he
planned on a clandestine drag, he'd best get to it.

The dogs snoozing at his feet didn't even crack an
eye at the spark of the match, the sounds and the
scents so common to them their noses merely twitched
as they settled deeper into slumber. John closed his
eyes and let the smoke drift through his lips slow and
easy.

Just one last cigarette, he promised himself. *Just
one more, then I'll quit.* He took another deep drag.

The door opened behind him. The dogs jumped up.
In the confusion, he managed to drop what was left of
his precious cigarette to the floor and grind it dead
beneath his boot. The smoke in his mouth was another
story.

His wife stepped in front of him and sent the dogs
scurrying with one single flip of her hand. She'd never
warmed up to the Dalmatians, or any petlike creatures
for that matter. Bear and Bull were terrified of her,
though she'd never laid a hand on them in her life.
Perhaps being Dalmatians allowed them to recognize
the heart of Cruella in any woman.

"Are you coming to bed?" she asked.

He nodded.

She sniffed the air, once, twice, then folded her

arms over her chest and tapped her foot. Bear, who had just begun to slink back up the steps, whimpered, turned tail and ran.

"Were you smoking?" He shook his head. Her eagle eyes sharpened. "Then why is there smoke coming out of your nose?"

John crossed his eyes and looked down. Sure enough, smoke leaked out his nostrils. He gave up trying to hide it and released the evidence.

"John." She rubbed her eyes as if her head ached. "One day home and you're smoking already?"

"That was the last one. I swear."

"That's what they all say. Should I get you a patch or something?"

John scowled. He hated the thought of wearing a nicotine patch. He'd always insisted he could quit smoking any time he wanted to. He just didn't want to. The common excuse of the lifelong smoker, he knew, but a very good excuse all the same.

The problem was, he still didn't want to quit. He had to.

"No patch. I can quit on my own."

"Yeah, I can see how well that's going."

"Ellie, I—"

"Eleanor."

Annoyance sparked hot and prickly. "What the hell's the difference?"

She turned up her nose. "A syllable. But it's mine."

Was she *trying* to piss him off?

John stood. He'd been sitting in one position too

long and a foot had fallen asleep. When he swayed, Ellie let out a cry and grabbed his arms.

"Are you all right? Does your chest hurt?" She lifted one hand and patted him there.

"I'm fine. My foot fell asleep is all. Relax."

"Oh."

His wife released her breath with a huff, and he frowned. She was so unlike herself, he wasn't sure what to do anymore. He hated being unsure. He never had been before; now he seemed to be all the time.

"I—I could help you to bed." Ellie kept her hand on his chest, then lifted her eyes to his.

John's belly fluttered. It had been so long since he'd felt desire he'd almost forgotten the flare, the heat, the need. No wonder young men were ruled by it.

But he was an old man—or at least old enough to know better. He'd just had a heart attack, and while his doctor told him normal activities were okay, he hadn't had sex in so long he didn't think it would be considered a normal activity.

Ellie's fingers smoothed his collarbone, dipped beneath his shirt and stroked. His body responded as it hadn't in months and he found it hard to think; all he could do was feel.

He'd never believed it when other men said their interest in sex waned as they grew older. He and Ellie had always had plenty of interest in each other by the light of moon—and any other time they could manage. They had six kids to prove it. But about three months ago, John *had* lost interest. Right about the time his best friend Mose's wife had given birth at the age of forty-seven.

Oops.

The pregnancy had been a nightmare—risky and terrifying—but everything had turned out all right. If you called a son and a grandson born a month apart all right.

But John had taken the lesson to heart. He couldn't do to Ellie what Mose had done to his wife. Hell, he didn't want to do it to himself. So he'd stopped touching her. And the longer he didn't, the easier it became.

There were ways to prevent pregnancy—though none of them was foolproof, as Mose had so morosely informed him when John had pointed this out. The only sure thing was nothing.

His fear was irrational, but that didn't make him any less afraid. In fact, the older he became, the more that he knew, the more he seemed to fear things that had never bothered him before.

"John?" Ellie murmured, then she kissed him.

Panic flared along with his desire. Nevertheless, for a moment he kissed her back, lost in the taste of her, captured by the magic that had always been his Ellie. Suddenly, abstinence wasn't so easy anymore.

One time couldn't hurt. Just one more time.

Ellie trailed her mouth along his jaw, then whispered in his ear, "Let me help you to bed."

Help. One tiny word reminded him of all he had so easily forgotten.

Only an old man needed help. What an old man did not need was another child.

His belly clenched as his chest went tight. He tore himself from her arms. "I don't need help!"

As soon as the words came out of his mouth he wanted to snatch them back, because her face, which had been dreamy and soft, so much like it had been so many times before, became tense and hard.

"Ellie—"

She smacked the heel of her hand against his chest, and when his breath caught, she paled. "Oh, John, I'm sorry. Your chest, does it hurt?"

She reached for him, and he stumbled back before he could stop himself. "I'm fine. Forget it."

Her lips tightened and two bright spots of color appeared in her white face. "All right. Are you coming to bed? It's late."

He didn't know what to say. If he went to bed now, he wasn't sure if he'd be able to keep himself from touching her. When he'd had his heart attack all he'd been able to think about as the pain intensified and the darkness overcame him was that he didn't want to leave her. He loved her so much.

John was torn, more uncertain than he'd ever been in his life. He wanted to touch her, but he was afraid. What if he couldn't anymore, or worse, what if he could?

Either way, he was doomed.

"Maybe I should sleep in the guest room for a while."

She gasped, staring at him as if he'd slapped her. John reached for her, but she'd already turned away and stepped into the house. The slam of the screen door held a finality he didn't much care for. His hand drifted back to his side.

He could not continue to sleep in the same bed with Ellie and not go back to the way things had been. But things were different.

And the sooner both of them realized that, the better.

KIM'S DOOR rattled at 7:00 a.m. Even though she'd felt safer on the second floor behind closed doors, with Brian near at hand, having the object of many a nightmare dropped on her pillow did not make for pleasant dreams.

Groggy, at first she thought someone was knocking. But when her head cleared a bit, she saw the tiny gray paw shoot beneath the door, curl upward and jiggle a bit. Precious just might be too smart for anyone's good.

Kim let her in only after checking to make sure there were no gifts waiting on the other side of the door or perhaps hidden in her mouth. The kitten curled around Kim's feet, rubbing her head against Kim's ankles. Begging for food, or showing true love? Kim had a pretty good idea.

"All right, all right. I'll get your breakfast."

Kim glanced around for a robe, then remembered she'd left everything downstairs when she'd fled the invasion. She'd been too shaky then to worry about what she was wearing. Now, staring down at her bare legs and practically translucent T-shirt, she blushed.

No wonder Brian had looked at her last night as though he wanted to swoop in and have a taste.

She'd thought he meant to kiss her, breaking his own foolish rules, and she'd tensed—both wanting the kiss and fearing it, too. Because if he touched her as she wanted him to, would he then expect her to talk about the past?

She couldn't. Not even for the promise of the best oblivion she'd ever known.

But he'd turned away and disappeared into his room without even saying good-night, and Kim had decided that she was merely projecting her needs and wants onto him. She'd convinced herself in the quiet loneliness of another fitful night that the desire in his eyes had only been the magic in the moonlight or a trick of her mind.

As if she'd conjured him, Brian appeared in the doorway of his room. Dean had helped him change again into fresh sweatpants and a clean T-shirt. Today Kim was glad. The less temptation the better—for them both.

"'Morning,'' he said, his voice rough, as though he'd slept a little or smoked a lot. The sound trilled along her skin like a warm, summer wind.

Her nipples hardened, pressing against the worn cotton of her shirt. Goose bumps rose on the bare flesh of her thighs. She crossed her arms over her chest, the movement only making her more self-conscious. She didn't bother to answer his greeting, afraid she'd say much more than she should.

"I have an appointment in an hour for these." Brian lifted his splints.

"Oh. Okay. I'll get dressed."

"Great!"

He sounded far too enthused. Maybe she hadn't been projecting so much after all.

Uncomfortable silence descended. Neither of them moved. Kim felt she should say something more, but she wasn't sure what.

Precious shot out of the room, skidded across the hallway and slammed into the far wall. She shook her head, lifted one paw and rubbed her ear; then, without sparing them a glance, she stuck her tail in the air and walked down the stairs as if the embarrassing moment had never occurred. Kim wished she could be that nonchalant whenever she made a fool of herself.

Brian snorted. Kim smiled, and just like that the unease dissipated. She saw what life might have been like if she'd stayed instead of run, and it wasn't bad. In fact, waking up to Brian, a cat, perhaps a dog, even that blasted sheep, held a certain appeal. And that thought brought about the usual need to be anywhere but there.

"Shower," Kim mumbled. "Coffee. Preferably coffee in the shower."

Brian didn't answer, merely raised a brow as she fled downstairs in the wake of her kitten.

CHAPTER TWELVE

KIM PUT ON the coffee, then showered and dressed in plenty of time to make scrambled eggs and toast. She managed not to burn the eggs; however, their taste was reminiscent of dry grass. She'd always thought wrecking scrambled eggs was pretty hard. But she managed it.

So they ate toast and cereal. Brian didn't seem to mind. In fact, he didn't say anything, just opened his mouth and swallowed what she fed him like an eager baby bird.

Despite her failure with the eggs, the time was peaceful and relaxed. Back in Savannah Kim was always running late by the time she got to the office. This caused her to begin the day frazzled before she even dealt with any of the craziness associated with her job. Knowing she and Brian did not have to run out the door and race into town, Kim found herself enjoying the simplicity of the morning.

Precious chased dust motes through the golden slants of sunlight spraying through the kitchen window and onto the floor. The back door was open and in another patch of sunshine Ba sprawled, belly skyward, hooves cocked like a big black dog.

From another part of the house drifted an oldies radio station—eighties, her favorite. Brian hummed along to the Bee Gees as he read *The Agricultural Journal*.

If the pace in Savannah was lethargic, the pace here was downright bucolic. As it should be.

A short time later Kim ushered Brian into the waiting room of the orthopedic surgeon, located in an office building attached to the hospital. Since Brian had the first appointment of the day, the waiting room was deserted. Kim checked him in, filling out the forms, after asking him the questions.

"Are all the doctors' offices in this building?" Kim handed the nurse the clipboard.

"As far as I know." The woman's gaze swept the papers and she gave a slight nod at finding everything completed to her satisfaction. "Easier for everyone that way."

Easier for Kim, too. She would stop by the OB-GYN and make an appointment for her delinquent mother. She might not be an ellie-phant, but Kim wasn't going to forget what she'd promised, either.

She shook her head, remembering Dad's confusion over Mom's indignant reaction to his joke. The changes in her mother's body were in a large part to blame for her behavior. Still, Kim had to admit she wouldn't have liked being called an elephant, even in jest. She was seeing her mother's side of things more and more as each day passed.

"Thanks, Mrs. Riley." The nurse glanced up from

the clipboard with a big, Barbie-like smile. "You and your husband can come back now."

Kim blinked. "Oh, I'm not—"

But the nurse had scurried off to open the door that led from the waiting room to the exam rooms.

She snapped her mouth shut. *Mrs. Riley.* How many times had she imagined being called that? And why did the same sense of fear, joy and anticipation bubble within her now?

Because the temptations were mounting. Staying with Brian and taking care of him had turned into living with Brian and lusting after him. Doing a job had turned into being a wife—in theory, anyway. What would tempt her next?

"Kim?" Brian stood in the doorway; the nurse hovered behind him.

"You don't need me, do you?" she blurted.

The nurse frowned. Brian shook his head, shrugged. "It's not like you can hold my hand." He wiggled his splints and winked.

Kim gaped. In that moment he looked exactly like the young boy she'd been unable to resist. In some ways Brian was different, so remote and solemn she couldn't fathom her continued attraction; then he would say or do something that reminded her of every single reason she had adored him.

Temptation beckoned once more. She could stay, help him pick out colors for his casts, pretend to be his wife and continue to be seduced by everything she had put behind her. Or she could do what was best for them both.

"I said I'd make an appointment for my mom with the OB-GYN. I'll take care of that while you're in there."

"Okay."

The door closed, removing him from her sight. Kim found it much easier to breathe when Brian wasn't staring at her as if he wanted to kiss her goodbye. Or maybe she was just projecting again.

She slipped out of the room and moments later located the office of the local OB-GYN. Kim stepped inside and froze.

The place was full of women in every stage of life and pregnancy. Children of all shapes and sizes tumbled across the carpet. The noise level rivaled a McDonald's Playplace.

"That's it," Kim mumbled. "I'm going to stop drinking the water."

Now she understood why the orthopedist's office had been empty. Everyone in town was here—or at least the female population and any children under twelve. Didn't they have school?

"Oh, my God! Kim! Is that you?"

Kim had been contemplating escape, but now it was too late. Becky Jo Sopol had seen her.

Though Becky Jo was a few pounds heavier, a bit pale and tired, she was still the perky, blond beauty she had always been. With wide blue eyes and creamy skin, she presented the picture of innocence, even though she was anything but. Whenever Kim and Becky Jo had acted up—cut class, skipped school, swiped a cigarette from Kim's father's stash to share under the bleachers—and gotten caught, Becky had batted her blues and walked, while Kim took the fall.

Kim hadn't minded. She'd always been searching for trouble—until she'd found Brian and discovered what trouble really meant.

"I heard you were home." Becky Jo jiggled the baby in her arms with the absent air of a mother of four. "But why are you *here?*"

Although the children continued to laugh and cry and argue, everyone else became quiet. Kim's gaze swept the room, to discover far too many eyes on her. Several of the faces struck familiar chords, but Kim had been gone so long and tried so hard to forget so many things she could put names with none of them but Becky Jo.

"Kim?" Becky Jo prompted when she continued to stare at everyone mutely.

"I—uh, well, I'm—you see, Brian—"

"Brian?" Her friend's innocent eyes went shrewd. "What about Brian?"

"Oh, I just heard this morning," said a woman who, from the size of her middle, appeared eight years pregnant. "He fell off the barn roof."

A collective gasp swirled about the room. Some of the children stilled and glanced at their mothers, no doubt wondering what on earth they had done this time. Seeing the women occupied elsewhere and not bearing down on them, they resumed whatever anarchy they were engaged in.

"Is he all right?" questioned an older woman, who peered at Kim from behind inordinately thick glasses.

Kim needed another few seconds to recognize Señora Stonefield, the high school Spanish teacher.
When she did, she quickly looked away, hoping the
señora wasn't the kind of woman to hold a grudge.

In retrospect, the whoopee cushion she'd placed on
her teacher's chair before general assembly had probably not been the best idea.

"*Two* broken wrists," the incredible pregnant
woman informed them in a stage whisper.

She struggled to sit up straighter, winced, gasped
and put a hand to her stomach. The others held their
breath. But after a moment, she shook her head and
collapsed back in the seat, legs splayed out in front of
her. In that position her belly rose up like the back of
a whale breaking the ocean's surface.

No wonder the woman was camped in the doctor's
office. She was going to pop at any minute and give
the community's children a lesson in childbirth they
could probably do without.

"What does Brian's fall have to do with you,
Kim?"

There was no moss on Becky Jo Sopol. Never had
been.

"Well, he fell. And I—well, really I didn't, but then
I had to—"

"She's living with him."

This time even the children went quiet and stared.

Kim glared at Chatty Cathy, as she'd dubbed her in
her mind. Much better than Huge Hannah, she ratio-
nalized, which had been her first choice.

"Do I know you?" she asked. "Because you seem to know a hell of a lot about me."

The woman gaped; so did several of the others. Becky Jo smirked. No one seemed to know what to say now. *Good.*

One of the things Kim did not miss about a small community—was there something she *did* miss?—was the seemingly telepathic ability to know everyone's else's business.

Though Savannah was a small town in theory, in practice it was pretty big. That Kim was a stranger, and a Yankee to boot, had allowed her to escape a lot of the censure and gossip. Once a Yankee, always a Yankee, and therefore outside the notice of the folks who had lived there forever. Another reason she loved the place.

Something tugged on Kim's jeans. She glanced down and a sudden, shocking wave of longing broadsided her. About eight years old, blond hair in braids, freckles on the nose, the child was the image of Becky Jo, except for the lighter blue of her eyes.

"You swore," the child informed her.

"I did?"

"H-E-double toothpicks. That's a swear."

"You're right. Sorry."

"My dog died."

Kim frowned at the inexplicable change in subject. But when the girl's eyes filled with tears, moisture brimming over and dripping down her cheeks like a flash flood, she cast a panicked glance at Becky Jo, who shrugged.

"Sorry," Kim repeated. Her mind searched for something, anything, to say. "I'm sure he's in heaven. With God."

Kim wasn't sure of any such thing, but it sounded good, and the child stopped leaking.

But instead of being comforted by Kim's words, she appeared confused. "What's God gonna do with a dead dog?"

Kim didn't have an answer for that.

"Never mind, Cindy," Becky Jo admonished. "Go watch the video with your sister and brother."

"That show *sucks.*"

Kim blinked at the vehemence in Cindy's voice. In her opinion hearing *sucks* from the mouth of a little girl sounded worse than H-E-double toothpicks from an adult.

She waited for the explosion from Becky Jo, but none came. If Kim had have spoken like that to her mother, or Becky Jo to hers, they'd have had their ears blistered along with their backsides.

"The video is what you get," Becky Jo said calmly.

"It's stupid, stupid, stupid. I wanna watch *Jerry Springer.*"

Becky Jo blushed and glanced furtively at the other women. "I keep falling asleep with the television on. You know how it is with a new baby."

"Why don't people like transvestites? They're pretty."

Becky Jo mumbled something that sounded much worse than H-E-double toothpicks and got to her feet. Cindy, no dummy by a long shot, ran behind Kim.

"She's going to beat on me," the child cried in a dramatic falsetto. "Save me."

Kim half expected her to clasp her hands to her breast and beat her sooty dark lashes. She couldn't help but smile. Until Becky Jo thrust something into her arms.

"Hold this a minute."

Kim bobbled the baby, earning a collective gasp and several glares from the assembly. Thankfully the child was fast asleep and didn't start to wail.

"School's out for teachers' convention," Becky Jo muttered, "and I've had about all I can take of togetherness." She turned her attention to the ducking, bobbing Cindy. "I've never laid a hand on you in your life, Cynthia Jane, though I haven't put it completely out of my head yet."

Cindy froze. "'But—but—if you don't beat on me we can't be on the show 'Mothers Who Are Very, Very Sorry.'"

Becky Jo snatched her daughter by the arm before she could duck behind Kim again. "I tell you what, if you don't go watch the video, we can rehearse the show 'Daughters Who Are in Big, Big Trouble.'"

The two of them moved off toward the corner television, where a purple dinosaur danced and sang in the middle of a classroom full of smiling cherubs. Kim had never seen that many children that happy to be in school. Maybe she could interest Jerry Springer in the topic—real life versus the world of Barney.

The baby hiccupped in her sleep. Kim held her awkwardly away from her body, not wanting to cuddle too close. She was terrified that if she did she just might break down completely. Once in a lifetime had been quite enough for her, thank you.

However, the perfection of the child's skin, the shadows of eyelashes along the half-moon of her closed eyelids and the pink bowed mouth mesmerized her.

"Kim? You're so pale." Becky Jo had returned and now peered quizzically into Kim's face. She laid a hand on Kim's arm but made no move to take the baby back. "Are you sick? Is that why you're here?"

"No, I'm fine. Tired, that's all."

"Are you…" She lifted her eyebrows, glanced down at the baby, then back at Kim.

"No." Kim shook her head fast and hard. "Oh, no."

Just the thought made her dizzy again. If there was one thing she feared more than Brian discovering the truth, it was that.

"If you aren't sick, then what are you doing here?" Becky pressed.

Kim dumped the baby back into her friend's arms, then glanced around the room. Mothers talked quietly with their children; ladies without children talked quietly with one another or read *People* magazine. Though no one appeared the slightest bit interested, Kim could tell by the pointed way they ignored her that they were all very interested indeed.

Kim drew Becky Jo farther away from the room at large, though the place was so full there wasn't anywhere private to go. "I need to make an appointment for my mom."

"*She's* sick?"

"No."

Kim didn't elaborate. Her mother wasn't sick. What she was, was no business but theirs.

Country concern was what Becky Jo would call such questions, and she'd be both surprised and dismayed to hear that Kim just considered her nosy. Kim liked to keep her private life private. In Gainsville there was no such thing.

The receptionist beckoned, so Kim murmured, "Excuse me," and took care of business, hoping all the while that Becky Jo would be called to her appointment before Kim finished and she could slip out of the room without further conversation. No such luck.

When Kim turned away from the window, she nearly stumbled over Becky Jo and two more children.

"This is Carrie and Joey."

"Uh, hi."

The two smiled with gap-toothed innocence, then as soon as Becky Jo's back was turned they began to punch each other in the arm with drumbeat precision.

They reminded Kim of her and Dean at that age. Of course, their mother would never have permitted the punching to go on as long as it had. She'd have slapped them both up alongside the head while admonishing them that "Hitting wasn't nice."

Kim smirked. The more she thought about certain occurrences in her past, the funnier they got—while others only appeared sadder from a distance.

"Is Brian really all right?"

Kim dragged her gaze from the children and back to Becky Jo, who was jiggling the wide-eyed baby. Kim wasn't sure, but she didn't think all that jiggling could be good for the digestion. As if to prove her point, the baby burped and white gook sprayed from her sweet little mouth, plunging through the air and landing on the floor with a wet splotch.

Becky Jo didn't even look down. With the precision of a laser beam, her foot covered the spot and ground it into the busy pattern of the carpet. She raised her eyebrows and cocked her head, waiting for Kim's answer.

"Um, oh, Brian. Yeah, he seems to be all right. I just dropped him at the doctor to get his casts."

"*You* did?"

"Someone had to."

"Are you and Brian back together?"

"No!"

The receptionist glanced up at the force and volume of Kim's denial; so did three-quarters of the room. Kim cleared her throat, gave everyone an apologetic smile. *No* seemed to be her word today.

Perhaps sensing the conversation in the waiting room could turn even louder, the receptionist summoned Becky Jo to her appointment.

"You know what?" Becky Jo motioned to the immensely pregnant lady. "Take Julie."

The receptionist frowned. "You were first, Mrs. Sopol."

"I know. But she's been doing her breathing exercises for five minutes now. You remember how she almost dropped that last baby out in the frozen-food section? The doctor better take a peek.''

Alarm widened the receptionist's eyes and she hurried over to Julie. ''Let me help you up.''

No small feat, but several huffing, puffing minutes later the two women disappeared beyond closed doors.

Becky Jo plopped the baby into the *señora's* lap, wagged a finger at her three other children and grabbed Kim's arm. She steered Kim into the hall and waited for the door to shut behind them before she spoke.

''You're my friend. Always will be, no matter what. Friends are forever in my book.''

Kim frowned. She didn't deserve Becky Jo's devotion, wasn't sure what to do or say in return. But Becky Jo didn't wait for any response on Kim's part.

''Doesn't matter how long since you've seen 'em, how little you've heard from 'em or what they might have done. But Brian's a good guy, and he doesn't deserve to be hurt again.''

''I have no intention of hurting him.''

''Then why are you living with him?'' Becky Jo whispered furiously.

''You make it sound like we're having mad, passionate sex on the kitchen table.''

''It wouldn't be the first time.''

Kim blushed. She'd once shared a lot with Becky Jo—perhaps too much.

''He still loves you.''

Kim laughed. ''No, he doesn't.''

The idea was ludicrous. Brian might want her; hell, she wanted him, too. But sex wasn't love. She knew that better than anyone.

"Wake up and smell the manure, Kim. If friendship lasts, love lasts longer. And the kind of love you and Brian had doesn't just go away no matter what either of you has done."

Kim's mouth opened, then shut. She wasn't sure what to say. She'd never considered that Brian might still love her. How could he?

The door opened. "Mrs. Sopol?" the receptionist urged.

"Coming." Becky Jo patted Kim on the arm. "You think about what I said."

Kim could only nod. She had no energy left to argue. She barely registered when Becky Jo disappeared and the door closed, leaving Kim blissfully alone in the hall.

She couldn't get her mind around the possibility that Brian might still love her. Even if he did, it wouldn't matter. Just as her loving him didn't matter. She couldn't have him.

Brian deserved better, and she knew just how to make him realize that.

"MODERN MEDICINE is unbelievable." Brian admired his shiny new casts.

Kim grunted. She'd been doing that a lot since picking him up at the doctor's office and stuffing him back into her Miata.

"You know with these I can take a shower, go swimming, even wash a cow if I want to."

"And why would you want to?"

He grinned. "Because they're there?"

She didn't smile; she didn't laugh. She didn't even roll her eyes or say "har-har." But Brian was too excited about modern medicine to care at the moment.

"You remember what casts used to be like? Heavy and white. You couldn't do a damn thing when you had one on."

"Which might have been the point."

He ignored her, holding his arms out in front of him and turning them this way, then that. "I could have gotten black and red. But since it's football season, I thought blue and orange would be better."

Kim glanced at the neon-orange cast circling his right forearm. "How could you resist?"

"Exactly. Dean is going to love these."

She returned her attention to the road. "What's that saying about men and boys and the price of their toys?"

"Got me."

Kim muttered something that sounded suspiciously like "H-E-double toothpicks," and spun the sports car from the road onto his lane. Gravel sprayed in their wake.

"What's eating you?"

She'd been acting strange all day, come to think of it. This morning she'd practically run for the shower, but when she'd come out, they'd shared a peaceful, pleasant breakfast. The ride to town had been okay.

Then she'd made an excuse to leave him at the doctor's office alone. Was she *trying* to make him crazy?

Kim parked her car, leaped out of the driver's seat and headed for the house. If he didn't know better he'd think she was avoiding him. But why? He hadn't touched her—lately.

"Hey," he shouted out the half open window. "We forgot to buy groceries."

Kim disappeared inside, leaving Brian to get himself out of the car. Luckily, the sturdiness of the casts enabled him to accomplish more with his fingers. He was clumsy and slow, but he managed to open the car door and exit under his own power.

Just in time to hear Kim scream.

Ba, who had been trotting over to greet him, skittered and balked. Brian didn't have time to soothe her; he was already running for the house. He left her staring after him, head cocked like a Labrador retriever.

Brian opened the screen door and Precious shot out squalling as loudly as her mistress. The kitten's feet scrabbled for purchase on the smooth wood of the porch. She dug in and leaped.

Just then Ba decided to come to the rescue, loping toward the house. The cat landed on her back. Ba bleated, bucked and began to spin madly.

Instead of jumping free and running away, the kitten arched her back like an imitation of a Halloween cat and held on. The sheep leaped around the yard like a rodeo bull.

Brian's head spun, as well. With Kim yelling from one side and Ba *baaing* from the other, he wasn't sure what to do. Another panicked shriek from the house made his decision for him. Though he'd like to stay and watch the show, he hurried inside.

He should have known what had happened just by the tenor of Kim's screams. Nevertheless, he stood openmouthed in the kitchen doorway. Kim was perched on the counter as what appeared to be a drunken mouse ran circles around the kitchen table. Every time she yelled, the mouse changed directions. Why it didn't run away from the sound, back to the basement or even into the hallway, Brian couldn't figure.

The rambunctious rodent circled too close, and Brian snatched it up by the tail. Kim stopped screaming as if a switch had been thrown.

Brian let his gaze wander from the dangling mouse to the trembling woman. "Why didn't you come back outside if there was a mouse in the kitchen?"

"There *wasn't*. Precious ran in and dropped it on my foot."

"Boy, does she love you."

Kim winced, swallowed and looked away. "Can you get rid of that, please?"

"Oh, sure. Sorry."

He walked to the front door. Ba and Precious had disappeared, though he heard furious bleating and irate caterwauling from the back of the house. Apparently the party wasn't over.

Brian tossed the mouse outside and returned to find Kim still on top of the counter.

"You can come down now."

"I don't think so."

"You going to stay up there forever?"

"Maybe."

"Just so you know, the mouse was already up there."

"What?" Her gaze darted to and fro.

Brian crossed the room and pointed to the toast left over from that morning. Half had been nibbled away, and there were tiny mouse calling cards all over the place.

"Uck!" Kim jumped down.

She landed on her feet, but the force of the leap tossed her nose first into Brian's chest. He grabbed her shoulders, awkwardly because of the casts, and helped her stand up straight.

Blue highlights shone in the ebony silk of her hair. The scent of Kim—warmth, energy, both the sweetness and the spice of life—tantalized. The muscles beneath his fingertips danced. He felt her tremble. She was so on edge she was making *him* nervous.

"Hey," he murmured. "It was just a mouse."

"Just?" Her laugh sounded like a sob.

He should let her go, but he couldn't seem to make his fingers obey. He wanted her; he shouldn't. He loved her; he couldn't.

Brian lifted his hands, meaning to ruffle his hair in frustration and popped himself in the nose with his electric-orange cast.

"Shit," he muttered.

She took one step back, quirked a brow at his klutziness, but let it go without comment. "I suppose you're going to tell me next that the mouse was more afraid of me than I was of it."

Brian wanted to rub his throbbing nose, but he was afraid he might knock himself out if he tried—so he let it hurt. He was very good at letting it hurt.

"Well, it was."

"Doesn't matter. Irrational fears don't listen to rational explanations. When I see a mouse, I can't think straight. My skin crawls, my hair tingles and I scream, even though I know screaming won't do any good."

Her gaze met his, and the memory passed between them of another time screaming had done no good. He wanted to pull her closer but she'd only run away. Instead, very carefully, he brushed a strand of loose hair away from her face. His fingers drifted across her temple and her eyes closed.

"Just because you're touching me doesn't mean I'll talk," she murmured.

"Just because I promised not to talk doesn't mean I won't remember."

She opened her eyes and smiled sadly. "I know."

The love he'd tried so hard to kill pulsed to life, heating his skin, slowing his blood, tainting his thoughts. Before he knew what he was doing, he'd leaned over and brushed his lips across the place his fingers had touched.

She leaned into him; her arms went around his waist, and for a long, long time the two of them stood in his kitchen. Neither said a word, but it was the best conversation they'd had in years.

"I SHOULD FIND Precious," Kim said.

"She's with Ba."

"Then I should hurry."

His laughter rumbled against her cheek. The soap-and-water scent of his skin brushed her face. The heavy weight of his casts rested against her back. Longing rippled through her with an intensity that made Kim shudder.

She wanted to remain in his arms forever, so she had to pull away. She couldn't hurt Brian again. She had to make him see that she wasn't worthy of his love.

What was it all those gospel singers sang?

Oh, yeah. The truth shall set you free. She certainly hoped so.

"There something I have to tell you."

Brian's eyes widened. "Okay."

He sat at the table and stared at her expectantly.

Suddenly more nervous than she'd been when Precious had bestowed her latest present, Kim paced the room. "As near as I can figure it, when I left, you worked too much and withdrew from everyone who'd let you."

"So? Did you think I'd go merrily along, partying like there was no tomorrow."

She closed her eyes and confessed. "I did."

"You did what?"

"I tried to forget the only way I knew how." She opened her eyes and saw his confusion. "I was empty, Brian. So damn empty."

Her breath caught on the sob that nearly escaped.

He held out a hand, but she shook her head and stayed out of his reach. If he touched her now, she'd never be able to get through this without crying.

"I had to fill my time, my heart, my mind, myself."

"With what?" he whispered.

She wanted to run, but she'd run enough, and she had to tell him. She had to make him see that spending his life loving her was a waste of perfectly good love.

"Music, dancing, laughter, though I didn't feel like laughing. Tequila worked pretty good. But there was something that worked a whole lot better."

"What?"

The memory of those days hit her so hard she clenched her hands. Loneliness, emptiness, despair. Searching never finding. Needing always wanting.

Kim forced herself to look Brian in the eyes when she told him the truth. "Men," she blurted. "The dumber and prettier the better."

He blinked as if she'd said she'd invited little green Martian men to supper.

She waited for him to get up and walk out, or to tell her to get out. He did nothing, merely frowned and stared at her some more.

"Brian? Did you hear what I said?"

"My wrists are broken. My hearing's just fine." He tilted his head. "So there are a lot of pretty dumb men in Savannah?"

"That isn't funny."

"Do you see me laughing? I'm just trying to figure out why you're so upset."

She gaped. Could he possibly not understand what

she'd said? Did she have the courage to spell
things out?

Brian beat her to it. "I withdrew from everyone.
You went searching for someone."

"Anyone," she muttered.

He shrugged. "We all handle devastation in our
own way, Kim. I only have one question."

She cast him a wary glance. Whatever his question,
she was certain the answer would hurt them both.

"Did it help?"

Her eyebrows shot up. That was one question she
hadn't expected and didn't want to answer.

It hadn't helped. Because none of them had
been him.

CHAPTER THIRTEEN

THE PHONE RESCUED Kim from the unanswerable question. Brian answered, then passed it to her. "Your mother."

She grabbed the receiver. This might be the first time she'd been overjoyed at a phone call from Mom.

"The doctor's office just called to confirm my appointment in an hour. I didn't know I had an appointment in an hour."

"Oh!" She'd forgotten. "Sorry. There was a cancellation and I took it. I'll be right over."

"Never mind. I'm not going."

"Mom. We've been over this. You're going." Kim hung up before she had to argue anymore.

"Your mom okay?"

"Fine. She just hasn't had a check up in several light-years. I'm going to make sure she gets one. Today."

"All right. We can finish this later."

That sounded like a threat, even though Brian leaned against the counter with lazy grace and smiled with more ease than Kim had seen in him since coming back.

For a moment she was struck by how handsome he

was, and the familiar longing consumed her. Not that she lusted for him only because he was beautiful. He was strong and sweet, responsible and funny—everything she missed. The problem was she not only lusted, she loved.

"Later," she echoed. A goodbye, not a promise. "I—I'll get groceries on the way back. What do you like?"

"Surprise me."

How could he be so nonchalant? How could he behave as if nothing had changed? As if what she'd just revealed meant as little to him as what they'd for supper last night? Could that truly be the case? And if so, what did it mean? Could she allow it to mean anything?

Kim stepped onto the porch and stopped dead as Ba bucked through the yard, Precious clinging to her back.

"Hey!" she shouted. "Drop that cat!"

"It wasn't Ba's idea." Brian appeared at the screen door. "Precious jumped on her."

"Make them stop."

Brian squinted at the cavorting sheep. "Yeah, right."

"I mean it! Someone's going to get hurt."

Oh, dear God, she sounded like her mother. When had that started?

"I think they're playing," Brian said, and his voice held a note of wonder.

Set to charge down the steps, grab the ewe by the ears and rescue her baby, Kim hesitated.

Ba stopped leaping. Her sides heaved and her head hung low. She appeared done in. Precious could have jumped down and been away. Instead, she continued to perch on the sheep's back, reaching forward with sheathed claws to bat at Ba's twitching ear. Ba folded one leg underneath herself and leaned forward.

"Oh-oh." Kim tensed, afraid Ba meant to flip the kitten onto the ground and pulverize her.

But the ewe lay down; the kitten tumbled off, then promptly curled into a ball between Ba's outstretched hooves and fell asleep. Ba nuzzled the orange-white-and-gray speckled fur. Kim had never seen her behave with such gentleness and care.

"They're in love," Brian murmured.

Kim couldn't bring herself to look at him, terrified he'd be looking at her with the love he spoke of so freely in his eyes.

Instead, Kim did what she always did when she was afraid. But this time she ran to her mother.

An hour later, Eleanor left the doctor's office with a prescription, her daughter and the truth.

Life as she knew it was over.

"I was right, wasn't I?" Kim held out her coat. "You are."

"Shh," Eleanor warned, and glanced at Señora Stonefield. The woman listened avidly, as did the rest of the packed house.

Kim frowned and pulled her nearer the door. "The *señora* was here this morning."

"She's here every Thursday." Eleanor slid into her jacket.

"Is she sick?"

"No. She spends every Thursday in that chair. She says the place has better shows than *Jerry Springer*."

"What is it with *Jerry Springer* around here?" Kim muttered.

"The winters are long."

Kim opened the door. Eleanor went through. They met in the hallway.

"So I was right?" Kim pressed.

"Yeah."

"I don't understand why you're so upset. It's not the end of the world."

"It's the end of my world."

"But why?"

Eleanor shook her head and stalked away. She didn't want to talk right now; she wanted to think.

How was she going to tell John? What would he do? Would it be out to pasture for her? Or worse?

Kim climbed into the driver's seat. She appeared concerned. The novelty of that was outweighed by uncertainty. If Kim was worried about her, Eleanor must be behaving more strangely than even she was aware of.

Making no move to start the car, Kim turned toward her. "Explain what's so terrible about menopause, Mom. I really want to know."

"Besides feeling crazy half the time?"

"The meds should take care of that. You'll feel good as new in no time at all."

"But I won't *be* good as new."

"Why not?"

"Because I'm defective and old."

"Old? You're fifty. These days that's middle-aged." Kim shook her head. "And defective? Where do you get this stuff? Menopause is a natural occurrence."

"Your father isn't going to think so."

"What does this have to do with Daddy?"

"When cows can't have calves, what does he do with them?"

Kim rolled her eyes. "You're not a cow."

"No, I'm an ellie-phant."

"You know, I thought the joke was in poor taste myself, but let it go already."

Eleanor didn't bother to dignify that with a response. "I wouldn't be surprised if he goes out and finds a younger model the minute he hears."

"You're being irrational. Daddy *loves* you."

"He told you this?"

Kim's brow creased. "Well, not in so many words."

"That's what I thought."

"You've lived with the man for over thirty years, had six children, and you don't think he loves you?"

"I think he *did*."

"I think we better get that prescription filled on the way home so you can start tonight."

Eleanor's lips tightened. "You're saying I'm crazy."

"If you think Daddy doesn't love you, then yeah, you're crazy."

"You know he hasn't touched me in months?"

Kim clapped her hands over her ears. "Too much information."

Eleanor reached over and pulled Kim's palms away from her head. For an instant she felt like a mommy, and the longing made her dizzy. Would she forever miss what she could never have again?

"*You* wanted to talk about this. Your friend's mom thought you should know all about menopause, and she's probably right. But let's talk about how it feels to have one of the most important things in your life taken away and there's nothing you can do about it."

Kim gave her a wary look. "What's been taken away?"

"One of my greatest joys was having kids and raising them. I was good at it."

Or at least I was until I messed up with you, Eleanor thought.

But she kept her mouth shut. One thing the two of them never discussed was what had gone wrong between them. Kim had a way of shutting down and running off whenever things got sticky. No doubt another black mark on Eleanor's maternal scorecard.

Silence fell between them. Eleanor laid her head back against the seat and closed her eyes. "No one needs me anymore, and now no one ever will."

"You believe that the only thing you have to offer is being someone's mother?"

Eleanor didn't bother to open her eyes. "That's all I've ever had to offer, and now it's done."

"You're really pissing me off, Mom."

Her eyes snapped open. She glared at Kim, but her daughter had always been beyond any evil eye Eleanor could manage.

"This is why I never wanted to learn what you had to teach me," Kim muttered. "You thought all there was to life was being someone's wife or mother."

"And you thought being a wife and mother was a life sentence and not a life."

Kim flinched. "That's not true."

"What is true?" Then, because Kim's lips tightened mutinously, Eleanor put a hand atop her daughter's and urged, "Tell me. Please. I want to understand."

Kim searched Eleanor's face. What she saw there must have convinced her that her mother *did* want to know the truth—even if it hurt. The time had come to settle a few old questions.

"I felt pushed—into staying here, living the same life as you had. Even in school, girls were cheerleaders and not basketball players. We took home ec, not shop. We were supposed to become teachers, nurses or secretaries, never professors, doctors or lawyers." She spread her hands. "Telling me I couldn't only made me certain that I could. Telling me I should only made me certain I shouldn't. I'm sure having five older brothers had something to do with my attitude. But I wanted more, or at least the chance to try."

"I didn't mean to push you. It was just…I'd dreamed of having a little girl for a long, long time. I wanted to share what I knew. It was one of the few things I had to give.''

''And I didn't want to be like you,'' Kim murmured. ''Working as hard as any field hand, so many kids, so close together. You were always tired, forever busy.''

''I was a mom. It's part of the job description.''

Kim took a deep breath, hesitated.

''Tell me,'' Eleanor insisted. ''It's time we got this out. Both of us.''

Kim gave one sharp nod of agreement. ''Every time I fell, you told me I was too big to cry. When I asked to be rocked, you had somewhere else to be. Whenever I hugged you, you always pulled away first.''

Every word was like a needle to Eleanor's already sore heart. But she couldn't deny what she knew to be true.

''I was overwhelmed. Excited to have a girl, but a sixth child...'' Eleanor sighed. ''I have so few memories of when you were a baby. I was hanging on by my fingernails then. By the time I felt more in control, you were out of diapers and I wondered what had happened. The proverbial, Where did the time go?''

She shook her head. ''You were different from your brothers. The way I handled them didn't work with you. When I held the boys, they pushed me away. So I learned not to hold on too long. If I wasn't on the ball, they rolled over me. I learned to be quick, get ahead, get on top of things or I was sorry. But I ended up being sorry anyway.''

''Why?''

"I wasn't the mother you wanted."

"I wasn't any prize of a daughter, either."

"I thought so."

Kim laughed. "You did not. I was a pain in the ass, Mom. I know it—you know it. All of Gainsville knows it."

"Well, if we're telling the truth…"

They shared a smile.

"None of us gets the mother we want," Kim said. "But if we try, we might get the one we need."

Kim held out a hand. Eleanor took it, then pulled her daughter into her arms and held on tight. She almost forgot her life was over, because something wonderful had just begun.

THE FOOD BEGAN to arrive five minutes after Kim left. He was surprised it had taken this long. News usually traveled faster than Amtrak in Gainsville.

Casseroles, banana bread, Jell-O molds. Cake, cookies, pie. There was no way Brian and Kim could eat everything the ladies of the town brought by.

Along with the food came offers of help from the men. Beau Radly would spread manure. Jerry Potter could pick up and deliver feed. Lou Ferrenge would send his son, Stew, to do whatever Brian could think of. Patrick Sopol planned to spell Dean at the milking whenever Dean needed him.

Considering Brian had pretty much kept to himself ever since he'd taken over the farm, he couldn't fathom the outpouring of generosity. He was still scratching his head when Dean showed up.

"It's called being neighborly, moron. If you weren't such a social reject, you wouldn't have to ask."

"Takes one to know one."

"Gee, did you need all day to think that up?"

Brian would have punched him in the arm, just to be neighborly, but in his current condition a friendly tap could cause serious damage.

Then Dean's dad climbed out of the cab of Dean's pickup and all Brian's humor vanished beneath the wave of guilt that overwhelmed him every time he saw John Luchetti.

Dean's grin disappeared, as well. "Dad wanted to come over and talk."

A chill ran down Brian's back. What could Kim's dad want to talk about? He'd never wanted to talk before—a fact for which Brian had been eternally grateful. He was just lucky John hadn't beaten the crap out of him on principle after he and Kim had run away.

Panicked, Brian watched Dean desert him for the barn. John crossed the yard, climbed the steps and took a seat on the porch just as Ba skidded around the corner, her new best friend on her back.

John stared at the animals, then raised one brow in Brian's direction. "Cat jockey?"

Brian snorted. "Maybe. They seem to like each other, and since Ba doesn't like much—" he shrugged "—I decided to ignore them."

"Your farm has always been interesting, Riley. I'll give you that."

Brian wasn't sure what to make of "interesting," so he ignored that, too.

Ba trotted over and butted Brian in the hip. When he tried to rub between her eyes, Precious attacked his cast, then fell on her head. Ba immediately lay down so the kitten could climb back on.

"Well, if that isn't the darnedest thing," John muttered. "I've never seen a sheep like that."

"You and me both."

"You could probably sell her for a pretty penny."

"Sell her?"

"Well, you aren't going to eat her, are you? I know we're farmers, but I've always drawn the line at eating pets."

Brian stared at John wide-eyed. "Eat Ba?"

"Baaa!"

John blinked. "If I didn't know better, I'd think Barbara there understands what we're talking about."

Brian glanced at the sheep, who appeared to be staring at him with reproach. "I didn't say it," he whispered.

Ba stuck her nose in the air, then trotted off toward the barn, taking Precious with her.

John patted the pocket of his shirt, glanced around as if searching for someone, then withdrew a cigarette. "You don't care if I smoke."

The words weren't a question, but Brian answered anyway. "Uh, no, sir. But—"

John squinted at him through the haze of smoke he'd already exhaled.

"No, sir," Brian repeated.

"Take a load off," John offered, as if this were his house and not Brian's.

Brian did as he was told. No sense avoiding the inevitable, or making the man any more angry than he already was. Though to be honest, John didn't look mad. He looked…peaceful, content, darned near joyous, in fact, as he sucked on his cigarette and blew smoke rings at the afternoon sky.

The weather was fine—doubly so for October in Illinois. The sun shone brightly in a sky of purest blue, and the breeze that had held a chill that morning did so no longer.

"Don't suppose you've got anything to drink around here."

"Uh, sure. But I have a hard time playing host with these." He held up his casts.

"Go Bears," John said dryly.

Brian spread his arms. "It seemed like a good idea at the time."

"It always does." John got up. "I'll be right back."

Seconds later he returned with two bottles of beer and handed one to Brian. Brian didn't think John was supposed to drink either, but *he* wasn't about to mention it.

"Thanks." He took a long swig, managing the bottle with some difficulty, then he took another and waited.

John seemed perfectly content to drink, smoke and stare at the sky. So Brian let him until he could stand the silence no longer.

"How are you feeling?"

"Damn good right now. You?"

Nervous. Guilty. Embarrassed.

"Fine," Brian said quickly.

"We could play checkers or cards, but—" John tipped his beer to indicate Brian's casts.

"Yeah. I seem to knock things over more than I pick them up."

"Well, that's what Kim's here for. Where is she, anyway?"

"She took Mrs. Riley to the OB-GYN."

As soon as the words were out of his mouth, Brian wanted to snatch them back, because John sat up so fast his chair nearly tipped over, and he spilled beer on his shoe.

"What?"

"Uh, I thought you knew."

Duh, his mind mocked, *obviously not.*

"I knew they went somewhere, which I thought was weird, considering. But with my wife lately—" he shook his head "—*weird* has taken on a whole new meaning. What did Kim say?"

"Just a checkup. That's all."

"Ellie—I mean Eleanor—" John rolled his eyes.

Brian wasn't sure what was up with that, so he kept quiet.

"She never goes for a checkup."

"That's what Kim said."

John took a hard pull on his cigarette, which he'd smoked down to the filter. He didn't seem to mind— or even notice. "If it's only a checkup, then why did Kim drive her there?"

"To spend some time together?"

John snorted and got to his feet. He flicked the remains of his cigarette over the railing. The butt landed on the autumn brown grass and began to smolder. Brian didn't have the guts to mention that, either.

"Tell my son I borrowed his truck."

Alarmed, Brian jumped up. "But—"

"I'll be back. I've just got to go into town a minute."

Brian's mouth opened, then closed. He'd been sitting here waiting for the explosion with his name on it, expecting it, even wanting it, because then he'd no longer have to fear the tongue-lashing or worse that he'd deserved for eight years. But John appeared in no hurry to give it to him, and Brian couldn't wait any longer.

"I thought you wanted to talk," he blurted.

John stopped, then slowly turned. "And I thought you broke your wrists and not your fat head."

Being used to Dean's idea of affection, Brian didn't even blink at the sarcasm. "Sir?" he asked.

"Enough of that 'sir' stuff already. It's John. And we've *been* talking since I got here."

"Oh," was all Brian could manage.

"You thought I meant to have a serious talk? Maybe about Kim?"

Brian's throat was dry, so was his beer bottle. When had that happened? He managed a nod.

"I'm not much for talk. Never have been. I figure if people don't know how you feel, then you haven't been showin' 'em right. I should have kicked your ass back then. Would have, but you were so busy kicking your own, I didn't have the heart.''

Heart? John Luchetti? Since when?

''I'm not sure what happened between the two of you.'' He held up his hand when Brian opened his mouth, though what Brian planned to say he wasn't quite sure. ''And I don't wanna know! You still love my daughter, don't you?''

Brian didn't answer. What could he say? The truth might get his ass kicked as easily as a lie.

John didn't appear to need any answer. For a man who wasn't much for talk, he couldn't keep his lip zipped today.

''She loves you, too.''

''No, sir, she doesn't. I don't think she ever did.''

John smacked himself in the forehead. ''I'm dealing with a half-wit.''

''I see that you and your son have the same idea of sweet talk.''

John's green eyes narrowed, and Brian suddenly understood why the Luchetti brothers feared this man in a temper. Though John usually projected the cantankerous yet unflappable demeanor of a born farmer, there lurked beneath the surface a spark of temper ready and willing to ignite. Kim had been like this once, too. Back when he'd thought she loved him.

''What gave you the idea Kim didn't love you?''

''She left. That isn't love.''

John mumbled something that didn't sound like sweetheart and patted his pocket again. He scowled when he came up empty.

"She loved you then—she loves you now. I know my baby girl. She's afraid."

"Of what?"

"That's for you to find out."

"Swell," Brian muttered.

"Nothing worth having is easy. Every farmer knows that."

John climbed into the pickup. Without so much as a goodbye, he turned the truck around and headed for town, leaving Brian with plenty to think about.

Kim had always been closer to John than anyone else, until Brian. He was quite sure that John *did* know his baby girl, but did he know the woman she had become?

If Kim had always loved him, did in fact still love him, then maybe there was a chance to have back all they had lost—or at least what was left of it.

CHAPTER FOURTEEN

JOHN TORE INTO the parking lot of the clinic and wasted no time locating the office of the only OB-GYN in Gainsville. His heart was pounding far too fast for his age and his condition. But at least he was at the hospital already—just in case.

He stood in the hall. He did not want to go in there. Back when he and Ellie were having kids, very few men in Gainsville went where no man had gone before—specifically, into the delivery room. They waited outside like the cowards they were until the screaming was done and the babies were clean. As a result, John had never stepped foot in the office of a doctor who dealt only with women—and he didn't want to.

But he couldn't stand the suspense any longer. He was scared. Something was wrong with his wife, and he was afraid he knew exactly what.

John shoved open the door. He wasn't sure what he expected, maybe mauve carpet and rocking chairs, pastel wallpaper and lullabies to replace the Muzak. What he got was the same bland office decor he'd seen too many times before.

"Mr. Luchetti!" An elderly woman with glasses so thick her eyes appeared magnified waved to him from the chair next to the empty receptionist window.

John winced. He'd hoped to dash into a vacant room, ask for his wife, find out the truth and escape with no one the wiser. A foolish hope since everyone in Gainsville knew the office of the OB-GYN was where all the gossips congregated.

Ellie usually avoided town, doctors and gossips. She had no patience for any of them. That she'd come here at all only proved she'd had little choice.

The lady, who appeared to be eighty if she was a day, continued to wave at him.

"Ma'am." John nodded politely, even though his face felt on fire.

"I'm the *señora*," she informed him as if he should know her.

His memory not what it used to be, John just smiled and nodded some more.

"I had your daughter in Spanish 100."

John nearly groaned. He remembered her now. An irate phone call half in Spanish, half in English, something about a whoopee cushion and detention. Ellie had grounded Kim for two weeks, which only meant Kim had to shimmy down the drainpipe a lot.

He'd most likely been too lenient with her, partly to make up for Ellie being so strict and partly because Kim had been too much like him. Thinking back, he should have been more of a father and less of a friend. But what was that old saying about hindsight?

"Nice to see you," he murmured, and craned his neck searching for the receptionist.

"She's helping the doctor," the *señora* said.

John smiled, shuffled his feet, stretched his neck.

"You trying to find your wife or your daughter?"

"Both."

"They left a long time ago."

He frowned. Then why hadn't Kim returned to Brian's?

"Your wife seemed upset."

Double damn.

"She did?"

The señora nodded eagerly, then lowered her voice to a conspiratorial level. "Your daughter said, 'Are you?' Then later your wife said, 'Yeah.'"

The sweat on John's back turned cold. "Do you know where they went?"

"They didn't come home?"

John shook his head, unable to speak for fear he'd whimper.

"Your wife had a prescription. They might have gone to the pharmacy."

"Thanks," John said, then he ran.

Moments later he entered the grocery store and made a beeline for the pharmacy in the back.

"You just missed Eleanor," Ron Goldsmith, pharmacist, informed him.

"You filled a prescription for her?"

"Sure."

"What was it?"

Goldsmith's welcoming smile became a frown. "Now, you know I can't tell you that, John."

"She's my wife!"

The volume of his voice caused several customers to pause in their examination of adult diapers, laxatives and condoms. From all indications, John could have done with a higher working knowledge of the latter.

"That doesn't matter," Ron whispered. "Her medications are as private as her medical records. I can't tell you a thing."

"You're about the only one in town who can't," John muttered and stomped away.

"Hey, John!" Annabelle Hauser, head cashier at the Gainsville Drug and Sundry for the past hundred years, hailed him. "You just missed Kim and your wife."

"That seems to be the story of my life today."

Annabelle tilted her head and her huge, bleach-blond-beehive tilted, too. John watched the mass warily, wondering if it all tumbled down, would it tumble off, as well? Gossip hinted that Annabelle was as bald as a cue ball beneath that beehive. Her lack of eyebrows, unless you counted the ones she'd drawn on that morning, lent truth to the fiction.

"Is Eleanor all right, John?"

With no small amount of effort, he turned his gaze from Annabelle's beehive to her face. "Why?"

"She's acting...different."

"How so?"

"Well, she and Kim were..."

Excess powder and rouge sifted off Annabelle's face like flour from a sieve as she frowned in concentration.

"Arguing?" John supplied. "Fighting? Choking each other in the canned-goods section?"

"No. They were holding hands."

"You're sure they weren't arm wrestling?"

More powder fell as Annabelle scowled. "I may be old, but I'm not blind. They were holding hands, laughing and shopping together. It was downright spooky, considering those two. Made me wonder."

"What?"

"Which one of 'em is dying."

John's chest hurt again. He thought he was having another heart attack, until he realized he was holding his breath. He let it out in a rush and leaned on the nearest wall until his head stopped pounding in time with his pulse.

"Do you know where they went?" he managed.

"Are you sure you're okay?"

"Annabelle! Where?"

"All right, all right. You don't have to shout. They went to the Edge of Town."

"The tavern?"

"Last I heard."

"Why?"

"Something about toasting—" she circled her hands in an uncertain gesture "—something."

"With ears like yours, that's all you got?"

She stuck her nose in the air. "More than you knew when you came in here."

"Not by much," he grumbled.

She shrugged. "No new knock-knocks today?"

"I'm not in the mood."

"Impossible. You've told me a joke every time you've walked in here for the past ten years."

"And you've never laughed once."

One penciled eyebrow lifted. "I was supposed to laugh?"

"Har-har." He patted his shirt pocket. Empty. "Give me a pack of the usual before I go, Annabelle."

She gave him a funny look, but she did as he asked without question. If she wasn't old enough to be his mother, and possibly bald, she could be the perfect woman. If John wasn't crazy in love with his wife.

Outside he managed to light up, even with his hands shaking so badly he almost lit his thumb on fire. Then he drove across town with the window of Dean's truck wide open, chill wind in his hair, across his face, because he couldn't afford to return the truck smelling of smoke.

He felt like a teenager again—tooling around, hiding his smokes, woman trouble on the mind. It wasn't half as fun as he remembered.

John flicked his ashes out the window. What in hell was going on with Ellie? Was the news bad or was it good? Was it both or somewhere in between?

Whatever had happened, or was yet to happen, John resolved to be the husband Ellie needed no matter what.

Far beyond the edge of town, the tavern appeared. The place should be named the Edge of the Interstate, instead, but that title just didn't have the same down-home flavor.

The bar had once been a stone farmhouse in the middle of one of the largest single family farms in the area. Then the federal government, in all its wisdom, had built an interstate smack-dab through the barn. What was left of the family had taken the money and run to Phoenix—where all old farmers seemed to go.

In Phoenix there were no worries about rain, snow or tornadoes—just the heat—and if you didn't have to fret over your animals or your crops, heat was a fine, fine thing. After you spent fifty years at a livelihood dependent on the weather, Phoenix was a paradise to aspire to amid the uncertainties of Midwestern farm life. For some guys, but not for him. John preferred the elements, the seasons, the adventure of the unknown. He always had.

He ground his cigarette into the dirt next to a thousand others and glanced around the parking lot. No sign of Kim's car here, either. They were gone. He'd just step inside and see what he could find out—if anything.

A warm, scented wave of smoke hit him in the face. He wouldn't have to worry about explaining away why his shirt smelled like cigarettes. After five minutes in here, everyone did.

"Hey, John!" hailed the owner and bartender, Ezra Duncan. "Long time no."

John scooted his behind onto a bar stool at the same time Ezra shot a beer down the counter. John caught it and lifted the mug to his lips. He swallowed and discovered that a dry mouth, muddled mind and messed-up life could make beer taste like...

He didn't want to analyze what it tasted like. Grimacing, John put the glass down without taking another sip.

"You just missed your wife and daughter."

John rubbed his eyes. The smoke was burning them. That had never happened to him before.

"I've been missing them all over town," he said. "Any idea where they went after here?"

"Home is my guess."

"You didn't hear?"

"Not me."

He probably had, but Ezra was as closemouthed as a priest when it came to confessions at the bar. Probably because he'd been a priest once, which made his present occupation downright curious.

That he and Aaron were pals was understandable, given Aaron's experimentation with God and their common bent for saying very little, remaining very calm and helping anyone who would let them. But other than that, there was not much to compare between John's slim, albeit wiry, son and this six-feet-five-inch, 280-pound black man.

"What were they doing in here?" John asked.

"The usual."

"Drinking?"

"Soft drinks." Ezra picked up a towel and began to polish the glassware.

"They came in here for pop?"

"And a game of darts."

"Ellie?"

"She tried, but she hit Ruddy." Ezra pointed at the bull moose that hung on the wall above the dartboard. A dart stuck out of his nose. "They had a pretty good laugh over that."

"Uh, sorry," John said.

The moose was a souvenir of Ezra's first trip into the world after he'd left the priesthood. He loved that dead head and decorated it for every holiday. Right now orange pumpkin lights were strung between the impressive antlers.

"You can understand why I took the darts away after that."

"But they weren't drinking?"

"Kim said she was driving. Your wife ordered Beam and Seven, then changed her mind and ordered just Seven."

John didn't like the sound of that. But then, he'd liked the sound of precious little all day.

"I didn't think they got along," Ezra murmured.

"They don't. Or they didn't." John threw up his hands. "I don't know."

"Maybe God smiled." After taking in John's blank look, he continued. "God smiled and wiped the tears from their eyes. Or maybe the anger from their hearts."

"I find that hard to believe."

"Stranger things have happened."

"You sure?"

Ezra grinned. "Walking on water, parting the sea, wine from water. Should I keep goin'?"

"No, thanks."

John tapped his fingers on the side of his glass but left the beer right where it was. Now that he thought about it, his son never brought up God anymore. Not the way Ezra did, and John had to wonder why.

He didn't understand his quiet, sober, gentle son. Aaron had never given him or Ellie a lick of trouble, and while he should have been grateful, John had started to worry about Aaron. Especially when the boy went all the way through high school without ever bringing home a girl.

In the end, having his son turn to God had been something of a relief. Not that John would ever stop loving him, but certain things were difficult to explain to a Midwestern farming community.

However, Aaron had not become a priest and he'd never explained why. John wondered. Ellie worried. Dean mumbled and Evan cajoled. But none of them had ever asked the inevitable question.

Why not?

John ran his thumb down the condensation on the side of his glass and peered at Ezra. "Can I ask you something?"

"You can ask. Doesn't mean I'll answer."

John thought for a moment on how best to phrase his question, then gave up and blurted it out. "How come you stopped being a priest?"

One of Ezra's heavy, muscular shoulders lifted, then lowered. "Thought I could help a lot more people right here."

John glanced around the room. Besides him, there were two other customers. Considering it was a Thursday afternoon in October, the place was hopping.

"Here?"

"Souls come in lost. And here I am. When I was a

priest, I was preachin' to the choir." He winked. "So to speak."

"Do you think that's why Aaron came home?"

Ezra's open, smiling face closed. "You know I'm not going to tell you anything that Aaron's shared with me, John. That wouldn't be right."

"I know." John stared into his beer.

"Have you ever asked him yourself?"

"I figured if he wanted me to know, he'd tell me."

"What if he's thinking, 'If my dad cared he'd ask?'"

John scowled. "Did he say that?"

Ezra shook his head. "You're old school. I understand that. Men don't cry. Men don't hug. Men don't ask or tell. My daddy was just like you. And you know what he said to me on his deathbed?"

John winced. Since his heart had sent him to his knees and then to the hospital, any talk of deathbeds was talk he didn't want to hear.

But Ezra wasn't the kind of man to be stopped midstory, even if no one had asked to hear the rest. "He said, 'I wish that I'd been different, but I didn't know how.' Not everyone gets a second chance. Why don't you mend some fences while you still can?"

"I've been mendin' fences all my life. I'm lousy with a hammer."

Ezra shook his head. "Go home. You must be chasing your wife all over town for a reason. I can only hope it's to make her eyes less sad."

The cold sweat reappeared on John's spine. "You said she was laughing."

"On the outside. I've had enough experience to know what crying on the inside looks like."

John cursed, threw some money on the bar and took Ezra's advice.

ELEANOR WAS getting worried. The cows had gathered at the barn door and no one was there to let them in for the evening milking.

No sign of Aaron or Evan. Dean's truck, Dean and John were missing, too. She'd called Brian's, but there was no answer. In five minutes she was going to have to start the milking herself. Not that she didn't know how, but honestly, there were four men living on this property. Where was it written that she had to milk the cows?

Eleanor was just pulling on her boots when Dean's truck careered into the lane and stopped with a lurch in front of the house. She stepped onto the porch. The setting sun blinded her a moment, and she raised her hand to block it out.

"You don't have to drive like a maniac," she reproached her son. "The cows aren't going anywhere."

Her husband jumped out of the truck. Eleanor peered into the shadowy cab. "Where's Dean?"

"Damn!" John kicked the tire. "I forgot him at Brian's."

"Forgot him? How?"

"I was searching all over town for you."

"Why?"

He stuck his hands into his pockets and stared at

the ground. Uncomfortable silence settled between them. What else was new?

"Get Dean." She descended the steps. "I'll start the milking."

"No!"

He reached for her, then yanked his hand back before they touched. Her hurt deepened. He didn't even want to touch her casually anymore.

"I mean…" He struggled, patted his shirt, and she saw the cigarettes peeping out of his pocket.

Eleanor snatched them free as both fury and fear bubbled in her belly. He might not want her any longer, he might not love her, but she loved him, and she was not about to watch him die in front of her this time.

"You went to town looking for me?" She held up the pack. "Right. You went to town to get these."

She upended them, scattering white sticks over the ground. Then she stomped on the cigarettes with her muck-encrusted boot, following that with a little dance, grinding each and every one into a splayed piece of paper and scattered tobacco with her heel. Because that felt so good, she jumped—up and down, up and down—atop his, so help her God, last pack of cigarettes.

She stopped when she became breathless, then kicked the pile for good measure.

"Are you through?"

He leaned against the truck, staring at her as if he'd never seen her before. Well, he'd probably never seen this *her*. Psycho Eleanor was someone she usually reserved for private parties.

When it's just me, myself and I, she thought, then giggled.

John frowned. He was so handsome standing there with his arms crossed over his chest, long lean body still fit and hard in all the right places. Eleanor tugged on her shirt collar. How long would it take for those new meds to start working?

"Through for now," she replied, and headed for the barn once more.

This time he grabbed her arm, and he didn't let go. "The cows can wait. We need to talk."

"Wait? The cows? Since when?"

"Don't be sarcastic, Eleanor. It isn't attractive."

"Then sarcasm fits right in with me, doesn't it?"

Confusion spread over his face before he shook his head. "Never mind. I know you went to the doctor. And I'm afraid I know why."

Eleanor's skin went from hot to cold in a heartbeat. He was afraid? Well, of course he was. What was he going to do with a wife past her prime?

She tugged her arm from his grasp and hugged herself. The remnant of happiness she'd enjoyed that afternoon with Kim dissolved. Though she was thrilled to have started a new relationship with her daughter, facing the end of the relationship with her husband took some of the shine off.

"This is all my fault, and I'm sorry," he said.

Eleanor's eyes stung. She wouldn't cry in front of him. She *would not*. He might dump her like a dead fish, but she wasn't going to cry about it. At least not until she was alone—forever.

"I never should have touched you. I knew better."

What was he talking about? Did he mean he'd never loved her? Her chest hurt. She stumbled toward the porch.

He caught her around the waist. "What's the matter?"

"Dizzy," she muttered.

He helped her sit on the top step. Then he began to pace. "This isn't going to be easy. But you can handle it."

Eleanor dropped her head between her knees. At the moment she didn't feel capable of handling anything. "Just get it over with, John. Say what you came to say and go."

His boots appeared in her line of vision. "Go? Where? To get Dean?"

She forced herself to sit up and meet his eyes. "No. Go wherever it is you plan to go when you leave me."

"Leave you? We're having a baby. Why would I leave you?"

Her mouth fell open. After a moment, John reached over and pushed her jaw shut with one finger.

"You had me worried the way you were acting. Then you go to the doctor? You *never* go to the doctor." He scratched his head. "I was half-afraid you were dying. But the *señora* told me what she'd overheard between you and Kim. Then there was the prescription and Ezra said you ordered white soda. Now you're dizzy." He patted her shoulder—hands big and awkward, yet somehow gentle and sure. "I should have figured it out. But you never acted crazy any of the other times. I guess when you're older, things are different."

Eleanor's mouth moved a few more times before she found the words. "You want another baby?"

His gaze flicked to the setting sun. He took a deep breath, and when he looked at her again he was smiling. "Sure!"

Her worst fear realized, Eleanor gave up trying and burst into tears.

John danced about—reminding her of a little boy in need of a bathroom. He patted her back, his hands clumsy but endearing. She was going to miss him so much.

"It's okay…it's okay," he muttered. "I know women get like this when they're pregnant. We're in it together. I'll even come into the delivery room this time. I promise."

She had to stop him before he started knitting booties and naming the mythical child.

"I'm not pregnant," she choked out.

He stopped midpat. "No? Then what—?" He yanked his arm away. "What in hell's goin' on, Eleanor?"

Though her hands shook, she rubbed them over her face, dispersing the tears. Her palms were icy cold; she let them rest against her swollen, aching eyes for a moment. Then she forced herself to look him in the face.

"I went to the doctor because I felt like I was losing my mind. I was hot—I was cold—I was forgetful. I wanted to slap everyone silly just for coming near me."

"PMS?"

Eleanor narrowed her eyes. He was such a *man*. PMS was their excuse for everything.

"No." She took a deep breath and got it over with. "Menopause."

Now his mouth fell open. "But, but, you're only—"

"Fifty." She shrugged. "Just *lucky* I guess."

"The prescription?"

"Hormone replacements should help the hot flashes and night sweats. Calcium for osteoporosis." Her face heated just talking about old-lady ailments.

"The white soda."

"This whole thing makes me sick."

"But…why?"

"I doubt there'll be any more babies, John."

Although the doctor had pointed out they needed to be careful. She could still get pregnant. Eleanor glanced at John's gray, shocked face. If he was leaving her, careful wasn't going to be necessary.

"I'm sorry," she murmured.

He started to laugh—a bit hysterically, she thought. Alarmed, she reached for him, but he sat on the step below her, put his arms around her waist and laid his cheek against her stomach.

"Thank God," he whispered. "Thank God."

Eleanor stared at the top of his head, uncertain what

to do, what to say. But John, who had never said much about anything, suddenly seemed inclined to talk.

"I was so afraid to touch you."

"Afraid?"

He nodded; his five o'clock shadow made a scruffing sound against her jeans. Tenderness consumed her and she ran her hand over his hair.

"After what happened to Mose and his wife, I was afraid for you. After my heart attack, I was afraid for me. I didn't want another child and the only way I knew to make sure that didn't happen was to make sure I didn't touch you at all."

"Then why did you think I was pregnant?"

He lifted his head, sat back against the stair, but kept his hand on her thigh. "Remember the last time we…?"

A bright flash of memory came to her. The middle of a hot summer day, alone in the house, living room floor… The last time had been one of the best times.

"Oh, yeah," she murmured.

He chuckled. "That was three months ago. About a month after that you started acting—"

"Insane?"

"Uh-huh. I put one and one together—"

"And got three."

He shrugged. "A mathematician I'm not."

"I thought you didn't love me anymore."

He started, stared. "Not *love* you? Not love *you?*" His voice got higher and louder with each repetition. "You and Brian are two of a kind."

"Brian doesn't think you love him, either?"

"Har-har. He doesn't think Kim ever loved him."

Eleanor rolled his eyes. "Well, he did fall on his head."

"My thoughts exactly."

"Do you think they'll work things out?"

"Hell with them." John slid onto the top step, his hip bumping hers, then settling in close. "Will we?"

"This entire mess happened because we don't talk enough, John. I know people our age just don't, but that doesn't make it right."

"I'm not very good at *Jerry Springer* type confessions."

"You got one?"

"Yeah." He ran his hand over her head, tangled his fingers in her hair. "Thirty years later and I'm still in love with my wife."

"Do you realize you've never once told me that?"

"I showed you."

"You haven't lately," she grumbled.

His palm settled on the back of her neck, and he drew her toward him. "I can fix that."

Eleanor's heart fluttered the same way it had for over thirty years. He touched her cheek with his worn and weathered thumb, then gave her everything she'd ever wanted all over again. "I love you, Eleanor."

She smiled, fisted her fingers in his shirt and pulled him close, closer still. When his lips were only a breath away, she whispered, "Call me, Ellie."

CHAPTER FIFTEEN

"OH, MAN, why don't they get a room?"

Startled out of her reverie by Dean's annoyed voice, Kim peered into the dusk. Her parents sat on the porch steps smooching. From the way they were plastered to each other, they'd been at it a while.

Kim smiled. Mom must have told Dad the truth, and as Kim had predicted, it didn't matter. From the looks of things they'd worked out the little problem about who still loved whom, as well. Too bad life and love weren't that easy for everyone.

But there were some things that could not be forgotten or forgiven—regardless of what Brian had tried to make her believe that morning. Love could not heal all wounds, no matter what the poets and the songwriters said.

Dean muttered and grumbled as she parked the car in front of the house.

"You know, you ought to be glad they love each other," Kim pointed out. "There are a whole lot of parents who don't. Makes for dysfunctional families."

Dean raised an eyebrow in her direction.

"Oh, yeah. We *are* dysfunctional. How did that happen?"

"All families are dysfunctional, Princess. If they weren't, no one would ever leave home, and they'd always be coming back."

Kim raised an eyebrow this time.

"Oh, yeah. That's us, too."

Since their parents had stopped making out and now stood together on the porch, arms around each other as they waited for Kim and Dean to get out of the car, the two of them did just that.

"Sorry, son," their father called. "I meant to come back and pick you up."

"Save it." Dean strode toward the barn, where his cows milled a bit frantically at the door.

"After you're done with the milking what say you and I take a gander at that robotics information?"

Dean stopped, shook his head as if he hadn't heard right, and turned. "What?"

"The more I think about it, the more interesting it gets. Let's talk."

"Talk?" Dean repeated, as if his dad had said, "Paint ourselves blue all over."

"Yeah. Talk. You say something—then I say something. In a normal voice. We don't shout."

"Like that'll happen," Dean muttered.

Their dad frowned, but when Mom stepped on his toe, hard, he shrugged and let it go. "All sorts of things might happen if we try. Maybe the time has come for me to relax a bit."

Kim gaped. Her mother gave a pleased exclamation. Dean shook his head again, and this time stuck his finger in his ear and wiggled it for good measure.

"Relax?"

"Retire. Or at least semiretire. Your mom and I have decided to do a few of the things we've never done."

"Like what?" Dean appeared skeptical.

"Like talking and walking and going to Tahiti. The robotics would come in handy then."

"I thought you were leaving the place to Aaron," Dean sneered.

"I thought so, too. But I've had a change of heart." He patted his chest. "Or I might have to if I don't make some better choices. You and I may not always see eye to eye, Son, and that's okay."

"Since when?"

"Since I had a few good scares and started to look at life more clearly." Their father waited for an answer, but when Dean continued to stand in the yard and gape, he smiled. "We'll talk later. Right now me and your mom need to do some talking of our own."

They disappeared into the house.

"Talking." Dean snorted. "I believe that as much as I believe the Saturday-afternoon nap story they told us when we were kids."

"Or the one about the two of them showering together to save water." Kim laughed.

Dean joined her, until he realized who he was laughing with and stopped. Kim sighed. They'd never gotten along, but why couldn't they start?

Talking about the past with her mother that afternoon had filled some of the emptiness inside her. Could working things out with Dean fill even more?

If not for her, then maybe for him. Sometimes Dean appeared to be the emptiest person she knew.

When her brother stalked into the barn, Kim followed. He glared at her. "What do you want?"

"I thought I'd help."

"You?"

"Isn't there *something* I can do?"

"I don't know, is there?"

He wasn't going to make this easy. But then, with Dean nothing ever was.

He opened the back door and cows lumbered inside. A dozen or so continued into the milking parlor and he hooked them up to the machines. Kim grabbed a machine and, after watching what Dean did, tried to do it, too.

The cow, who reminded her of Max when he had to pee, danced about so much Kim's foot nearly became a pancake. After several minutes of chasing the udder, Dean walked over and grabbed the machine out of her hand with a disgusted exclamation. "I can do it quicker myself."

"If you'd just show me how to make her quit prancing, I could do it."

"Really?" He smirked. "Okay."

Dean leaned his shoulder against the cow's rear, shoved her into position. Every time the animal tried to move, he shoved her right back. With deft movements, he attached the machine to the cow.

Straightening, he smirked. "Think you can manage that?"

Kim stuck her chin in the air and tried. The first

time she shoved at a cow's behind with her shoulder, the animal turned and stared at her with placid eyes.

"Harder, Princess. She weighs about fourteen hundred pounds, and she's not a wimp like you."

"Can you be more annoying?" she muttered.

"Probably."

Kim gritted her teeth, put some feeling into the shove. And the cow shoved back so hard Kim flew into the wall. Her teeth clicked together, narrowly missing her tongue. The machine in her hands sprang free, clanging against the floor so loudly most of the cows skittered.

Dean cursed. "You're going to make them so crazy they'll give sour milk."

"Can that happen?"

He crossed the small room. Kim offered her hand, and he picked up the machine, instead, then did the job she had bungled.

Turning, he stared down at her. "Get lost, Kimmy. I've been doing fine without help for a long time now."

Kim refused to be deterred, since that was what he was after. She got up, rubbed her bruised backside, then sat on a stool in the corner and watched. She didn't need Dean to tell her that she was no good at dairy farming and a piss-poor farm-wife. She'd already figured that out for herself.

He ignored her through the cycle. But as he went about hooking up another set of cows, he stopped and glared. "What?"

"What did I do to make you hate me?"

He blinked. "Hate you?"

"Dislike me, then. For as long as I can remember, nothing I did was ever right enough for you. I'd like to know why, and what I can do to make things better."

"Don't you have enough people fawning over you, Princess? You need me to adore you, too?"

"I'd just like you to be my friend."

He turned away. "I'm no good at being a friend."

"That's not true. From what I hear you've been the best friend Brian could have had. I'm glad you were here for him when I couldn't be."

Dean finished attaching another machine to another cow. "Couldn't be? Or wouldn't be?"

Kim stiffened. "I'm talking about you and me, not me and Brian. What did I do to make you so angry? How can I fix it?"

"You can't." He went back to work.

"I'm not leaving until you tell me. This has gone on long enough."

Dean sighed, straightened and rubbed the small of his back. "Fine. You want to know what you did? You were born. Cute and tiny. Daddy's angel. You were sweet—I was sour. You were petite—I was a great, hulking brute. You laughed and everyone laughed with you. I acted up just to get someone to look at me. You were smart—I was dumb. Should I go on?"

She nodded, amazed at the rush of words, as much as the words themselves.

"In this family I was the black sheep." He gave a

hollow laugh. "Which explains why I like Brian's sheepdog so much."

"You were the black sheep? I thought the black sheep was me."

"Right, Princess. *You* never fit in."

"I didn't. Not here." She opened her arms wide. "I was the girl. The princess. You guys never let me play with you. You were always doing chores, laughing and roughhousing together. No one would let me take a step off the porch."

"We'd have crushed you flat, and Dad would have skinned our hides."

He had her there. "Where did you get the idea that you were dumb?"

"I barely made it through school. You were destined for college from day one."

"You wanted to go to college?"

"No. All I ever wanted was this." He rested a hand on a bony, bovine rump. "Farming is what I was born to do, and I love it."

Kim was confused. "Then what are you mad about?"

"Hell if I know." He ran his fingers through his hair. "I feel like I've been mad all my life. Aaron was calm and quiet. He was God's chosen, for crying out loud. How do you compete with that?"

"Why did you have to compete?"

"You try being boy number four in a crowd of five. Compete or get trampled."

Kim had always thought they were just having fun without her, when in fact they'd been trying to wrestle into the lead in some competition she hadn't even known about.

"Then we have Bobby and Colin. They're fricking action figures come to life. Evan is…" He shrugged, spread his big, hard hands. "He's a… What is he?"

"Babe magnet. Eye candy. Just a gigolo."

Dean's lips twitched. "You always did have a way with words." He sobered almost instantly. "So Evan is a charter member of the Gainsville Stud Club, and I can barely talk to a woman without stuttering. Do you know I've never met one who didn't ask me about another Luchetti brother within two minutes of our first hello?"

"Then you haven't met the right woman."

He rolled his eyes. "Animals don't know how to lie or cheat. They don't compare one man with another because of how he looks or talks or walks. The only thing that lasts forever is the land."

"What about love?"

"You and Brian were in love. How long did that last?"

She flinched. Dean didn't notice. He was staring out the single, tiny window of the milking parlor in the direction of the setting sun. The expression on his face made her curious. There was pain there, memories, too.

"Did someone break your heart?" she asked.

He scowled. "I've got no heart, Kim, or haven't you noticed?"

"That's what you want everyone to think, but I'm starting to wonder."

"Don't. What you see is what you get. I'm an ass-hole."

"Hmm. I always thought so. But now I'm not so sure."

Dean faced her, and any softness that had been in his eyes was gone now. "Bite me, Princess. I've bared my soul enough for one day."

"You've got no soul."

"Now you're catching on."

He released the cows and continued to work, ignoring her again. But she'd learned more about Dean in the past few minutes than she'd known her entire life.

"Do you want to talk about it?"

"About what?" he shouted, making the cows skitter.

"Whatever's making you miserable."

"Are you going to talk to Brian? Are you going to work it all out?"

"No."

"Why not? Explain to me how you and Brian could have it all, then you could walk away without a backward glance."

She didn't answer, because she couldn't. Some confessions were better left unsaid; some secrets were not only hers to tell.

Dean tossed the washcloth into the bucket so hard the water sloshed over his boots. "How, Kim?" The cows shifted and lowed uneasily at the tone and volume of his voice. "Did you ever love him at all?"

He wasn't just asking about Brian. Something else

was wrong here. Kim stepped toward him, hand out-stretched. "Dean, I—"

"Leave me alone." He turned away, running his palm over one of the cows that danced nervously and mooed. The animal calmed immediately. Dean had always had that gift.

Kim slipped out, but not before she heard him murmur, "I do better alone."

As she drove back to Brian's, she ached for the brother who couldn't seem to find any good in himself.

The Luchetti family curse.

BA AND PRECIOUS fell asleep on the porch at Brian's feet as darkness spread over the farm. He could hear the cows in the near pasture, the sheep on the hill; the pigs snored, so did Ba. He wasn't alone, yet he felt lonelier than he had for a very long time.

He should have known that having Kim back in his life, even for a little while, would make him ache for her every minute she was away. Nevertheless, he was preparing to do something that would no doubt make her run back to Georgia before the sun even rose on tomorrow.

The chill of an autumn evening skated over Brian's bare arms. The days of sitting on the porch until bedtime were done until summer. He stood, scooped a warm, limp Precious off Ba's back and went inside, where he left the sleeping kitten on the couch. She looked so cute and cuddly lying there that he hurried upstairs before he decided to let her sleep on his bed.

Kim had returned with the groceries, bubbly, happy.

Seeing her like that had reminded him of the reason he had fallen in love with her. Kim was life and laughter against the darkness. She always had been.

She'd only had time to say she and her mother had talked before Dean had tromped in and demanded she take him home so he could milk his cows. He'd been fit to be tied when he'd come out of Brian's barn to discover his dad had made off with his truck. Since John had never caught up to Kim and her mother, it was anyone's guess where he'd ended up. Brian hoped Kim wasn't out searching for the man half the night.

Because tonight was the night.

They could no longer dance around what had happened in the past. He'd been wrong to agree to keep quiet. They were both broken inside, and the only way to heal was to face what they'd lost.

He'd just stepped into his parents' room when the crunch of gravel and the sweep of headlights across the front of the house announced a visitor. Brian glanced out the window and recognized Kim's car.

She parked next to his truck and climbed out, stiffening as Ba trotted down the steps. But for the first time the ewe ignored her, heading for the back porch and the bed he had made for her there. Kim didn't know it, but Ba had just given her a huge compliment by ignoring her. The sheep had accepted Kim as family. Would Kim ever accept that, too?

Downstairs the door opened, then closed. "Hey, Precious, baby. Open your mouth. That's a good girl. No mice for an entire day. Maybe you got them all, hmm?"

Brian smiled. Little did Kim know he'd tossed five furry friends outside since she'd left that morning. Precious was a mouser to be reckoned with—farm-cat gold, though he doubted Kim would agree.

Kim jogged upstairs, paused just outside his room. "Brian?" she whispered.

"I'm here."

Her startled gasp caught at his gut. She'd sounded just like that—surprised, shocked, excited—the first time his palm had touched her skin where no one else's ever had.

She appeared in the doorway, silhouetted by the harsh, bare lightbulb in the hall. "What are you doing in the dark?"

"Don't," he said as she reached for the light.

"Why not?" she asked, but her hand fell back to her side.

He hoped that the semidarkness would entice secrets, confessions, a sense of what they'd once shared. But he couldn't tell her that.

"My eyes ache," he said, and that was true, too.

She crossed the room quickly. The light from the hall gave just enough illumination for him to see her face. The face he'd dreamed of a thousand times before.

She put her hand to his forehead. Her fingers were cool, but then, he was hot.

"You don't have a fever."

Her hand lowered. He snatched her fingers and held on as best he could.

"Not that kind, anyway," he murmured.

She smiled, uncertain. "What's that matter?"

"Nothing. Everything." He shrugged. "The usual."

She tried to tug free, but he wasn't letting go that easily. Not this time.

"I suppose you want to hash over what I told you this morning," she said.

"What was that?"

Her eyes widened. "You know."

He thought back. "Oh! Your search for someone." She opened her mouth; he jumped right in. "Anyone. I remember. What else is there to say?"

"You don't want to ask me anything?"

"No. Wait a minute. Yes."

He still held her hand, so he felt the tremor run through her. She stared at the floor and not at him. Did she think he was going to be as harsh with her as she no doubt had been with herself? He put his fingertips on her shoulders, and she glanced up, startled and wary.

"Did it help?" he murmured, repeating the question she'd never answered. "Did they make you forget that we lost our baby?"

She jerked her head back as if he'd slapped her and struggled to get away. Brian's fingertips slipped free, and he caught her around the waist, pressing his cast into her back and pulling her body flush with his.

"Let me go!" She pushed on his chest. "Let me go. You promised you wouldn't talk about that."

"I did. But then you promised to love me forever."

She stopped struggling and stared into his face. Hers was white and strained.

"Did you ever love me at all?" he whispered.

She blinked, but she no longer tried to get free. "My brother just asked me that. What is it with you two?"

"Since when does Dean care if you love him?"

"Not me." She shook her head. "Never mind. I'm not talking about this with you, Brian. It won't do a damn bit of good."

"Nothing else does any good, either. We've both proved that. And you didn't answer my question."

"Did I ever love you? How can you ask that?"

"Leaving isn't love."

"It was for me. I couldn't be what you needed. Not then and not now."

"You have no idea what I need. Not then, not now," he repeated. "Just answer the question."

"Do you think I'd have let you touch me if I didn't love you?"

"Sex isn't love. I think we've proved that, too."

She pushed against his chest again, but less emphatically than earlier. "Let me go Brian. Please."

"No. I let you go once and I shouldn't have. I should have chased you down and dragged you back."

"By my hair?" she sneered.

"What would you have done?"

"I'd have run again. And again and again. I couldn't stay."

"Because you didn't want to be a farmer's wife?"

She paused, then shook her head. "No. Because every time I looked at you I saw her."

He sighed. "And you don't see her still? Every time you close your eyes?"

"Not if I'm drunk enough." She flung the words at him defiantly. "Not if I'm never alone."

He rested his forehead against hers. "Oh, baby, why? Why didn't you stay and let me help you? Why didn't you stay and help me?"

She hesitated; then, as if against her will, she leaned into him, and he gathered her close. "I couldn't help anyone. It was all I could do to breathe, and sometimes that was hard."

"You think I could breathe after I lost her, then I lost you? Wouldn't it have been better to grieve together? Face it and go on. Maybe if we'd had another baby—"

She tore herself from his arms and turned away. "*Nothing* can replace her." She hugged herself as if she were cold, and Brian saw that her hands were trembling. "No one."

"I didn't say replace."

The silence pulsed with sadness, despair, tension. Brian faltered, uncertain if he should press her now but afraid that if he didn't he'd never get another chance to learn the truth.

"You've never talked about it, have you?"

She stilled. "It? It?" Dropping her arms, she spun around. "You say that like we misplaced a shirt. We lost *it*," she mimicked as she advanced on him. "*It* was a baby. She died! My. Baby. Died.'' She punctuated each word with a poke to his chest.

He grabbed her hand, stared fiercely into her anguished face. "So. Did. Mine."

The truth hung between them. Brian held his breath. She either came back to him, or it was over forever.

Her eyes shone in the half light. A tear dropped onto the back of his hand.

"Brian," she whispered. "Brian."

Then she touched him and forever became now.

CHAPTER SIXTEEN

KIM LAID HER PALM along Brian's waist and a second later she was in his arms. Her mouth reached for his. The salt of tears mingled on their lips.

His? Hers? She didn't know. She didn't care.

What they had shared once had torn them apart; tonight it brought them together. The need to feel his skin against hers was overwhelming. She shouldn't touch him, but she was no longer able to reason or think beyond the moment.

Her hands slid beneath the hem of his T-shirt, and she ran her fingertips along the firm, solid ridge of his belly. Her thumbs dove beneath the waistband of his sweatpants and dipped into the hollow at his hipbone. His breath caught; so did hers.

She wanted to put her mouth where her hands roamed. Taste him where she'd tasted him before.

She tugged his shirt upward, broke off their kiss just long enough to yank it over his head, but the material got caught on his casts. She let him struggle while she ran her hands over his chest. The contortions made his skin ripple; his struggles were more erotic than anything she'd ever known.

Years of hard work had turned his lean muscles

large, and time had honed him into a different man than she remembered. But he was still Brian, and no matter what had happened or would happen, he would always be hers.

She knew that he liked to be kissed on the throat, savored the sensation of fingertips at the base of his spine. If she put her lips to his chest he would gasp; if she flicked her tongue across his nipple he would moan.

Kim slid down his body. And if she pressed her open mouth to his belly and suckled he would—

Go still beneath her touch and whisper her name.

His skin quivered against her lips. The sound of his breath warred with her own. She lifted her head, looked into his eyes and let him see that all she wanted was this.

He reached for her and his casts scraped her arms. She jumped at the unexpected sensation.

Cursing, he yanked them back. His fingers curled in upon themselves, nails clicking against the hardened plaster.

He made a sound of self-derision. "I want to touch you so badly I'm shaking. But I'm afraid I'll scrape you or bang you or hurt you."

His hands had always excited her. They were big, rough and strong, yet right now they were nearly useless. An odd surge of tenderness consumed her.

She lifted the heavy casts, kissed the tips of his fingers, then lowered them back to his sides. "Let me touch you," she whispered. "You won't have to do a thing."

He lifted a brow. "Nothing?"

"Well, one thing. But you won't need your hands."

He laughed; she joined him. Why did she feel as if everything was going to be all right?

Kim pushed aside the foolish thought. Nothing would ever be all right again. She'd learned that much. But she could have this, right now, with him.

How many times had she awakened with tears on her face, memories flickering, images of him and her, together, fresh in her mind? Too many to count, too many to allow her the strength to say no when he led her to the bed.

She sat down, but he didn't join her. Afraid he'd change his mind, she reached for him.

"No," he murmured, and took a quick step back.

Her heart thudded harder; her stomach jittered faster. "Brian, if you say don't touch me again I'll—"

"What?" His startled gaze met hers. "Oh." He shook his head, took her hand and urged her to stand. "Don't." Kissing her forehead, he placed her palm against his chest. "Touch me," he breathed into her hair.

"Very funny," she said, but she smiled. How could he make her laugh, twice now, in the middle of the most frightening yet exciting night of her life.

She lifted her mouth, but he stepped back once more. "Not here." He jerked his head at the bed. "I can't."

Suddenly, she remembered. This was his parents' room. Well, hell, now she couldn't, either.

She followed him across the hall. Moonlight spilled through the window and across his bed. The covers were tousled; the pillow still bore the outline of his head. She wanted to lie there with him; she wanted to sleep there, too. But not yet.

He crossed the room, looped his forefinger in the dresser drawer and yanked it open. "We should have used one of these before." He glanced at her, shrugged. "I'll need some help using one now."

She nodded. One mistake was foolish; two could only be termed moronic.

Brian reclined against the pillows. His eyes, no longer blue but silver, reflected the moon as he watched her. "I used to lie here and dream of the two of us together. Even if I'd just left you, and I could still smell your skin on mine, there was never time enough for me, for us. You remember how we were always hiding, sneaking?"

"Of course."

For her it had been exciting to hide and sneak. She'd been such a child.

However, she could also recall never wanting to let him go, clinging, getting a lump in her throat every time they said goodbye and waiting for the day they could make love in a bed and then sleep in each other's arms all night long. But that day had never come.

"No hiding anymore," he murmured. "No sneaking tonight. Be with me. Touch me. Please?"

The day that had never come was suddenly here. Needing to be free of every restriction, real and imagined, Kim reached up and removed the band from her hair, ran her fingers through the braid, let the tresses flow freely down her back.

He smiled as if he understood her need. Knowing Brian, he did. "I've wanted you here, in this bed, for so long. I'm afraid I'm going to wake up and you'll be gone."

"I'm real, Brian." She crossed the room, reached out and ran her fingers over his hard, smooth chest. "See?"

"Take off your clothes."

She snatched her hand back. "What?"

"I can't. And…I've never seen you without them."

Her cheeks heated. Furtive couplings in cars, barns, corners. What had they been thinking?

That they were in love and they had to have each other or die.

She did as he asked, unbuttoning her blouse, letting it slide to the floor. His eyes heated from silver back to blue again. He crossed his casts over his chest and continued to watch as every stitch of her clothing joined the blouse.

Her embarrassment faded. She wanted him to look at her. She wanted him to see. She wanted them to have everything they'd never had before.

His gaze traveled from her head to her feet, leaving heat in its wake. Steam along chilled skin, feathery touches in the night, both mist and magic. He said nothing, merely stood, hooked his thumbs in his sweatpants and dropped them to the floor.

She had never seen all of him, either. Brian was a

beautiful man—tall and firm, with ridges in all the right places, hard, yet somehow soft. Enticing, but dangerous, too.

Her skin tingled with the desire to press her body against all that long, strong muscle. When he beckoned, she joined him on the bed where he'd had so many youthful dreams.

His fingertips stroked her face; he tried to touch her hair and got it snagged at a rough spot on the cast. His curse destroyed a bit of the romance, but nothing could destroy the need she had to be with him.

"Hush." She untangled her hair, pressed her fingers to his lips. "Lie back."

He did what she asked. When she straddled him his eyes widened; when she took his hands and held them firmly to the mattress on each side of his head he raised a brow, but he didn't argue. What man would?

She kissed him everywhere she had ever wanted to, until the languid tension in his body had peaked to quivering need. Then she lifted her mouth a fraction and breathed, "Don't touch."

His lips curved in acquiescence as he brought them back to hers. Freely she took—his mouth, his skin, his soul. Freely he gave—his kiss, his body, his heart.

She never let him touch her at all. She took care of everything. Still, he consumed her; he surrounded and filled her, and the power of that made her weak.

Weak enough to let him touch the emptiness, to make the pain go away in a moment of such wonder and unity she was left shaking and stunned.

"Stay," he whispered. "Marry me."

And the temptation was so great she knew the time had come for her to go.

BECAUSE SHE WAS WEAK, Kim remained with him all night. She touched him every way that she wanted, let him touch her every way that he'd dreamed.

Each time he tried to talk, she distracted him. It wasn't difficult. They were both starved for the fulfillment they'd only found with each other.

She was terrified by her need to stay, by the depth of her desire to be his wife. But marriage meant truth, and she could not give him that, along with the children he deserved.

She was a liar and a coward, but that was no news to her.

However, it would be news to Brian, and she couldn't bear to see his face if he ever learned what she had done.

BRIAN AWOKE to the warmth of the sun on his face and the cool of an empty bed at his back. And he didn't suspect a thing.

Not even when Precious jumped onto the bed and deposited a mouse on his chest. The frightened rodent stared into Brian's eyes, trapped between human and feline.

Memories flickered. He'd seen that look before, and it hadn't been in the eyes of a mouse.

Brian shook off the odd thought and grabbed Precious by the scruff of the neck. Her affronted squall brought her little present out of its trance, and the animal leaped to the floor and scurried out the door.

Brian waited for a bang and a shriek from downstairs. When none came, he frowned. "Where's Mommy, Precious?"

A trickle of unease began at the base of his spine. Why was Precious bringing mice to him if Kim was around? He let the kitten go and got up.

After retrieving his sweatpants, he yanked them on and strolled across the hall. His shirt still lay on the floor near the window, so he scooped it up and put that on, too. The silence was starting to bug him.

Since Kim had left her clothes in the spare bedroom, though she slept up here, the emptiness of his parents' room wasn't the problem. But something was.

He went downstairs. His steps picked up speed as each room proved empty. He burst into the spare bedroom and knew immediately that she was gone. But how gone was she?

A quick search revealed the truth—no clothes, no suitcase, no Kim. He sat heavily on the bed. Precious dropped the same mouse on his foot. Absently he grabbed the kitten and held on while he flipped the mouse off and let it escape one more time. Then he held Kim's cat, which now appeared to be his, and let his mind whirl.

No note. No goodbye. Why was he surprised? This was Kim. Had he really expected her to stay?

Yes, dammit. He loved her; she loved him. What was so insulting about asking her to marry him that every single time he did it, she disappeared?

Lost, aching, furious, he walked in circles. He didn't know what to do. Should he stay or should he go? Chase her down or let her be?

The sound of a car door had him sprinting for the front of the house, foolish hope lighting his heart until he ran smack into Dean on the porch. Precious squalled and leaped from his arms, her back claws screeching along his cast like a buzz saw.

"So the princess ran off again."

"How did you know?"

"She called Mom and Dad from the airport this time."

Airport? It wasn't until the dizziness washed over him that he'd realized he'd continued to hope she'd only run as far as her mother.

"I take it from your face she didn't bother to tell you."

Brian didn't answer and Dean nodded smugly.

"She lasted longer than I thought. But I knew she couldn't hack it." Dean peered into Brian's face. "You didn't do anything stupid like fall in love with her again, did you?"

"No."

"Well, that's something."

"I didn't have to fall—I was there all along."

Dean cursed. "Are you crazy? How can you love someone who walked out on you? She thinks she's too good for you." Dean swept his arm out to indicate the farm. "Too good for this."

"That's not true."

"Did you forget that she left you behind without a

goodbye? Twice? Bright lights, big city, anywhere but here.''

"That's not what happened.''

"She was a selfish, spoiled brat. That hasn't changed.''

Brian couldn't lie anymore. "It wasn't Kim's fault. If anyone was selfish it was me.''

Dean snorted. "You keep saying that, but you don't have to protect her anymore. I didn't believe you then, and I don't believe you now.''

"I got her pregnant, Dean.''

Silence fell over the early morning. Ba came around the corner of the house, took one look at the two of them staring at each other and scuttled in the other direction. Precious was right behind her.

Dean's eyes narrowed. "Run that by me again.''

"I promised I wouldn't tell. Never. No one.'' He shrugged. "Still, I should have told you. Especially when you got so angry at her. But I was selfish. I wanted you to be angry along with me. So if you want to hate someone, hate me, Dean. I deserve it.''

"You deserve something, that's for sure.'' Dean rubbed his forehead in a gesture that was so like Kim Brian ached even more. "You let me believe she walked out and crushed you for no reason but selfishness.'' He frowned and glared at Brian suspiciously. "If Kimmy was pregnant, where's the baby?''

"Remember when we ran away?''

"How could I forget? I thought my dad was going to blow a fuse.''

Brian winced. His parents had been hurt that he'd

run off, hurt even more when he'd refused to share why. They had died never knowing the truth, and maybe that was for the best. There was no changing what had happened, no matter how much he might want to.

"We were going to get married," he continued, "but Kim lost—"

He stopped as he recalled her words. Their baby had not been misplaced; she had died, and they had buried her without a name in a place far away from here. Brian's eyes burned, but he fought the weakness. He would tell Dean the truth, and then maybe he'd feel better—though he doubted it.

"The baby died," he continued. "We came back. Kim was…different—quiet, sad, not herself at all. I thought she should talk about it, but she wouldn't. She couldn't even look at me anymore."

Brian paused, remembering how much that had hurt, how confused and lost and uncertain he had been. He'd wanted desperately to reach her, to help her, but he hadn't known how. They had both been so young, so foolish and, despite having each other, completely alone.

"One night I came to your house and I begged her to marry me anyway. What difference did it make? I loved her—she loved me. We'd have another baby. The next day she was gone." He laughed without humor. "How can the same thing happen to the same guy twice?"

"You got her pregnant twice?"

"No," he answered.

"You're sure?"

"As sure as I can be. I've gotta find her."

"You're going to run after her like a puppy?"

"No. I'm going to run after her like a man."

"Girlie man," Dean muttered. "I knew this would happen. I knew you wouldn't be able to keep your hands off her."

"If you're so damn smart, tell me why she ran again."

Dean hesitated, then shrugged. "You trapped her."

"Me?"

"With love, with sex, with a baby. She's got to want to stay, man, and I don't think she ever will. She's not cut out for this place, this life, and she knows it."

Suddenly Brian remembered the expression in the mouse's eyes that morning and exactly where he'd seen it before. Kim had looked like that all those years ago when he'd confronted her and begged her to marry him.

Trapped.

She'd looked like that last night, too, when he'd whispered, *Stay. Marry me.*

Dean was right. He couldn't make her stay here. He couldn't follow her there. All he could do was hope.

Brian sat down heavily on the top porch step.

But he had no hope left.

Dean climbed into his truck, then leaned out through the open window. "Brian? When you get those casts off your hands, I *will* beat the shit out of you." He started the truck. "Pain in the ass Kim may be, but she's still my little sister."

CHAPTER SEVENTEEN

EVERYONE WAS ASLEEP when she sneaked from her room, shimmied down the drainpipe and went into his arms. The night was dark and steamy with summer rain.

Running across the green grass, they slid a little in the mud of the lane that led up to the main road, then tumbled into his car.

They couldn't afford to be caught tonight. Not that they'd ever been caught before. That was what had brought them to this. If you didn't count love and youth and passion.

He kissed her and whispered, "Everything will be all right," and for a while it was.

They checked into a small, dark motel room. She was afraid; so was he. Something was wrong, and they didn't know what to do.

Then there were people everywhere. Strangers. So much noise and light. But he never left her, not for a second.

Too soon. Too small. A girl.

The murmurs reached her over time. Someone was crying, and that someone was her.

She held the baby; the child didn't breathe. She was

too tiny, completely perfect, exquisitely beautiful—and she looked just like her father.

She shoved the bundle back into the stranger's arms, and she never saw it again.

But the emptiness left by the loss of that child never left her.

Kim came awake with a gasp into the silent stillness of another lonely night.

She was shaking, sweating. The breeze through her open window was warm and smelled of the river and autumn. She ached for the scent of snow and falling leaves. What she wouldn't give right now for a hint of manure on the east wind.

Kim got up and padded to the bathroom, splashed her face, got a shock when she glanced into the mirror. She was as white as a Savannah ghost. Maybe she was dead and just didn't know it—like any good ghost— she certainly didn't feel alive, and she hadn't since she'd gotten on that plane.

She'd been back in Savannah for over a month. The first few weeks she'd hidden out in her apartment, not even telling Livy that she was back. She'd managed to miss her friend's wedding this way.

When the silence became too loud and her boredom too deep, she'd come out of her isolation and returned to the life she'd made for herself in Savannah.

But she no longer found any joy here—not in the place, her friends or her job. Not that she hadn't tried. She'd danced, but she couldn't laugh. She'd drunk, but everything tasted like dirt. So she'd immersed herself in cases during the week and taken Max to the park every weekend.

Nothing helped. Kim was miserable, and she didn't know what to do about it.

The dream was back, worse than before. The heat, the rain, the pain. Brian's fear, their love, her secret.

Kim wandered through her apartment and wished she'd brought Precious here. She'd have had to get rid of the glass. No doubt the kitten would have broken every pretty thing. But it would have been worth it not to be alone.

She sat on her veranda and stared at the city that had given her so much pleasure for so long. Savannah was just a place now. A place without him.

She stayed up late, staring at the shadows of old buildings, listening to the music drift from River Street, refusing to think, trying not to feel.

As a result, she overslept, awakening to irate pounding on her door. A glimpse through the peephole revealed Livy and Max. Since they had doughnuts, she let them in.

Max flung himself at her waist, nearly knocking her down. Before she could do anything more than run her hand over his electric-blond hair, he was off, taking the doughnuts with him.

"Freeze!" Livy commanded. "Hand over that bag or pay the price."

"You already paid the price, Mom. You said it was exbetent."

"Exorbitant," Livy corrected. "Come back here."

Max turned. His lips were painted with chocolate. Kim looked down. So was her nightshirt.

She covered the stain with her arm so Livy wouldn't notice. But a single glance at her friend's eagle eyes told her she was too late.

Kim shrugged. "What's a little chocolate between pals?"

Livy rolled her eyes. "Better you than me."

Impeccably dressed in a suit of royal blue for her afternoon court date Livy had not yet begun to show. But the glow of her skin and the happiness in her eyes would have tipped Kim off to the secret of her pregnancy, even if Livy hadn't told her the news the second she learned Kim had returned to town.

Kim was thrilled for Livy, thrilled for Max, even thrilled for Garrett, who seemed to be a decent guy despite his desertion of Livy the first time around. But these days, happiness only made Kim realize how sad she was.

Max stuffed the doughnut bag into Kim's hand and beelined for the open veranda doors again.

"I don't think so, buddy!" Livy snapped.

"Aw, Mom." He treated Livy to his kicked-puppy face. Kim snickered and got the same glare that Max did.

"We're too high up, Max."

"I promise not to lean out too far. I promise not to nearly fall. I promise not to die. I promise not to break anything, not even myself." He crossed his heart.

Livy bit her lip. Max pressed the advantage. "Daddy says you have to let me be a boy."

"Oh, really," Kim purred, and stared archly at her friend. "Daddy says, huh?"

"I know, I know. You've been telling me that for years." Livy threw up her hands. "Fine. But so help me, Max, if you fall off that balcony and die, I will kill you."

"You always say that," he mumbled.

"Gee, I wonder why."

But Max had already skipped off to the veranda before his mom could change her mind.

"You do say that all the time, you know?"

Kim led the way into the kitchen, where they could watch Max through the floor-length window next to the breakfast nook. She poured milk for Livy, then made coffee for herself.

"And your point would be what?" Livy asked.

"I don't have one." Kim set the doughnuts on the table. "Just an observation."

"Well, I'm going to make an observation. You look like hell."

Kim glanced up from her unenthusiastic contemplation of the doughnuts. "And *your* point would be?"

"*Why* do you look like hell, Kim? Why do you walk around in a daze? You've stopped going out. You've even given up brainless bimbo boys."

"Which you've been begging me to do for years."

"Tell me where you went," Livy demanded. "Tell me what happened there."

"Don't take your lawyer's tone with me, Livy Frasier Stark. It won't work."

"What will?"

Kim reached for the last chocolate doughnut.

"Touch that and die." Livy snatched the sweet from her hand.

Kim blinked at her empty fingers. "Remind me never to get between a pregnant woman and the last chocolate doughnut."

"Are we going to talk about doughnuts or you?"

"Doughnuts."

Livy gave her the glare she usually reserved for recalcitrant defense witnesses. "Spill it, Kim."

Kim hesitated. She'd never talked to anyone about that night. Was Brian right? If she did would the pain stop? Would the dream go away? Or would it only get worse?

"Tell me what's wrong," Livy pressed. "If I didn't know better I'd think you were scared of something, but you're the most fearless person I know."

"Me?" Kim laughed. "I sure had you fooled."

Livy frowned and set down the doughnut as Kim continued.

"Did you know I'm scared to death of mice? I'm scared of secrets and the truth. I'm scared of love. I'm scared of babies. I'm scared of memories and nightmares and—" Her voice broke.

She was terrified she'd never feel again the way she'd felt with Brian. And if that was true, what reason was there to go on?

"Gotta face those fears."

"Max!" Livy put a hand to her chest. "Aren't you supposed to be hanging off the veranda?"

"I came in for a doughnut."

"I think three is your limit."

He eyed the half-eaten one in front of her. "It wasn't yours."

"Do as I say, not as I do."

"You always say that."

Livy gave an aggrieved sigh. "Is there anything I don't always say?"

"Party on? Be free? Do what you wanna do?"

"That would be your gramma. Now, run along."

"But Kim's sad." Max came into the room and leaned against Kim's shoulder. His dark eyes were sad, too. "I used to be afraid of stuff. But Daddy taught me how not to be."

In spite of herself, Kim was intrigued. "How?"

"Gotta face it, then it can't hurt you no more. Don't like the dark—turn off the lights. 'Fraid of coffins—jump right in. Stuff that isn't there? Gotta own it in a story."

Kim lifted a brow at Livy. "I see now where the horror writer gets his ideas."

Livy shrugged.

"You're afraid of mice?" Max continued. "Gotta pick one up."

Kim shivered. "I don't think so."

"They won't hurt you. They're little and kind of cute."

"Not."

"'Fraid of babies? Maybe you oughta have one."

Kim shuddered.

"Max," Livy warned.

"I'm puttin' a lid on it. I just don't want Kim to be scared."

"Thanks." Kim gave him a quick hug. "I'll take it under advisement."

"Lawyers," Max muttered, and returned to the veranda.

"Sorry," Livy said as soon as he was out of earshot. "You know how he is."

Kim smiled. Everyone in Savannah knew how Max was. Precocious, adorable, brilliant, special beyond understanding. And usually right.

Face her fear and it would go away? Well, Max could forget about her picking up a mouse, but there was one thing she'd never faced. Considering her nightmare, maybe she ought to.

"I gotta go." Kim stood.

"What? Where?"

"Gotta face those fears."

"You're taking advice from an eight-year-old?"

"Which he got from his father."

"His father talks to people who aren't real."

"Hey, you married him."

Livy grinned. "I did, didn't I?"

Kim shook her head. She really had to get out of there.

MID-NOVEMBER WAS late for Indian summer. The trees in central Wisconsin were well past their peak, yet the day shone bright with sunshine, and the temperature was far above sixty. The single snowstorm of the year had nearly melted away.

Brian wasn't sure what had drawn him here. He'd only known that he had to come.

He parked his truck at the sign that pointed downhill, got out then followed the arrow. Moments later he stood at a tiny grave, complete with a tiny headstone. The only thing that was incomplete was the name.

Baby Riley.

The wind ruffled his hair, stirred the flowers he'd stopped to spend a fortune on. But he felt that the first time he visited his daughter in eight years he ought to bring something.

Brian laid the miniature pink roses atop the tiny patch of snow sheltered by the stone. Then he stuck his newly released hands into his pockets. What was he supposed to say? His baby didn't even have name.

Dean would have a field day with that one.

He spun away from the grave, the pain too deep to bear. This had been a mistake. He'd hoped that by facing what he'd never faced he might be able to move on. But there was nowhere for him to go but back where he had been. And he hated it there.

The farm that had been his lifeline was no longer. Everywhere he looked, she was there. Outside the chicken coop, with egg in her hair. In the barn, holding kittens to her face. On the kitchen counter, screaming as a mouse ran around and around. In his bed touching him everywhere, yet nowhere at all.

Nothing was ever going to be right again without her. But he couldn't beg for her love any more. Begging had never done either of them any good.

Brian reached the top of the hill. He wasn't sure what made him turn back, maybe the sound of a car door or the scent of evergreen on the wind.

His gaze went to his daughter's grave, and there she was.

SOMEONE HAD LAID pink roses in the snow. Who? No one knew about this place but her and—

Kim's head jerked up; her gaze darted around the cemetery. On the hill stood a man, and even from this distance, she knew that it was him.

Was this fate? Or destiny? Divine intervention? Kim glanced at the tiny headstone. Perhaps just an angel at work.

She could run again. Jump in her car and never come back. But she'd come to face her fears. And the biggest fear was him.

She couldn't run anymore. She couldn't hide. She couldn't lie or keep the secrets. She was so damn tired of being afraid.

Kim knelt and placed the small stuffed kitten against the headstone. She'd tied a big pink bow around the toy's neck. Strange how the shade of the ribbon and the shade of the flowers were the same. Or maybe not so strange at all.

Brian's shadow fell over them both. He didn't say a word and suddenly she had to. "I'm sorry."

He shuffled, impatient, annoyed. "I'm tired of hearing you're sorry, Kim. I want to hear why you can't love me."

"I do love you. That's why I'm sorry. You deserve better."

He cursed and she focused on the headstone, afraid to look into his face. "What I *deserve* is the mother of my child as my wife. Why is it that every time I ask you to marry me—" he snapped his fingers, and it was then she realized his hands were no longer encased in casts "—*poof.* You're gone the next day."

She glanced at him and gaped. He had the brightest shiner she'd ever seen. "What happened to your eye?"

He hunched his shoulders and looked away. "Your brother happened."

"What? Why?"

"I was sick of lying. I told him that I'd gotten you pregnant the baby died and that's why you left."

"I thought we weren't going to tell anyone."

"I thought a lot of things and none of them was true."

She sighed. "I can't believe Evan would exert himself enough to do that."

"Not Evan."

"Aaron?"

Brian snorted. "Right."

"Bobby or Colin came home? Why one earth would you tell one of them?"

"It was Dean, Kim. *Dean.*"

She blinked. Considered, then shook her head. "No way."

"Way. He had the courtesy to wait until my wrists were healed, and then he punched me in the nose."

"He's your best friend."

"And you're his little sister. As he so kindly informed me—with his knuckles."

Kim would never understand men. They got mad; they punched one another out; it was done and they were pals again. "So what does he look like?"

"Same's usual."

"You didn't hit him back?"

"What for? I deserved this."

"I thought you deserved a wife."

"I do. And the only one I want is you."

She was shaking her head before he finished. "Brian, I *suck* at being a farmer's wife. You've seen me. I try and try and I can't get it right. I break the eggs—I scare the cows—I burn the food, lose the baby."

"We didn't misplace her," he said softly. "She's right here."

Kim's eyes burned. "I know."

She ran her palm over the sharp autumn grass, then touched a pink rose petal with her fingertip. The softness, the perfection reminded Kim of her daughter's skin. For the first time she savored the memory.

After a moment she realized that the silence felt good; being here wasn't so bad, now that he was here, too.

Brian sat on the ground at her side. "I never stopped loving you, Kim."

The sense of peace evaporated on the unseasonably warm wind. She didn't want to hurt him anymore, but she didn't think she was going to be able to stop it.

"It doesn't matter," she managed to say.

"Love is the only thing that does matter."

"Love can't bring her back."

"Is that what you want?"

"Yes. I want her back, Brian."

"And that's the one thing I can't give you. But I can give you more children. We can fill up the house if you want."

"You think another child will make me forget the first one?"

"Of course not. But you've got to go on. We could have a life, if you'd let her death go."

"I can't."

"Why?"

"Because it was my fault!" she shouted. Heart pounding with both fear and anger, Kim breathed deeply until the urge to scream or cry or both passed. "She died because of me."

"What are you saying?"

The confusion in his voice did not quite mask the suspicion. Kim braced herself, then met Brian's eyes when she finally told him the truth.

"I didn't want to stay in Gainsville. I didn't want to marry you. At least not yet. I wished her gone—" Kim returned her attention to the headstone "—and then she was."

"You *wished?*"

Kim fought not to cringe at the incredulity in his tone. He couldn't believe she'd been so heartless and selfish. Which only made two of them.

She nodded. "Every single night, until it happened."

Brian laughed, startling her. "Wishing doesn't make something happen."

"I know that here." She tapped her head. "But here?" Kim touched her chest. "Not so much. That's why I couldn't stay. You wanted her so badly. Every time I looked at you I remembered that I'd resented her, resented you."

"You were eighteen and confused. So was I."

"No, from the moment you heard we were having a baby, you knew what to do, you knew what you wanted."

"But I didn't stop to think what you wanted, and that was my mistake. I had to take care of you both, to make everything all right. And in doing that, I trapped you in the life I wanted."

She had felt trapped. But she had no one to blame but herself.

"You were as trapped as I was, Brian."

"Not really. I was scared, but I was happy."

She smiled, remembering why she had loved him, why she loved him still. "You were so sure of everything. So confident, so certain. All you ever needed was your farm, a wife and some kids. Simple, beautiful dreams that I couldn't give you. Not then and not now."

"Fine. What *can* you give me? Love? I'll take it." He jumped up and held out his hand. "Let's go."

She stared at him, wary. "Go where?"

"Anywhere you want. Wherever you'll be happy. I love you. Screw the farm."

"You don't mean that."

"I don't? You think I'm going to let some grass and a few cows keep me from being with you?"

"It's not the farm. It never was. You haven't been listening to me. I can't give you children, Brian. And you deserve them."

He let his hand fall back to his side. "Can't or won't?"

"Both. To go through that again…" She stared at the grass as a cold sweat sprang up on her skin. "Just the thought paralyzes me."

Silence fell between them for several moments. Then Kim murmured, "Do you remember when they made me hold her?"

"Yeah," Brian whispered.

One of the paramedics who had answered Brian's frantic 911 call had also been a midwife. She'd insisted that Kim needed to hold the baby or she'd never get over the loss. Kim had never gotten over it anyway.

"When I held her…I wanted her, and all I could think of was that it was too late. I'd been selfish, and she was the one who paid. I can't forgive myself for that, Brian. Can you?"

"I should forgive you for being a child and frightened? I should forgive you for something that wasn't your fault? No matter what you might think when it's dark and you're all alone, you didn't kill that baby, Kim. Miscarriages happen all the time."

"Exactly." Kim jumped to her feet and faced him. "What if it happens again and again?"

"What if it doesn't? You can't live your life hiding from the bad what-ifs. Why don't you go looking for the good ones? What if I take a chance? What if I find a life? What if love really can heal?"

"Is there nothing I could do or say or confess that you wouldn't forgive?"

"No."

"You're a better person than me."

He threw up his hands. "It isn't about me forgiving you. It's about you forgiving yourself. And as much as I want to help you, with that you're on your own."

He tempted her with the promise of the future she'd denied. Could love heal? Nothing else had been able to.

"Why did you come here today, Brian?"

He remained silent so long she didn't think he would answer. Then he stepped closer and he slipped his hand into hers. The warmth of his fingers against her chilled skin felt so good, so right, she couldn't pull away—she could only hold on.

"We never put her to rest. We never said goodbye." He pointed to the headstone. "She doesn't even have a name. It's as if she never existed, and we both know that's not true."

"What should we do?"

The breath he took shook in the middle, but when he spoke his voice was strong. "We should name our little girl. We should tell everyone about her. We should change that headstone, have a funeral, say goodbye. And then—"

He turned her to face him, took both her hands in his. "Then we should get married, share a name and face everything we're afraid of together."

"What are you afraid of?"

"That I'll wake up one morning and you'll be gone again."

She flinched.

"But I'm willing to take the chance, because I love you. I want that simple, beautiful life I dreamed of, and I think deep down you want it, too."

She stared into his face, uncertain yet hopeful. If he was by her side, she might be able to find the courage to try.

"The only thing I'm sure of is that I want you."

The light in his eyes accepted her promise and made promises of its own. "Should we live on the farm or sell it and move to Savannah?"

"You can't sell a farm that's been in your family for the better part of a century."

"Sure I can. A big For Sale sign in the yard, and within a week they'll be building condos on the lawn."

Kim winced. "I don't think so. And while the idea of mice in the bed and sheep on the porch and chickens squawking at dawn's early light gives me the heebie-jeebies, there's something that's worse."

"What's that?"

"Life without you."

He grinned and lowered his mouth to hers. Their

kiss was long and thorough and ended only when the wind picked up and stirred Kim's hair.

She pulled away. "Did you smell that?"

"Manure again?"

"No." She punched his arm. "It smelled like—"

She closed her eyes. The wind had smelled of spring in the heart of the autumn. Rain, new grass, roses and...

"Hope," she murmured. The wind had smelled of hope. She opened her eyes.

Brian knelt next to the headstone. His hand shook as he ran his fingertips along the letters.

"Hope Riley." He glanced at her. "What do you think?"

The answer came on the wind and this time there was no question.

Hope lived in the air.

EPILOGUE

HUGE, LACY SNOWFLAKES drifted from a navy-blue sky. John Luchetti raised his face to the night and smiled. Everyone knew that Christmas Eve snow was magic.

An ear-piercing shriek made him pause with his hand lifted, ready to knock on the front door of the Riley farmhouse. Before John could recover, his daughter appeared. Wearing her wedding dress, she carried a broom in one hand. John got out of the way in a hurry. Ba, who had been sleeping on the porch for quite a while, from the depth of the snow on her back, didn't even open her eyes.

The door flew open and one perfect slap shot later a mouse came flying out. Precious, the cat, followed and the chase was on, the fleet kitten-cat scrambling over new fallen snow.

John lifted a brow at his daughter. "Mice are pretty hard to ferret out in the dead of winter."

Kim snorted. "Tell it to the great mouse detective. That's the third one this week she's dropped at my feet." She swished her broom. "But I showed 'em."

"I wish your mother had never taught you how to get rid of mice. You're a menace."

"But only to mice." She gave him a kiss, then waved at her mother, who waited in the truck.

"Are you ready?" he asked

"As I'll ever be."

She reached back into the house, lost the broom to grab a small overnight bag, then gathered her dress over one arm. Beneath the ivory silk and satin, she had on clodhopper farm boots.

John shook his head. "What happened to the little girl who wore high-heeled fancy shoes?"

Kim jiggled the bag. "Wait until you see what I've got in here."

The drive to the church was filled with chatter. Things certainly had changed. His wife and his daughter were now closer than any of them could ever have imagined. Kim came to Ellie for advice; Ellie went to Kim to talk. They were pals, and while John missed the connection that he and his girl had shared, he had to admit that it had been time for his wife and daughter to work things out.

A lot of problems had been worked out over the past several weeks, and some needed more time. His relationship with his sons, for one thing, was still not all he wished for it to be. But he was trying.

John parked his truck at the back of the church. Though the wedding was family and close friends only, the tiny parking lot was nearly full. They were the last ones to arrive.

Inside, Kim kicked off her boots and pulled from her bag the tallest, fanciest shoes John had ever seen.

She grinned as she slipped on the crystal-clear pumps; their five-inch heels appeared made of gold.

"I had to order these from New York and they nearly cost as much as a prize bull." She winked. "But some things are worth it."

And some things never changed. Though Kim might live on a farm and be marrying a farmer, she would never be a true farmwife, just as Ba would never be a true black sheep and Precious would never be a true mouser. But it didn't matter, as long as everyone was happy.

John smiled and patted the breast pocket of his rented black tux. The cigarette was there, and he felt better just knowing that.

He scratched his arm. The patch was there, too. He'd finally given up and given in, agreeing to wear the patch if he could keep one cigarette in his pocket, just in case.

Ellie's eyes met his. She smiled, winked and scratched the place where her own patch lay. She'd gotten sick of taking the pills and opted for a long-lasting patch. Which made Ellie and him two of a kind these days.

With all the upheaval, they hadn't made it to Tahiti yet. He was still spending his days, and his nights, convincing Ellie she was needed, wanted and loved. He planned on devoting the rest of his life to that task.

Music began in the sanctuary. Kim caught her breath.

"You okay?" he asked.

"Better than okay." She picked up her bouquet of

miniature pink roses. "I love him. Always have, always will."

She put her face to the flowers, inhaled the fragrance, and a whisper of sadness passed over her face. John and Ellie exchanged glances.

Brian and Kim had sat every available family member down and told them of the daughter they'd lost. After taking care of a few legalities, they'd held a memorial service at the grave site in Wisconsin. From that day forward, Kim and Brian had changed. They'd looked ahead and not behind; they'd planned for a future and they were making it happen. John was proud of them both.

With Kim between them, John and Ellie started down the aisle. The sanctuary was decorated for Christmas. Holly and ivy were strung from the rafters and the pews, poinsettias graced the dais and a huge tree covered with glass ornaments filled one corner. John understood why Kim had insisted on a Christmas Eve wedding. New life, hope is born, the world starts over again.

The only friends missing were Kim's friend Livy and her family. But Livy's doctor had nixed the trip at the last minute. Nothing serious, but better safe than sorry.

All the Luchetti brothers save Bobby were in attendance. Everyone was a bit worried at the inability to get in touch with him, but at least Colin had made it home—just in time, as usual.

Dean stood next to Brian, serving as his best man. All seemed to be forgiven between them now. In fact,

Dean's defense of Kim had started the two of them on
the road, if not to friendship, at least to tolerance. Anything was better than the way it had been.

Brian stood straight, strong and tall in his black suit.
His gaze never left Kim during her walk down the
aisle. He looked at her as if his world lay in her eyes.
John glanced at Kim. She looked at Brian in exactly
the same way.

He and Ellie handed their daughter into Brian Riley's care, then they took their seats in the front pew.

"You think they'll be all right?" Ellie whispered,
her eyes moist with tears as she watched their baby
take her vows.

"Knock-knock," John answered.

"Not now."

"Knock-knock," he repeated.

"Oh, fine. Who's there?"

"Ellie."

"Ellie, who?" she asked warily. "And so help me
if you say *phant* I will kick you right here before God
and everyone."

He shook his head and returned his attention to his
daughter just as Kim gazed into Brian's face and
smiled with utter joy.

"Ellie need is love," John murmured.

THE RECEPTION was held in the basement room at the
Edge of Town. Most of the county came. The neigh-
bors were nosy; there was no help for that.

Kim would get used to it. She had to. She planned
on living here for the next fifty years—give or take.

While the thought would have once made her run screaming from the room, the town, the state, now it gave her a measure of peace. The farm that had once reminded her only of the past now represented a whole new future.

Her father selected the music for the first dance, then saluted Kim with a wink. As the strains of "Love Is All You Need" filtered through the smoky, noisy interior, Kim leaned her head against Brian's chest and thought that John and Paul had known what they were talking about. But then, that had never really been in doubt.

The last several weeks had been both the most challenging and the happiest of her life. She still sucked at being a farmwife, but with the help of her mother and a renewed friendship with Becky Jo, she was managing. And, as Brian had pointed out, he'd done just fine without a farmwife for a whole lot of years, why rock the boat now? To be honest, he made a better one than Kim ever could.

She'd sold Livy her half of the law firm. Since her friend was married to a future millionaire—Garrett's next book, according to his agent, was going to hit the *New York Times* Best-Seller List and stay there for so many weeks they'd lose count—Livy could afford it.

"When does school start?" Brian murmured.

"Three weeks."

Kim had decided, at Brian's urging, to take the money from Livy and go back to school. Gainsville wasn't short on bars or doctors, but it was definitely slim on lawyers.

"That'll give us plenty of time for the honeymoon."

"Honeymoon? We can't leave the farm. The cows will explode. My chickens will stop laying. Who will take care of Ba and Precious? There'll be mice all over the house and—"

He stopped her tirade with a kiss. The crowd whooped.

They'd decided to wait until they were married before they slept together again. Even if that was closing the barn door after the cows were gone—

Kim smiled. She seemed to be making quite a few allusions to the barnyard these days.

Well, whatever. As a result of their agreement, every time Brian looked at her, touched her or kissed her, she wanted to crawl all over him and rip his clothes off.

He lifted his head. He was breathing as heavily as she. "The honeymoon I had planned involved staying at home in bed for as long as we could manage."

"Works for me." She yanked his mouth back to hers.

Later that night, as Brian made love to her for the first time as husband and wife, the last of the emptiness inside Kim dissolved. As he lay with his head on her shoulder, she twined her fingers in the tight curls of his hair the way she always used to.

She felt healed as well as whole, and it was because of Brian, because of love. He'd given her such a beautiful gift—love no matter what. She wanted to give him something wonderful, too.

"But I'm still afraid," she whispered.

He shifted and pulled her into his arms instead of the other way around. "Of what?"

"What if—"

He put his fingers to her lips, stifling the words.

"What if she's perfect? What if she's beautiful?" He kissed her nose. "What if he's strong, tall and brilliant? What if you never take a chance and never find out what could be?"

He was right. She had to take a chance. She had to face her fears. She had to find her courage.

Kim took a deep breath, picked up the box of condoms from the bedside table and tossed it into the trash. "No guts, no glory?" she asked.

"You took the words right out of my mouth."

Nine months later.

FROM THE ANNOUNCEMENT page of the *Gainsville Gazette*:

Brian and Kim Riley are proud to announce the birth of their daughter.

Glory.

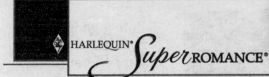

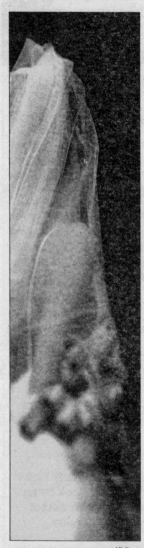

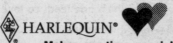
HINTBB

The Healer
by Jean Brashear

Diego Montalvo's life changed forever after the
Special Forces mission that nearly killed him.
Now a *curandero*—healer—whose healing tradition
calls into question everything that cardiac surgeon
Caroline Malone believes, he may be her key to
regaining the career that's her life. Except,
success in healing means losing each other.
Because he can't leave his home in West Texas…
and she can't stay.

**Look for more
Deep in the Heart
Superromance titles
in the months to come!**

**Heartwarming stories with
a sense of humor,
genuine charm and emotion
and lots of family!**

**On sale starting
January 2003 from
Harlequin Superromance.**

*Available wherever
Harlequin books are sold.*